No one does it like Tracy Bloom!

'Deft and witty'
Sunday Mirror

'Warm, witty and wise'
Daily Mail

'Likeable, funny and relatable'
Heat

'This hilarious book will sweep
you up in its sheer brilliance'
Marie Claire

'Feisty and fabulous'
Milly Johnson

'Pure joy!'
Katie Fforde

'Laugh out loud'
Adele Parks

'Guaranteed to put a smile on your face'
Debbie Johnson

'Just the pick-me-up I needed!'
Jo Thomas

'Hilarious! A must-read for anyone who's ever
been on the wrong side of a relationship'
Coleen Nolan

'Warm, and extremely funny'
Reels and Reads

'Uplifting, life-affirming and most of all funny'
Bee Reads

Readers' five-star love for Tracy Bloom

'So, so, so funny, I genuinely laughed out loud'

'No doubt about it . . . at least a 6 out of 5!'

'Peppered with fantastically humorous episodes . . . a joy'

'It wasn't long before I was so engrossed in it that I couldn't put it down'

'Funny, totally relatable and made me laugh out loud'

'Tracy Bloom has the lightest of touches with the deepest of understanding'

'Where has [Tracy Bloom] been all my life'

'I really loved this book, so funny and life-affirming'

'Hilarious, touching and really laugh out loud!!'

'A fab read which you don't want to put down'

'Just like catching up with a good friend'

'Utterly brilliant'

'Great story, not least because it made me realize I'm not alone'

The Secret Santa Project

Tracy started writing when her cruel, heartless husband ripped her away from her dream job – shopping for rollercoasters for the UK's leading theme parks – to live in America with a brand-new baby and no mates. In a cunning plan to avoid domestic duties and people who didn't understand her Derbyshire accent, she wrote *No-one Ever Has Sex on a Tuesday*. It went on to become a No. 1 bestseller and publishing phenomenon. Since then, Tracy has written many more novels and been published successfully around the world. She now lives back home in Derbyshire with her husband and children.

To keep in touch with Tracy, follow her on social media.

𝕏 @TracyBBloom
🄵 /tracybloomwrites

The Secret Santa Project

TRACY BLOOM

HarperCollins*Publishers*

HarperCollins*Publishers* Ltd
1 London Bridge Street,
London SE1 9GF

www.harpercollins.co.uk

HarperCollins*Publishers*
Macken House, 39/40 Mayor Street Upper
Dublin 1, D01 C9W8

First published by HarperCollins*Publishers* 2024
1

A catalogue record for this book is available from the British Library

ISBN: 978-0-00-861914-5 (PBO)

This novel is entirely a work of fiction.
The names, characters and incidents portrayed in it are
the work of the author's imagination. Any resemblance to
actual persons, living or dead, events or localities is
entirely coincidental.

Typeset in Sabon LT Std by Palimpsest Book Production Ltd, Falkirk,
Stirlingshire

Printed and bound in the UK using 100% Renewable Electricity by
CPI Group (UK) Ltd

MIX
Paper | Supporting
responsible forestry
FSC™ C007454

This book contains FSC™ certified paper and other controlled sources
to ensure responsible forest management.

For more information visit: www.harpercollins.co.uk/green

*For all the very special people I've met through work
But mostly for Richard Swainson
Miss the chats, miss the laughs, miss you*

Chapter 1

1 December

Diane knew she should feel lucky to live and work in London, especially during the festive season, with its sparkling lights, magical displays and historic monuments lit up like Christmas trees. But Diane didn't feel lucky. Especially not today, on the first day of December, as she headed into work across Westminster Bridge, the wind biting her frozen cheeks, red double-decker buses splashing the previous night's rain over her ankles, and a million stressful thoughts in her head as to how the hell she was going to pull off Christmas this year. There was just so much to do between now and the big day. Shopping lists, food lists, card lists, visits lists, lists lists . . . bloody lists! When had Christmas become just one massive list of stuff to do on top of all the other massive lists of stuff to do? As she pushed open the century-old oak doors to the Bermondsey Council building and walked past the pathetically decorated tree in the foyer, she made a mental note to add to a list somewhere to book her supermarket Christmas food delivery slot and to make sure her husband could pick up their daughter from university.

But first and foremost, coffee – essential to get through any day working in the Accounts Department at Bermondsey Council. She strode down the corridor to the alcove containing the recently installed coffee machine, scrabbled around in her pocket for her coffee card and slotted it into the hole.

Then Diane kicked the coffee machine very hard.

'For crying out loud, what does a woman have to do to get a crappy coffee out of this crappy machine, for goodness' sake!'

'Are you sure you have enough credits on your card?' came a voice from behind her.

She turned round and saw Kevin from HR, smiling with his head on one side, talking to her as though she was an elderly relative, despite the fact she was only just old enough to be his mother – possibly.

'Why can't we just have a kettle like we used to?' she asked him.

'Something to do with taxable benefits,' he said. 'And Facilities management didn't have a code for maintenance, and the cleaners came to us up in arms because they were sick of washing up dirty coffee mugs, despite the fact they'd put twenty-five signs up in the kitchen telling everyone they would be murdered if they didn't wash their own. But the straw that really broke the camel's back was when Tim from downstairs punched Matt from Security because he caught him nicking some of his milk out the shared fridge. At the resulting tribunal Tim said bringing his own milk into the office was causing him significant anxiety through fear of other people taking it, which had led to his aggressive behaviour. He's currently off sick with stress.'

Diane snorted. She didn't have time for this. 'So, because of all that pathetic behaviour, the kettle has been taken away and now we have rubbish coffee that costs a fortune, with crappy dried milk in plastic cups!' She looked at Kevin. 'I'm going to buy a kettle and put one in my office.'

'No, no, can't do that,' said Kevin, shaking his head.

'Why not?'

'Only insured for kitchen equipment in the kitchen.'

'I'll bring my own kettle in then, and put it in the kitchen.'

'No, can't do that, I'm afraid. The recommendation from the tribunal with Tim was that kettles should no longer be allowed in the building.'

'Bloody hell!' exclaimed Diane. 'How am I supposed to work without coffee!'

'Why don't you have one of my credits and you can give me one back another time?' He took her defective card out of the machine and replaced it with his own. 'How do you want it?'

'From a kettle?'

Kevin did not reply.

'Black, no sugar,' she said eventually. 'Thank you.'

He handed over the coffee. 'So I'll be up with Jolene at about half past nine, after I've done the basic induction.'

Diane stared back at him. 'Jolene?' she said, shaking her head.

'Your new graduate trainee. Starts today. I did email you.'

Diane continued to stare blankly. She took her phone out of her suit pocket and did a quick search. Kevin did the same. They stood opposite each other frantically tapping at their phones.

'You did,' breathed Diane.

'In October,' muttered Kevin, 'and last week.'

Diane shook her head. 'Bollocks,' she muttered under her breath. 'Why did you give it a subject title of "Graduate Training Scheme"? I just thought it was one of those hideous, covering-your-arse-type emails that had nothing useful in it.'

She looked up at Kevin, who was smiling in a weird way at her.

'Look, Diane,' he said, touching her arm lightly. She stared at his hand. Was this some weird new HR ritual? 'Diane,' he repeated softly. 'I know that you celebrated a big birthday last year and, well—'

'Do you mean my fiftieth?'

'Well, yes.' He looked around awkwardly, as though he didn't want anyone to overhear their conversation.

'What's that got to do with anything?'

'Well, it's just that, well – how do I put it? – well, they sent me on a menopause- awareness course—'

'They sent *you* on one? Why you? Why not me? You are unlikely to experience it, are you not?'

'It was about awareness in the workplace. You know, about being sympathetic to women who may be suffering and what symptoms to look out for, and I just want you to know that your outbursts of anger and rage, alongside signs of forgetfulness, well, if there is anything I can do to support you, I'm here. That's all I'm saying.' He squeezed her arm. She pulled it away sharply and drew herself up to her near five foot ten inches in patent leather heels. She tapped her immaculate platinum-blond updo and then smoothed down the pencil skirt of her perfectly fitted black suit.

'My outbursts of anger and rage, as you call them, are not due to me going through the menopause. My anger and rage are entirely caused by the idiots I work with and *not* my own biology. My anger and rage are down to the fact that my colleagues have decreed that I'm not allowed to have my own bloody stupid kettle. And as for forgetfulness, I cannot read all the twenty thousand emails your department churns out needlessly every five minutes, so when it's important you had better start making sure they stand out. How dare you blame the biological make-up of a woman rather than your own incompetence?'

Kevin quivered. He took a step back and swallowed. 'I'm sorry,' he whispered.

'So you should be,' Diane hissed back. 'Bring her to my office at ten o'clock. We'll do our best to have something organised for her by then.'

'OK.'

'What's her name again?'

'Jolene.'

'Jolene?'

'Jolene.'

'Jolene.'

'Jesus, Mary and Joseph,' muttered Diane, and stalked off, grabbing the coffee out of Kevin's hand as she went. 'That's all I need.'

'The mayor is chasing you,' was the news that greeted Diane when she finally got to the Accounts Department office, lukewarm coffee in hand. 'He's rung four times already this morning,' Jerry told her as she hung up her coat.

It was a long oblong office off the main corridor in the crumbling building that housed the vast majority of the inmates at Bermondsey Council, which looked after around twenty square miles of the city of London. They had windows, which was a plus. There were four desks and a meeting table scattered around the room, and a long line of filing cabinets standing against the back wall. Quite what was in them nobody really knew, since no one had used a filing cabinet since 2012 and now all documents were stored in the sky somewhere. However, opening them would require someone to decide what to do with their contents and nobody really knew whose decision that was. Consequently they remained closed, like graves to a bygone era of accounting.

'What did he want?' Diane asked Jerry, pausing outside the door to her own office, which occupied one end of the oblong.

'He wants to know if we have anything in the budget left to be able to throw a Christmas party for some kids in the area,' replied Jerry. 'Of course, he doesn't

6

actually mean a party. What he means is, he wants a photo op, given we are heading towards elections. A few pictures of him with grateful children splashed over the front of the *Gazette* wouldn't do him any harm, would it? Especially after being photographed dropping his kids off at private school in a Range Rover.'

Jerry – highly dependable, if opinionated – was Diane's number two in the department. She didn't know what she would do without him.

'Did you tell him about the Cost of Christmas project?' she asked.

'I did,' replied Jerry. 'I told him that we were about to review if we can even afford fairy lights on the tree in the park next year. So it didn't seem likely there would be any money to throw a community party.'

'What did he say?'

'He said you can't place a value on putting smiles on young people's faces during the festive period.'

'It's bugger all to do with putting smiles on children's faces and everything to do with putting a smile on his face when he gets re-elected.'

'I said you'd call him back,' Jerry said. 'Sorry. You know he won't listen to me.'

'No, no, that's fine. I'll call him. See where he thinks we can conjure up this mythical money. Maybe he has something in his budget he can sacrifice. Print me off his accounts and let's see if we can find something.'

'Sure,' said Jerry. He paused then asked her an unusual question. 'So, what are you up to this weekend?'

Diane looked up at him in surprise. She and Jerry didn't often exchange personal life pleasantries, despite the fact they'd worked together for over five years. She knew the basics, of course. Born in Missouri, USA, he'd moved to London in his late twenties for the culture and because he thought it would be easier to come out as gay. Owner of a UK passport due to his British mum, he'd done evening classes in accountancy and had worked at several councils across the city. He had amazing knowledge of the processes within local government, making him a very valuable member of Diane's team. Also, single men were very handy to have in the department as they didn't mind working late or coming in early. That is, so far as she knew he was single. He didn't talk much in the office about his private life, which is why she was so startled by the question.

'Oh, the usual,' she replied. 'Housework, food shopping, trying to get my teenage daughter to communicate with me whilst she lives it up at uni. You?'

'Nothing much,' replied Jerry. 'Might try and take in a play and there's a new exhibition I must see at the Tate. Sunday I'll probably treat myself to brunch at Borough Market seeing as I've finished my Christmas shopping.'

'What!' exclaimed Diane. 'Seriously? How do you do that?' She put her head in her hands. She really didn't need to hear that someone had finished their Christmas shopping.

'It's easy,' said Jerry. 'It's called having only one sibling, only one parent still alive and not being in a relationship. Simplifies Christmas no end.'

Diane looked up at him. He looked as distressed

about the smallness of his Christmas as she felt about the magnitude of hers. Time to get off Christmas and back to work.

'Now, I have to go to a meeting,' she told Jerry, 'but Kevin will be arriving shortly with our new graduate trainee—'

'New graduate trainee! Since when?'

'Since Kevin decided to half-tell me in emails buried by a landslide of emails covering personal injury liability and working hours directives. Anyway, can you look after her this morning? Conjure up some reading material. Organise a laptop for her. Stuff like that. Or get Yang to do it.'

Diane looked over at Yang, who had been sitting opposite Jerry the whole time. He had headphones on and was staring at a spreadsheet on his computer as he bobbed his head rhythmically up and down. Yang was nearly twenty years younger than Jerry and pretty much his exact opposite. Yang was wearing a yellow checked shirt covered by a navy V-necked sweater that stretched over his slightly rotund belly. His wire-rimmed glasses completed the look of a young man trying and failing to be fashionable. This contrasted heavily with Jerry's suit trousers, slim-fit collared shirt, ironed to perfection, and the shiniest leather brogues Diane had ever seen.

'I've got Yang looking at the autumn statements, which will take him all day, so I'll sort the trainee,' said Jerry. 'Where is she going to sit?'

'Barney's not in today, so she can sit at his desk for now. Call Facilities and ask them if they have a desk they can bring up.'

'Sure,' nodded Jerry. 'What's her name, by the way?' He picked up a pen ready to write it down.

'Jolene,' said Diane.

'Jolene?' he asked, looking up.

'Jolene,' replied Diane, nodding.

'Joleeeeeeeene,' sang out Jerry, unable to help himself.

'I'm sure she's never heard that before,' said Diane, raising her eyebrows. 'God, I hope she's not some basket case. We've got enough to do without having to babysit some twenty-something who thinks that the world of work owes her a good time rather than being the thankless tedious grind that it actually is. Speaking of which, I'll see you after the Sanitation Board Meeting.'

Chapter 2

It was 9.30 a.m. and Jolene was alone in a small room, wearing headphones and staring at a screen on the first day of her new job as a graduate trainee working for Bermondsey Council. This did not bode well. She'd been so excited before she left home. She'd changed her outfit several times whilst trying to get advice via a Zoom call from her uni friends scattered all over the country. Not that they were much help. Dress-code conformity was not their strong point, particularly in the workplace. A group of outliers, they had bonded over their shared loathing of school, where, without exception, they had been bullied and harassed for not conforming to the views of the dominant tribe of skinny, blonde, short-skirted, spray-tanned, contoured-up-to-their-eyeballs girls that seemed to rule every school in the country. Jolene, with her lumpy figure, her pink plaited hair and her colour-clashing, Disney-sprinkled wardrobe, had never been more delighted to find an abundance of men and women like her, when she'd got to uni. She had found her tribe . . . finally, and it had been heartbreaking to leave them when she graduated. But there they all were, at the other end of the Zoom call that morning, and had approved her choice of a 'discreet' red and green shirt with the tiniest of Mickey Mouse silhouettes wearing a Christmas hat. It was 1 December, after all, and Disney and Christmas were Jolene's two favourite things.

Her mum had shown some slight concern over her chosen outfit as she waved goodbye from their South Croydon home in the depths of outer London. She'd looked her up and down as she often did at the sight of Jolene leaving the house.

'Just try and remember to not be too much,' her mother said.

'Too much of what?' replied Jolene.

'Just too much. You know what I mean. Be yourself, but maybe operate at fifty per cent for the first few days – just whilst they get used to you.'

'Sure,' nodded Jolene. She wasn't really sure what her mum meant. All she knew was she was so excited to meet who she was going to be working with and get to know them and be part of a team. So very, very excited!

And yet here she was in the office, on day one, commencing learning about the health and safety practices of Bermondsey Council in a tiny office on her own, not a soul to be seen.

Kevin had whisked her through the HR Department where a smattering of pallid-looking employees raised their heads and scanned her up and down, much as her mother had done on the doorstep. He'd said they'd use his boss's office to get some peace and quiet, but the main office was as quiet as a graveyard so she really didn't think it was necessary.

'Where is everybody?' she'd asked, when Kevin arrived back with a coffee in a plastic cup, having left her alone for at least ten minutes staring at the walls.

'Oh, a lot of people work from home on a Friday. You know, since Covid.'

She didn't know. Why would anyone in their right mind choose to work from home? Alone.

'I just bumped into your new boss, actually,' he continued. 'They're not quite ready for you yet so I'll take you through the welcome pack, then you can sit and do the health and safety video.'

Not quite ready, thought Jolene. That sounded hopeful. Maybe they were organising a welcome committee. She glanced out at the dormant HR office. Accounts was bound to be livelier than this. More up for it. She bet any money they were just putting the finishing touches to the Christmas decorations in the office. Unlike HR, who didn't seem to have started yet.

By 10.15 a.m. Jolene was sitting in the corner of the Accounts Department, wearing headphones and staring at a screen, having been told to study the council website. As if she hadn't fully researched that in preparation for her extensive interview some weeks ago. Kevin had delivered her to the department where she was supposed to meet her new boss, Diane, except she wasn't there, and apparently someone called Jerry was supposed to look after her, but he wasn't there either, so she had been left with someone called Yang, who looked like he was in his early thirties and had a lovely bright yellow checked shirt on.

'I'm Yang,' he said. 'Sorry, everyone else is out at the moment. Jerry said to tell you to familiarise yourself with the council website if he wasn't back, but he won't be long. He just got called in to see the mayor about Christmas or something. Anyway, take a seat. Can I get you a drink?'

Jolene shook her head. The coffee from the machine had been really bad. She couldn't face that again. She slowly put on the headphones that Yang had indicated, which could have been handcuffs as she was again confined to a world where only she existed in front of a screen. She'd sat there for five minutes, which gave her time to take in the dismally dull surroundings: again, no Christmas decorations to be seen, not even an Advent calendar. Jerry had eventually arrived back full of apologies, saying he'd been summoned to the mayor's office. Jolene said that sounded exciting and Jerry said it was about as exciting as the fifth movie in any film franchise. That cheered Jolene up. She thought that was really funny, although perhaps she'd laughed too hard. Yang took off his headphones and asked what was the joke and she told him, and he'd raised his eyebrows as if to say it was a typical Jerry joke. He then said, 'I like your shirt,' nodding at Mickey Mouse in his Santa hat in repeat on her green shirt. She was glad to have his approval as it seemed no one else was making any kind of festive efforts. Jerry then explained that they weren't aware that she was joining the department until that morning, which was why she was sitting at Barney's desk and researching the council website until they got organised. Barney's chair was very low and Jolene deduced he must be a short older man, given the height of the chair and framed photograph of an old woman eating an ice cream taking pride of place on his desk.

After Jolene's twenty minutes of further study of the pest-control section of the website, which she thought might come in handy at some point, a woman came bustling through the door, red in the face, unfolding a scarf from around her neck.

'Sorry I'm late,' she gasped.

Jolene took her headphones off, hopeful that the woman might talk to her. She was youngish, maybe late twenties. She was pretty, with dark straight hair, but she didn't make the most of it. She wore a short skirt and opaque tights with knee-high boots and a pink cardigan over a white T-shirt. She looked extremely harassed and stressed. Yang took off his headphones and looked at her, concerned.

'Everything all right?' he asked.

'Where do I start?' said the woman. 'Apparently Grace needed to take her Nativity costume in today, only she didn't tell me, did she? What does she think I am? A mind reader? She's not even told me what she is, so I had to wing it and take in a pillowcase and a tea towel and pray she was a shepherd.'

'Poor shepherds,' said Jerry, shaking his head. 'By far the worst costume of all the Nativity characters. Imagine a sack, and a tea towel over your head? My worst nightmare.'

15

'She isn't a shepherd, she's a donkey,' said the woman.

'I take it back,' replied Jerry. 'Grey fur – too hot and would wash any complexion out.'

'Oh, hello,' said the woman, suddenly noticing Jolene.

'I'm Jolene,' said Jolene, getting up and offering her hand.

'Hello, Jolene. I'm Stacey,' replied the woman.

'It's an HR screw-up,' explained Jerry. 'Jolene is our new graduate trainee. We only found out this morning.'

'What!' said Stacey, spinning round to face Jerry. 'Are you serious? Really? Graduate trainee? They're going to get me to train her up and then sack me, aren't they? I can see it happening now. Just because I don't have a degree. I'll be first out. I just know it. This is all I need. I'll be gone by Christmas!'

Jolene watched as Stacey sat down at her desk and put her head in her hands.

'Don't be silly,' Yang said to Stacey gently. 'They won't get rid of you. It'll be fine.' He put a reassuring hand on her shoulder.

'It's all right for you to say,' she said, turning to him. 'You've got a degree, and you've passed all those accounting exams. I'm always going to be first one out when push comes to shove.'

'I haven't passed any accounting exams,' said Jolene. 'I'm sure I'm not here to push you out of a job. That's not how it works, is it?'

Stacey looked at her as her shoulders drooped. 'Is this your first job?' she asked.

16

Jolene nodded.

'It's exactly how it works. You'll see. Is that Mickey Mouse in a Santa hat on your top?' Stacey asked.

'Er, yes,' Jolene replied. 'I thought, seeing as Christmas is coming, it would be all right to wear it.'

'Christmas is coming!' said Stacey, wide eyed.

'Yes,' said Jolene. 'It's 1 December.' She looked around, feeling slightly bewildered. 'Did you open your Advent calendar this morning?'

'Er, no. I don't have an Advent calendar,' said Stacey. 'I don't want to be reminded with a sickly sweet, low-quality chocolate-shaped bauble every single morning that it's Christmas.'

'But,' said Jolene, confused, 'Christmas is great. I love Christmas.'

Stacey stared at her as though she had landed from the North Pole. 'Lucky you,' she said, shaking her head. 'I'm very happy that it brings you such joy.'

'Doesn't it bring you joy?'

'No.'

'How come?' Jolene had never met anyone before who didn't like Christmas.

'Where do I start with how bad Christmas is for my life?' said Stacey, with a sigh, leaning back in her chair. 'Sorry, what was your name again?'

'Jolene.'

'Jolene?'

'Jolene.'

'Joleeeeeeeene,' sang out Jerry, unable to help himself.

Jolene grinned at Jerry. She liked it when people did that. It was like having a personal jingle.

17

'Jolene,' said Stacey, 'I'm a single mum to a seven-year-old daughter, so really Christmas just equals disappointment. My daughter will be disappointed because I can't afford the presents she really wants. Then she'll be disappointed that yet again I can't afford a real tree, because she longs to smell a Christmas tree in our house. Then there's a whole world of disappointment to come from her shitbag father. She will sit by the window of our flat on Christmas Eve hoping to see her father arrive, even though he never has before. Then there will be the absolutely hideous Christmas lunch at my mum's, when I'll take all the food round because she'll be too drunk to cook, she'll ask me for money the moment I get through the door, whilst my two waster brothers sit on the sofa doing sod all except smoke dope. Now tell me why I should look forward to Christmas,' Stacey asked Jolene. 'Christmas, the most stressful, most depressing time of year that ever existed.'

Jolene stared at Stacey. She didn't know what to say. How awful that Christmas could bring despair like this.

'I'm so sorry for your loss of Christmas,' said Jolene, startled.

Stacey stared back at her again as though she had grown reindeer antlers. Her phone suddenly started to buzz in her hand. 'Bloody hell, it's the school. What's she done now? I only left her half an hour ago.' She pressed a button on her phone and held it to her ear.

'Hello, Stacey Bentley speaking.'

She went quiet and listened. First nodding and then shaking her head. Then she sighed.

'I can't leave work now. I've only just got in. And I don't have a donkey tail to hand, despite what she might have told you, so just tell her she needs to improvise . . . Did she now?' Stacey reached down, picked a large tote bag up off the floor and looked inside. She pulled out a lunch box with Barbie on it. 'I'll pop it over now,' she sighed. She ended the call.

'The little minx put her lunch in my bag so I'd have to go back.' Stacey shook her head, looking defeated. 'I'll be half an hour,' she said to Jerry. 'I'll work later one day next week and put Grace into After School Club.'

Jerry nodded. 'Just so you know, the team meeting has been shifted to Monday, and don't forget that Christmas is on the agenda.'

'Brilliant!' said Stacey. 'Just to add insult to injury. Cannot wait!' She grabbed her coat and scarf.

Jolene watched her leave. All she could think about was how someone could possibly hate Christmas that much.

'You'll be attending the team meeting too,' Jerry told Jolene.

'Oh, great. What happens in those?' she asked.

'We talk about department budgets, mainly. It'll go over your head for a bit, but you'll get into it.'

'And Christmas?' asked Jolene. 'You mentioned Christmas?'

'Well, it is that time of year,' he replied.

'I could have a think about Christmas, if that would be helpful?' she offered.

19

Jerry looked at her puzzled, as though he couldn't understand why she was showing any enthusiasm.

'If you like,' said Jerry. 'Sure. Look, I'm really sorry, but I've got to go to another meeting. Ask Yang about Christmas. He'll fill you in.'

Yang had put his headphones back on the minute Stacey had left the room. She wondered what he was listening to. Maybe it was Christmas music.

She gave him a half-wave, hoping to get his attention. She didn't. She got up and waved her hand in front of his screen. He jumped and then removed his headphones.

'Can I help you?' he asked politely.

'Jerry said I could ask you about Christmas.'

'What about Christmas? I mean, I don't actually celebrate Christmas. You know, being Chinese and all that.'

'Oh, right, yes of course. Of course. Sorry. Must be so weird having it all around you and not taking part. Do you feel left out?'

'No, not really,' said Yang. 'We do our own thing on Christmas Day.'

'Oh, what's that then? If you don't mind me asking.'

'Well, typically we eat Chinese food. My mum and dad have a restaurant in China Town so we tend to go there.'

'How cool. Do you have crackers?'

'Er, no. Just fortune cookies.'

Jolene nodded. 'Bit like crackers, I guess.'

'I suppose.'

'Well, you pull them apart and they have something written inside. No toy, though.'

'Or paper hat. Or snapper,' said Yang. 'Look, I've got to get this spreadsheet checked by lunchtime, sorry.'

'Oh God, yes, sorry. So you can't tell me about Christmas then?'

'No, sorry. Sorry.' He put his headphones back on.

Never mind, thought Jolene. She could think about Christmas all by herself, no problem. She went back to her seat. Maybe she could even change Stacey's low opinion of it. Had to be worth a shot. She scrolled her mouse across the screen, clicked off the council website, found PowerPoint and opened up a blank sheet. Things were looking up. Her first day and she was being paid to think about Christmas.

Chapter 3

'You were a bit harsh on the new girl,' Jerry said to Stacey as they sat together on the top deck of the bus later that evening and stared out at the inky-black night sky.

'I know,' said Stacey. 'I feel bad now but, well, she's got everything I haven't, hasn't she? A degree, her freedom and all that excitement over Christmas. I just couldn't stomach it. I mean, I dream of enjoying Christmas but it's just one big fat pain in the backside, as far as I'm concerned.'

'Well, bah humbug to you,' said Jerry. 'I'll say hello to the Grinch when I next see him, shall I?'

Stacey shook her head. 'I know I sound like such a misery but Christmas is already ruined for me.' She turned to look at Jerry. 'Freddie got engaged.'

'Grace's dad?'

'Yeah, and it's all over bloody Instagram. He took her to Lapland and proposed. Can you believe it! I struggle to get child support out of him or even buy Grace a Christmas present, but he'll buy a woman he met online six months ago a diamond ring and take her to see Santa.'

'That's harsh,' agreed Jerry.

Stacey struggled to stop a tear falling down her face.

'And they're planning a super-quick wedding. Her parents are loaded, apparently. I reckon she's pregnant and she wants skinny designer-dress photos, not fat bloaty ones.'

'Oh, Stacey, I'm sorry,' said Jerry. 'That's a lot to deal with.'

'It is,' she sniffed. 'All I see is him swanning around having a great time, going here, there and everywhere, and I'm stuck at home. He never sees Grace, never offers to have her. He couldn't give a damn. And in the meantime, I'm rotting in a tiny flat at twenty-nine years old and my only dinner date is a seven-year-old with possible ADHD and a nut allergy. Don't get me wrong, I don't regret having Grace for one minute – I have no idea what I would do without her – but . . . but I *need* a life. I think I might be going slightly mad. I *need* to get out more. Just once every so often. I don't need to be a party animal – those days are gone – but I want to feel like I'm twenty-nine, not forty-nine, and go to Christmas parties and get hammered on cheap champagne and then snog someone under the mistletoe. Now that would really make my Christmas.'

'Sounds wonderful,' said Jerry.

'No sex, though,' stated Stacey. 'Absolutely no sex. Did you know that Grace was conceived on Christmas Eve?'

'No, you have never told me that.'

'I blame George Michael,' she continued. 'If he hadn't recorded "Last Christmas" I wouldn't have gone all weak at the knees and succumbed to Freddie's non-existent charms in Ellie's spare room.'

'Too much information,' said Jerry. 'But George Michael does have a lot to answer for, God rest his soul.'

Stacey nodded. 'They should ban sex at Christmas. All that slush and romance weakens your defences. December should be kissing only month. No one should be allowed to have sex at Christmas.'

'Well, there's a rule I would have no problems keeping.'

'Oh, I'm sorry,' said Stacey, turning to him. 'I forgot to ask about your self-inflicted celibacy.'

'No need to apologise. But you're right, the festive season makes it much harder not to have sex. Everyone else seems to be happily falling in love under fairy lights and mistletoe and then having sex to George Michael, but not me.'

'Has he still not made a move – seriously – coffee-shop man? How long has it been now?'

'Oh, four months, three weeks, seven days, four hours and thirty-five minutes, to almost quote the goddess that is Laura Linney.'

'Wow. I'm sorry. That is tragic,' said Stacey. 'How often do you see him?'

'Every single day after work. Ever since he walked through the door of my coffee shop and I complimented him on his brogues and we didn't stop talking for an hour and he said he hoped to see me again and I said I come here every day after work and then he said, well, I'll see you tomorrow then. And we shared a look. I'll never forget that look. We both knew he would definitely be coming to see me the next day. And he did. And the next day and every day since. I mean, who does that unless they're interested? I think I'm giving the right signals and the chemistry seems so good and we get on soooo well and we talk – we have the best conversations, honestly we do – but the moment I think he's going to make a move, ask me out on a proper date or something, he runs off like a startled rabbit. Like he's scared of something.'

'You could make the first move?'

Jerry went bright red.

'Oh, I couldn't,' he said. 'I just can't. I need it to come from him. I mean, if I ask him and he says no because I've read it all wrong, then he may never come into the coffee shop again and then I'd have lost him as a friend too.'

'You need to get them to play "Last Christmas" on repeat in the coffee shop, and if that doesn't get him to come on to you then you're done. There isn't a romantic bone in his body as far as you're concerned.'

'Maybe,' said Jerry. 'I fear I'm destined to be alone under the mistletoe for Christmas yet again, eating my Christmas lunch for one whilst pining for the man of my dreams.'

'You and me both, mister,' said Stacey, resting her head on his shoulder. 'You and me both.'

Chapter 4

Diane was staring at a screen at her kitchen table. Her finger poised over the mouse. She felt anxious and nervous. This moment could actually make or break Christmas. This moment could either mean a whole load of Christmas stress evaporated in a second or she would spend the next few weeks with an awful feeling in the pit of her stomach.

She checked her watch – 11.59 p.m. One minute to go until success or failure.

She heard the front door click. Leon back, trying to sneak in, thinking she'd be asleep. The door to the kitchen swung open and she noted the look of surprise-slash-horror that she was still up.

'Back late?' she asked as casually as she could.

'Oh, er, I went out with the cast for a drink after we were all done. It was Baz's birthday so I thought I'd better go along just to make sure he didn't get hammered and so couldn't make the matinée tomorrow.'

'And did he?'

'What?'

'Get hammered?'

'Of course he did, he's a raging alcoholic. If he wasn't so damn good at being a pantomime dame I never would have cast him. No one can wear a wig encrusted with replicas of the entire crown jewels as well as Baz can. Still, at least I know he's tucked up in bed. We shared a taxi home.'

'Just you,' she asked casually.

'Yes, well, me, Baz and Amy – you know, my assistant director.'

Diane took note of the use of 'my' rather than 'the'.

'Oh, you've worked with her before, haven't you?'

'Yes, a few times. You remember she worked with me at The Regents Theatre at the end of the summer.'

Diane did remember. Only too well. Something seemed to have shifted in their marriage since then. It was barely perceptible but it was something. He became actually a bit happier, a bit more relaxed. She knew she hadn't changed – she was still constantly mildly frustrated and resentful of what she perceived to be his much easier role in their marriage, which clouded many of their interactions. As they'd made the slow descent into autumn he had listened even less when she complained; allowed it to glide over him even more. It puzzled and vexed her. Why was he allowed to be happier when she felt as if she was getting more miserable?

'Bloody hell,' she said, slamming her hand down on the kitchen table as she glanced back down at her screen.

'What is it?' asked Leon.

'It's 12.04 a.m., that's what it is.' She frantically pushed keys on her laptop.

'Come on, you bastard,' she screeched at the screen. 'Stop winding me up and access the damn screen.'

'Can I help?' asked Leon.

Diane couldn't even look at him. It was all his fault. Coming home at midnight and distracting her. She thought she had it all organised. All planned, and now Christmas was ruined.

She gasped as the small disc in the middle of the screen stopped whirring and a new screen appeared, showing a raft of dates and times and lots of little boxes saying the worst words that Diane could possibly imagine.

'NOT AVAILABLE'.

Already, at 12.07 a.m., there were no food delivery slots available for the whole of Christmas week from the supermarket. This was a disaster of epic proportions.

'What's wrong?' asked Leon. She turned the screen to face him.

'I don't understand what that is,' he said.

Diane put her head in her hands in despair yet again. How could her husband have never seen a supermarket delivery schedule screen? He'd lived through a pandemic, for goodness' sake. It wasn't like he was a key worker or anything. Although she suspected Leon thought the role of theatre director was key. He'd sat on his arse all day every day, mostly running online rehearsals for shows that never happened. Keeping his hand in is what he had told her, whilst she slogged her way through countless council meetings, working out plans for opening buildings for vaccinations or what to do with the homeless. But had she never once got him to do the online food shop? What on earth had she been thinking?

She looked at him.

'That screen means we will have to go to a super-market in person, in Christmas week. Do you have any idea what kind of hell that is?'

'Can't you get a delivery?'

'That's what I've just been trying to do. They're all booked up.'

'Can't you try a different supermarket?'

'They'll be booked up too.'

'That's a shame.' He turned away.

'Perhaps we could go on the Wednesday really early in the morning – before it gets busy,' she mused.

'The Wednesday before Christmas?'

'Yes.'

'I won't be able to help you there. Wednesday is matinée day. You know how tiring those days are.'

Diane looked at him. Leon was directing *Snow White and the Seven Elves* in the West End. A fairy tale crossed with that most British of Christmas traditions, the pantomime. A very curious mixture of storytelling, singing, slapstick comedy and rampant innuendo. If you listened to Leon, it was the most exhausting thing he had ever directed, but it wasn't as if he was acting in the pantomime or anything. From what she could tell, he just watched at this stage. What was tiring about that?

'Well, maybe Tuesday then?'

'We'll see,' he said, running himself a glass of water from the tap. 'If I still have a full cast intact then I might be all right.'

Diane looked down at the list of jobs next to her. 'Book supermarket slot' was right at the top. Epic fail already. She scanned down the rest of the list.

'Any ideas for your mum and dad?' she asked Leon.

'What for?'

'Er, Christmas, of course.'

He shrugged. 'Not a clue.'

Diane breathed through her nostrils.

'What about your sister's kids?'

'How should I know?' he asked. 'How old are they again? Twelvish?'

'Fifteen and seventeen,' said Diane.

'Right,' nodded Leon. 'Won't cash do?'

'Your sister never gives Chloe cash.'

'So.'

'So, she makes an effort. So should we.'

'That's all well and good for her – she's not trying to stage a pantomime.'

'No, she's merely trying to save lives through her easy job as a surgeon in a hospital.'

'Are you being sarcastic?'

Diane said nothing.

'It's just such a busy time for me, Christmas.'

But you've got time to go for drinks after work practically every night and get taxis home with Amy, thought Diane.

Diane glanced down at her list again.

'When shall we visit your parents?' she asked.

Leon shrugged again. 'Can't we leave it until the new year?'

'Can you fetch Chloe from uni a week on Monday?'

'No.'

'But you don't have any performances on a Monday, do you?'

'Precisely. I need to sleep on Mondays during panto season. Can't you go?'

Diane would love to go. Quite frankly, their daughter coming home for Christmas was the only thing that Diane was looking forward to, regarding the festive period. Chloe all to themselves. The family back together. Who knew, it might even help build some much-needed warmth between her and Leon. She couldn't wait. She would have loved to have picked her up but there was no way she could afford the time off.

'I'm at work.'

'Can't you take a day off?'

'No. I've got a budget cuts meeting I cannot get out of. And you're not at work anyway. So I thought you could fetch her.'

'It will seriously kill me if I have to drive to Brighton and back. I'm just so busy,' replied Leon.

Diane looked down at her list of everything she needed to do to prepare for Christmas. It had forty-two items on it.

'Can't she get the train?' asked Leon.

'She's got to clear her room because they have some sort of conference in after New Year.'

'Well, let's have a think about that one then,' said Leon. 'I need to go to bed. I'm shattered.'

Diane watched him leave the room, abandoning her with the list of things to do for Christmas that he would no doubt avoid getting involved in in any way. He'd become very good at that – avoiding getting involved. She couldn't remember the last time he'd asked how things were for her. What was she thinking? What was she feeling? Was she OK? Maybe he didn't ask because he didn't want to know the answer. Or maybe he didn't care. Too wrapped up in what was going on in his life to think about how she was doing.

Diane picked up her pen and added number forty-three to her Christmas prep list.

43. Book day off a week Monday to pick up Chloe.

Then she added number forty-four.

44. Get up at 5 a.m. Wednesday before Christmas and go and do the food shop.

Chapter 5

Jolene couldn't have been more excited, if also slightly nervous, as she carefully unpacked her personal laptop from her bag the following Monday morning.

She'd spent the whole weekend preparing her presentation. She hoped her idea would go down well. In the absence of any clear direction on what they would be discussing regarding Christmas in the team meeting, she'd decided to think about how she could contribute to the celebration of Christmas within the department. She thought this would be a really good way to show she was a good asset to the team. That she was keen to get involved and fit in. And she was good at organising stuff like that. She'd been social secretary of her college and she'd done a great job of it. Everyone said so. She'd taken care to avoid the usual ways she envisaged that co-workers celebrate Christmas in London. Ice skating at Somerset House, themed party nights in Soho restaurants, listening to carols in St Paul's. Surely someone would have come up with one of those ideas already. No, she needed to complement whatever plans were already in place, not tread on the toes of someone who may already have organised something.

She'd looked in the mirror before she left. She'd put on what she deemed to be a subtle Christmas jumper today since she'd not spotted anyone else in the building wearing any festive attire on her first day. This one had silver snowflakes and gold baubles on it and was devoid of any Disney magic. Much more discreet. She'd save her more full-on Christmas clothing for closer to the big day.

'Morning everyone,' said Diane, once they had all gathered round the small meeting table in her office. 'When did you go for a Starbucks?' she asked Jerry, when she spotted his branded paper cup.

'I got it on my way in. I think I'm going to talk to the Union rep about getting the kettle in the kitchen reinstated. I'm going to be bankrupt and very fat by the end of the year if I keep going to Starbucks and buying their Eggnog Latte. I could sue! It's just outrageously priced, but outrageously good.'

'Can I try some?' asked Yang.

'If you like,' shrugged Jerry.

Yang took a sip and pulled a face.

'Does it have egg in it? It tastes weird.'

'I doubt an Eggnog Latte has egg in it, no.'

'I don't even know what eggnog is,' said Yang.

'Typically, in America, it's rum or brandy mixed with beaten egg, milk and sugar. But I suspect in Starbucks it'll be fake stuff and no alcohol,' said Jerry.

'So fake egg, fake milk and fake sugar and no alcohol – so not really eggnog then?' said Yang.

'No,' replied Jerry. 'Us Americans are pretty good at faking everything, including Christmas!'

'Right, shall we crack on?' said Diane. 'Good to see you back in, Barney. Did you do anything special with your day off?'

Barney leaned back slowly in his chair, blinking at Diane. As Jolene had correctly surmised, he was in his sixties: a short, rotund man in a short-sleeved shirt and a sleeveless jumper. Jerry had introduced them earlier, Barney greeting Jolene with a grunt and a pointed repositioning of the framed photo on his desk. Jolene had been moved to sit at the meeting table in the corner whilst they awaited news of her own desk from Facilities. The chair she had been given was hard and unsupportive, and she was already missing Barney's cushioned high-backed chair with headrest. She wouldn't complain, though. Especially not to Barney. She hadn't seen him smile yet.

Barney coughed. 'I went to the cemetery,' he said.

Jolene watched as everyone at the table looked at each other rather than Barney. There was an awkward silence.

'It's three years,' Barney finally said, looking down at the floor.

'Oh God,' said Diane, 'I'm so sorry. Is it really?'

'Barney, that's terrible. I'm so sorry,' added Jerry.

'Three years already?' gasped Stacey. 'Sorry, Barney.'

'I'm really sorry,' said Yang, momentarily putting his hand on Barney's shoulder.

Barney nodded, not raising his head.

'Er, I'm sorry too,' said Jolene. 'Whatever it is, I'm so sorry that you're sad.'

'Barney's wife, Linda, passed away three years ago,' Diane told Jolene.

'Oh gosh,' said Jolene, her hand leaping to her face. 'So sorry. So, so sorry.'

Yet another awkward silence.

'Right, well,' said Diane eventually, 'as I said, glad to have you back in, Barney.'

Barney nodded and took a sip from his tea mug.

'OK, so we'd better begin,' sighed Diane. 'Lots to get through, including Christmas. So shall we start with you, Stacey? This week's numbers on utilities, please.'

'Yes, yes, of course,' said Stacey, fumbling with a folder. She passed a spreadsheet round and proceeded to talk through it. Jolene desperately tried to follow what she was highlighting, but the acronyms came thick and fast, and she looked up at one point, at a loss as to what was going on. Diane caught her eye and she held her hand up to halt Stacey mid-flow.

'After this meeting, Stacey, will you take Jolene through this sheet separately, explain the KPIs and give her a glossary of the key terms?' she asked.

Stacey looked at Diane with her mouth slightly open. Then gave a very small sigh. 'Yes,' she said. 'Of course.'

'Gosh, thank you,' said Jolene. 'I am struggling to keep up.'

A multitude of spreadsheets containing a maze of numbers were passed around over the next hour. The foreign language continued to be spoken, interspersed with deep sighs and puffing of cheeks, so that Jolene assumed, whatever the pages of numbers told them, it was not good news. She made notes of anything that she was able to grasp, but she doubted any of them would make sense when she read them back.

Eventually they seemed to come to the end of the spreadsheet extravaganza. Diane turned round in her seat and dumped the sheets in her in-tray. Then rolled her sleeves and said the magic words.

'Right, let's get onto Christmas, shall we?'

Jolene perked up in her seat and smoothed down the snowflakes on her jumper.

'So, as you know, the leader of the council has asked us to review the budgets for next year as we need to find some serious savings. All sorts of measures are being looked at, but he's asked us particularly to do a review of what we're spending on Christmas this year and analyse if we think we're getting value for money.'

'Does that mean he's considering cancelling Christmas out of next year's budget?' asked Jerry.

'Yes,' stated Diane. 'I believe so. Unless we can prove that it's essential expenditure.'

Jolene gasped. Her hand even flew to her mouth.

'But you can't cancel Christmas,' she said.

She watched as Stacey gave a small smile, Jerry looked away, and Yang and Barney raised their eyebrows.

She turned to Diane for an answer, panic rising in her throat.

Diane stared back at her for a moment, then carried on.

'We will conduct a full and fair audit of this year's Christmas spend, assessing all expenditure to include the High Street lights and decorations, wage bill for erection and dismantling, electricity costs, the Christmas tree in the square, the light switch-on event, including marketing, security, fencing, litter collection, cost of celebrity switch-on . . .'

Yang burst out laughing. 'I'd hardly call the first person to get chucked off *Love Island* a celebrity,' he said.

'Oh, Henry was just unlucky,' Jolene couldn't help saying. 'He was the nicest one in there by far, just that no one fancied him.'

'Right,' said Diane. 'Thank you for that, Jolene. Where was I . . .?'

'Because he was ginger,' added Jolene. 'All the girls were very shallow this year.'

'Right, thank you,' said Diane. 'So would you say the thousand-pound fee we gave him to switch on the lights was a good use of taxpayers' money?'

Jolene had no idea.

'We spent similar on an expert who occasionally appears on *Antiques Roadshow*, last year,' said Stacey. 'I mean, who watches *Antiques Roadshow*?'

'I do,' said Jerry.

'Oh, right,' said Stacey. 'Sorry.'

'We don't have antiques in the States,' said Jerry flatly. 'You have no idea how lucky you are.'

'Anyway – moving on,' said Diane. 'Stacey and Yang, can you two set up and complete the audit? Get all the costs in and don't forget to include the out-of-season costs, such as storage and maintenance. And then you need to look at how we evaluate the return on our investment in Christmas. What does all that cost achieve? There will of course be tangible benefits, such as increased traffic to the High Street, increased revenue on switch-on night, but you will also need to look at more intangible benefits such as media coverage, satisfaction scores and anything else you can think of. Any ideas anyone?'

Everyone stared back blankly apart from Jolene, who looked at each of the faces in confused wonder.

'Jolene?' said Diane. 'You look like you've got something to say.'

'Well, er, it brings happiness, doesn't it? That is surely a major benefit.'

Everyone looked at her as though she had two heads. Apart from Yang.

'I mean, I don't celebrate Christmas, as you know,' he said. 'But I always thought that was the intention: to bring happiness.'

'Of course it is,' said Jolene. 'And . . . and . . .what better thing to spend taxpayers' money on . . . than bringing happiness?'

Diane, Jerry, Stacey continued to look at her as though a reindeer had just appeared in the building.

'She does have a point,' said Yang. 'Really no one can complain about spending council tax income on happiness, can they?'

Diane threw her head back and laughed. A hearty, throaty laugh.

'I can really see that justification going down a storm at the next council meeting. "Sorry, guys, we've got no money because we've spent it all on happiness,"' she said. 'Get a grip, Yang. You should know better.

39

No one wants to see a headline that we're all more cheerful because we put fairy lights up in the High Street. They want to see lower waiting times at hospitals, better school facilities, lower car parking charges. In any case, we can't put a value on happiness, can we?' Diane looked directly at Jolene.

'Is that because it is priceless?' she uttered, thinking that Diane was waiting for her to comment and she didn't know what else to say.

Diane blinked back at her.

'I guess it is,' she said quietly.

'Linda always loved the lights in the High Street,' said Barney, looking far into the distance. 'When they used to be good, of course,' he said. 'Back in the day they were amazing, a sight to behold. Not any more. They've hardly been worth having since the last time the budget was slashed.'

'Thank you, Barney,' said Diane. 'That's exactly what we need to try and assess. Are they worth having? So, Stacey, Yang, you get cracking. I suggest you get out and about and walk the streets. Take some inventory photos in situ. Get an assessment of the impact of the decorations. Might be worth going to some neighbouring boroughs. See how we compare. How do we stand up against our other councils? You should also talk to your counterparts in other areas, see what they're spending. That would be a useful comparison. Do you want to do that, Yang?'

'Sure,' said Yang, writing in his notepad. 'I'll phone Craig over at Westminster. He'll be able to give me some numbers.'

'Make sure they are actual figures, not just Craig figures,' piped up Stacey. 'You know what he's like.'

'What do you mean?' asked Yang, looking confused. 'What is he like?'

'Averagely good at his job. That's what he's like.'

Yang shifted uncomfortably in his seat. 'He's a really smart guy, actually. If you spoke to him you'd realise he's really nice.'

'Oh, yeah, really nice. He took the job I wanted.'

'I'm sure he didn't do it on purpose,' said Yang.

'Perhaps not. But he only got it because they wanted someone full time rather than flexitime. He had an unfair advantage,' said Stacey.

'What do you mean, unfair?' asked Yang.

'Because he's male, of course.'

'He can't help being male,' replied Yang, looking round the table for support.

'That's what they all say, these males,' said Stacey. 'They can't help it when they give a totally unfair advantage to all men in the job market by creating working conditions that totally exclude all the women out there who are desperately trying to have a career whilst also trying to raise kids. You have no idea how lucky you are to be born male,' Stacey said to Yang.

Yang bit his lip. 'I'm sorry for being male,' he said, swallowing. 'Truly I am.'

'I don't think you need to take it out on Yang,' interjected Diane. 'I keep telling my counterparts in other councils how offering more flexitime can work wonders for recruitment, but it's a slow process.'

'I know, I know,' said Stacey. 'I'm sorry. And I can never thank you enough for allowing me to work the hours I do. You get it. But that's because you've been through it. You understand that I can't leave after 4 p.m., even if it is the most important meeting ever. I can't leave my daughter at the school gate wondering where I am. It just winds me up that men don't get that. They still don't.'

'Well, we're not going to solve the problem of what men don't get at this meeting,' said Diane, gathering up her papers and tapping them on the table. 'Now, can you two, Stacey and Yang, play nicely and I'd like to see a full report on the value of Christmas on my desk before we finish for the holidays. The powers that be are looking to us to make a recommendation as to whether or not to cancel Christmas next year and use it as a major cost saving. So the review must be thorough and robust. Understood?'

'Yes, Diane,' they both muttered.

'Right. Is there any other business or are we all done?' Diane asked.

Jolene looked around desperately. Was that it? Was that the Christmas discussion? Surely not? That the department she had arrived in was looking at whether to cancel her beloved Christmas? This was a total disaster. And weren't they going to talk about what the department was going to do to celebrate Christmas? She so wanted to be a part of it all and it hadn't even been mentioned!

'Yes,' piped up Jerry. 'Speaking of Christmas.'

Jolene held her breath. Maybe this was it. Maybe this was the Christmas discussion she had been waiting for.

'We need to make sure the office is covered between Christmas and New Year so—'

'Please don't put me on over Christmas,' said Stacey. 'I might hate it but I at least want to spend it with my daughter.'

'I'll do it,' said Yang, looking furtively at Stacey.

'You did it last year, Yang. I'll do it,' said Jerry. 'I'll be on my own anyway, so I might as well get paid to be lonely at Christmas.'

'I said I'd do it and I'll do it,' said Yang firmly.

Everyone looked at the floor. There was an awkward silence.

'OK,' said Diane. 'Shall I call this meeting to a close?'

Jolene could feel her heart beating really fast. She was starting to panic. 'But . . . but . . . what about Christmas?' she said.

'We've done Christmas,' stated Diane.

'No, I mean, what about what we're going to do for Christmas? I mean . . . I was assuming that when you said Christmas was on the agenda then we'd be talking about how you . . . we celebrate Christmas – you know, as a team?'

'Oh,' said Diane, looking startled. 'Well, of course, yes. Well, we all have coffee together on our last day before we break up. Yes, we have Christmas Coffee, which you will of course be invited to. Oh, and we do all try to wear a Christmas jumper that day, don't we?' she added.

'I thought we decided to ditch that idea after last year,' moaned Jerry. 'It was such a pain finding one that matched anything I owned.'

'Christmas Coffee?' questioned Jolene.

'Oh, and we also said we'd have Eggnog Lattes this year,' said Jerry. 'Last year's mulled-wine-flavoured herbal tea really did not hit the spot.'

'I don't think I can drink that stuff,' said Yang, pointing at Jerry's cardboard cup.

'Can we claim it on expenses, because I can't afford fancy coffee at Christmas? Not with everything else,' said Stacey.

Jolene couldn't believe her ears. A Christmas coffee? That was their sum total of celebrating Christmas with the people they spend the majority of their lives with. This could not be right.

'Don't you go for an evening out or ice skating or something like that?' asked Jolene tentatively.

'We used to,' said Jerry. 'Then we could never get a night when everyone was free or agree on what we wanted to do, so we gave up.'

'It just got too hard,' said Diane to Jolene. 'Everyone is so busy. It's such a frantic time of year.'

Jolene felt like crying. Last year with her college friends, on the last day of term, they had all hired elf costumes and done a pub crawl around York before descending on a cinema that was showing her favourite film ever – *Elf*. It had been a brilliant night. One of the best. And now here she was, her first Christmas in the world of work and she wasn't going to celebrate with her new colleagues. Her absolute favourite time of year. All offices celebrated Christmas together in some way, surely? How could they dismiss Christmas so readily?

'Of course, if you'd like to organise something then I'm sure everyone would be willing,' Diane said to Jolene.

'Oh, yeah,' said Stacey, 'but just bear in mind that I can't get a babysitter for love nor money, and I can't afford anything fancy. I mean, there is literally nothing I would love more than going to one of those party nights laid on for Christmas – you know, one of those really fancy ones in a London landmark – but I just can't.'

'Yeah, and as I said before, I don't really do Christmas, so nothing too Christmassy, you know,' said Yang.

Jerry nodded. 'I don't do cheesy or tacky, so please no weird stuff with elves or anything. Actually, I think I might have a phobia of elves, so please just avoid elves, whatever you do.'

'And nothing that takes a load of time,' added Diane. 'Christmas is frantic when you have kids arriving home, relatives making demands, a husband who quite frankly is as useful as a chocolate elf. No, nothing that takes time up. I just haven't got time!'

'OK,' nodded Jolene, taking a deep breath. 'So cheap, not time consuming, not too Christmassy and no elves.' She paused. 'I think I have the perfect thing,' she said, opening up her laptop and turning it round to face the team.

They stared back at her open mouthed. She took a deep breath and began.

'I know I'm new at this whole workplace thing, but I thought we would be discussing how, as colleagues, we might celebrate the festive season, so I kind of did a bit of thinking myself.'

45

Her co-workers mostly looked confused and vaguely exasperated.

'I mean, it does seem now that in actual fact none of you are very keen on Christmas, but maybe you have forgotten the real meaning of Christmas. I mean, it is the season to be jolly, after all,' she pressed on.

Diane looked at her watch. Jolene thought she had better hurry along.

'Anyway, I had an idea. As my contribution to the Christmas celebrations. I thought maybe we could do something as simple as . . .' she paused before she pressed the button to display her first slide, '. . . THE SECRET SANTA PROJECT.'

Everyone groaned, apart from Yang.

'I thought I said cheap,' exclaimed Stacey.

'Bloody hell,' said Diane, putting her head into her hands. 'Not another present to buy!'

'We tried it a few years ago,' said Jerry. 'Do you remember? I put my tin of Christmas-pudding-flavoured tea bags straight in the bin. What a waste of time and money.'

'I remember,' said Barney, nodding. 'I got Clare, who used to work here. She was very upset with the chocolate-covered peanuts. How was I to know she had a nut allergy? She accused the whole department of trying to kill her.'

'Oh, I remember now,' added Diane. 'It was an utter disaster. Somehow Jack got missed out and got really upset. You found him crying in the loos, didn't you, Jerry?'

'That's right. Took me forty minutes to get him out.

I thought I'd never get the smell of urine off my clothes. We said never again, didn't we?'

'We did,' said Diane. 'Never again.'

'What is a Secret Santa Project?' asked Yang.

'Well, this is a bit different from the normal Secret Santa,' said Jolene, feeling her heart pounding in her chest. She flicked to the next slide. 'Just let me explain. It's not like the one you tried, which I'm guessing you all put your names in a hat, each picked one out and then bought that person a gift under a certain price limit?'

'Pwoaff,' said Barney. 'No one sticks to that. The chocolates I got I'd seen in Poundland and everyone was supposed to spend a fiver.'

'A fiver!' shrieked Stacey. 'Can't we all just go to Poundland?' She adopted a sulky frown. 'Jesus, this is all I need. I still haven't sorted Grace's donkey tail.'

'You don't even have to go to Poundland,' said Jolene. 'In this version, rather than buy a gift, you do some act of kindness for the person you pick out the hat. Doesn't need to cost anything at all. Christmas shouldn't be about spending money on pointless presents nobody wants. You must know each other really well and I bet you can all think of something that costs nothing but would bring one of your colleagues some Christmas joy.'

'I'd rather go to Poundland,' said Stacey flatly. 'I really don't have time for this.'

'You have time to go to Poundland and buy some cheap tat that absolutely no one needs, but you don't have time to think of something nice to do for a colleague?' said Jerry, turning on her. 'I don't want

47

some cheap body spray in plastic packaging that will live in a drawer until next Christmas, or some chocolate that tastes like soil, or a mug with a dodgy logo on it that will sit at the back of a cupboard until the end of time. If I get you,' he said, pointing at Stacey, 'I know exactly what I could do for you that would bring you a huge amount of joy.'

'What? How? How can you have thought of something already?' replied Stacey.

'Because I listen. I know you. I know what you need. Dead simple,' replied Jerry. 'I could probably make your Christmas and it would cost me nothing at all.'

'That's exactly it!' exclaimed Jolene, beaming at Jerry. 'When you know each other well it's dead easy to think of something that would bring real cheer to your lives. Not with gifts but with a kind thought. A gesture. A promise. Don't you think?'

Jolene looked round expectantly. Jerry looked up for it. He clearly got it. Stacey looked extremely pissed off, if a little curious that Jerry potentially held the key to making her Christmas. Yang looked worried. But maybe that was what his resting face always was. Barney had zoned out. He was gazing at the floor, twiddling his thumbs, clearly having decided he'd made his contribution to the conversation and any further input would have no impact at all so he may as well not bother. As for Diane? Well, Jolene couldn't tell. Diane looked deep in thought. Her brow was deeply furrowed under her perfectly made-up face. Perhaps she had thought of what would make her Christmas and it was nothing to do with expensive gifts or outings.

'OK,' said Diane eventually. 'Let's do it. You're in charge, Jolene. Make sure everyone is aware of the rules, set out your terms of reference, deadlines, etc. Let's have a go at seeing if we can make each other's Christmases, shall we?' She raised her eyebrows.

Jolene clapped her hands together in joy. 'Thank you,' she said. 'I'll manage it, don't you worry. Provide support, ideas, whatever it takes. Shall we do the draw now?' she asked, unable to contain her excitement.

'Yep – let's get it over with,' said Diane. 'See exactly which members of the team we're going to deliver Christmas joy to.'

Jolene wasn't sure if she was being just a tiny bit sarcastic.

'Great,' said Jolene, ripping a sheet of A4 paper off her pad. 'Six names, right?'

When she had written everyone's name on a scrap of the paper, she folded up the six pieces tightly. She put them in the middle of the table. 'So we each pick one.'

'What happens if you pick your own name?' asked Yang.

'Oh, I'm not sure,' replied Jolene.

'I'd keep quiet if I were you,' said Stacey. 'Save yourself a load of hassle. You'll have done yourself a favour pulling your own name out of a hat.'

'We'll just start again if that happens to anyone,' said Diane. 'Right, shall we get on with it? I do have another meeting to go to. I'll go first, shall I?' She reached out and grabbed a piece of paper. She opened it up and nodded, putting the piece of paper behind her on her desk without showing any emotion at all.

'I'll go next,' said Yang.

'Why you?' exclaimed Stacey.

'Oh, I'm so sorry, would you like to go next?'

'No, you carry on, Yang,' she said. 'Put yourself first.'

He awkwardly reached out and took another piece of folded paper. 'Oh shit,' he muttered when he read the name. He blew his cheeks out, looking terrified.

'Hope that wasn't me,' said Stacey, reaching for one of the remaining names. She opened hers.

'Bloody hell,' she said. 'Utterly impossible.' She glared at Jolene and folded her arms in a huff.

'Go on, Jerry,' said Jolene, giving him a nudge. 'Your turn.'

'Not sure I want to know, given the reaction of the previous two,' he said, unfolding his piece of paper. He shook his head slightly when he read it. 'Could be better, could be worse,' he said.

'Barney?' said Jolene.

He gave a huge sigh and selected one of the two pieces of paper left. He looked at the name then screwed it back up and put it in his trouser pocket. He returned to studying the carpet whilst twiddling his thumbs.

Jolene picked up the remaining piece of paper and unfolded it. She kept a poker face and folded it up again. She would have to wait and see what she could do with that one.

'Are we done now?' asked Diane rather impatiently.

'So just so I'm clear,' said Yang. 'We need to think of something that will make the person's Christmas. And it shouldn't be a physical present and it doesn't need to cost anything?'

'That's it,' said Jolene. 'An act of kindness. Something that will bring some Christmas joy.'

'Mm,' said Yang, deep in thought.

'I can't believe we're doing this,' said Stacey.

'Oh, and we should decide our deadline for exchanging our Secret Santa good deeds.'

Diane stared back at her. Jolene knew that look. Bizarrely, she often saw it on the faces of people she was talking to and she didn't really understand why. It was the look of someone losing patience very rapidly.

'How about over Christmas Coffee, on our last day? Let's do it then?' suggested Jerry.

'If it's something that is better done before then, then that's fine,' said Jolene. 'It doesn't matter. All that matters is that you do it.'

'OK, done,' said Diane, getting up and grabbing her things.

'Just one more tiny thing?' said Jolene quietly.

'What?' said Diane, raising her eyebrows to a whole new level.

'Merry Christmas.'

Chapter 6

'How did you get on?' Yang asked Stacey a couple of days later as she stomped towards him at the bottom of the High Street. She was wearing a thin coat and looked absolutely freezing. He longed to offer her his scarf or gloves but he didn't think she would appreciate the gesture. 'Was the park looking like a magical Christmas wonderland?' He gave her a grin, hoping she would grin back. But she didn't, she just grimaced.

'About as magical as anywhere that harbours the homeless in the depth of winter and is the drug-dealing centre of the borough,' replied Stacey, digging her cold hands deep in her pockets.

'Did you take some pictures?' asked Yang.

'Of the drug dealers?'

'No. Of the tree and the decorations and the Christmas signage?'

She shrugged. 'A few,' she said. 'Looks pretty sad, though. Especially in broad daylight. And I was a bit worried that the drug dealers might think I was the cops. So I was trying to be discreet.'

'I'm sorry. I should have done the park,' said Yang. 'I didn't mean to put you in danger.'

'Oh, I can take care of myself, Yang. Don't you worry. Those drug dealers mess with me, they'll regret it. I don't need you to look after me.'

Yang nodded. He'd said the wrong thing again. Whenever he tried to be kind to Stacey, she took it the wrong way. Like he was implying that she was a weak and pathetic woman. Which was the very last thing he thought. Why could he never get his sentences right when he was around her?

He looked at the notes on his phone. 'So you have pictures of the avenue lighting and the tree in the park?' he confirmed.

'Yes,' she sighed. 'For what good it will do anything.'

Yang knew doing this Christmas audit with Stacey was going to be difficult. Stacey was really good at her job but she didn't see the point in doing anything that might be a total waste of time. She valued her time way too much. Whereas Yang couldn't bear not to do anything properly. Even when he knew it might be a waste of time. He often wondered if he was mildly OCD in that respect, but he tried very hard to keep that under wraps, especially in front of Stacey.

'Right, shall we walk up each side of the High Street and take pictures of the decorations from both aspects?'

'If we must,' she said.

'Do you want to do the left-hand side and I'll do the right?' he suggested.

'Fine,' she sighed.

He crossed the road and walked up the street, taking

pictures of the lampposts with huge lit-up snowflakes on them interspersed with Christmas baubles. Christmas baubles? Now, there's a thing, he thought as he wandered along. Who on earth came up with the idea of baubles on a tree? What was that all about? Whilst he was pondering the mystery of baubles he walked past the open door of a bar, music blasting out, even though it was only three o'clock in the afternoon. He glanced across the street. Stacey was well ahead of him, occasionally raising her phone to snap pictures. He poked his head through the doorway of the pub. It was virtually empty, just a few punters perched on stools at the bar, but he could see a small stage at the back, set up with a mike. He should contact this place, he thought. He could do with some more gigs. Even if they would only give him the opening slot so he could play his Britpop covers on his acoustic guitar to next to no one. He didn't care. He loved it. When he played his guitar, something happened. He no longer cared for the opinion of anyone else, he just got lost in the music. He became the person he'd like to be in the rest of his life. Confident, relaxed, happy. No longer anxious and a bit miserable. He also liked to slip in his own tracks here or there. He liked to hear them in a large room, even if it was empty. Somehow, when he heard his own compositions in a venue, it was like hearing them for the first time. It gave him ideas, things to tweak, words to change. He could feel his imaginary audience and he took their feedback, helping him to make his songs better and better. In fact, his best song to date was one called 'Imaginary Girlfriend'. He sang it at every gig he did and imagined his imaginary girlfriend sitting at the back, giving him a secret smile. Perhaps if he got a gig here he could invite the team. Invite Stacey. Then she could see him at his best instead of the pathetic idiot he seemed to present to her most days.

He took a picture of the outside of the pub, which was called the Hope and Flowers, vowing to give them a call, and strode quickly up the street, realising Stacey might be waiting for him by the Christmas tree in the square.

She was. And she was tapping her foot.

'Thirteen pictures of unlit snowflakes,' she said. 'Is that enough?'

'Great,' he said, tapping notes into his phone. 'And what are we thinking in terms of impact?' he said, looking up. 'Are they achieving what they could be?'

Stacey looked around. 'Depends on what you want them to be achieving,' she said. 'If you think these sub-par Christmas trinkets are attracting more people to the depressing line of charity shops, betting offices and fast-food joints then I'm not sure you're right in the head. All the extra illumination is doing is lighting up the litter and graffiti better, if you ask me. But you know, who am I to say?'

'OK,' nodded Yang, looking around. 'Tell you what, why don't we try just asking a member of the public what they think?'

He turned to a man who was driving by on his mobility scooter.

'Excuse me, sir,' he said. 'I am from the council—'

'I wouldn't if I were you,' said Stacey, putting her hand on his arm.

Yang pressed on. 'Do you mind telling me what you think of the Christmas decorations this year?'

The man stopped. 'The council, you say?' he said. 'No, I don't mind telling you. What you doing wasting our money on this pathetic shit? No point, mate. No point at all. And cycle lanes. What are you bothering with them for when I can't use my mobility scooter in them? And the public toilets on Dig Street have been closed for over a year. A year – and you twats are bothering with this pathetic excuse for a Christmas tree. And council tax, bleeding council tax. You put it up every bleeding year and what the hell are you doing with it? It's not going on Christmas decorations, is it? Lining your bloody pockets, no doubt. Going in expenses for the good-for-nothing MPs we vote in. I want to know where my extra council tax is going, young man, before you even dare ask me about Christmas decorations.'

Yang looked at Stacey. Stacey had her arms folded and was grinning. She clearly knew better than to tell a member of the public that she worked for the council.

'I'm sorry to hear that you aren't happy with how the council is appropriating its funds. However, all these questions you really should take up with your MP,' he said to the man.

'My MP! And what good would that do? You can never get hold of them anyway. Useless good-for-nothings.'

'Well, they should all be doing a local surgery every week. You can talk to them there.'

'Me go to them? Why should I? They should come to me. Ask me what needs doing. They're only too eager to come knocking on my door, aren't they, when they want my vote, but the minute I want something. Oh, no, they're nowhere to be seen.'

Yang took a step back. Stacey was openly laughing at him now.

'So can I take it that you are not a supporter of spending money on Christmas decorations?' asked Yang.

The man looked at him. 'Oh, fuck off,' he said, and sped off on his scooter.

'Never, ever say you work for the council when you are out and about in the borough,' said Stacey. 'You should know that by now.'

Yang shrugged. 'I thought it would be good to see how people reacted to being asked. We should be asking the public, but maybe we need to think about how we do that.'

'Starting with not announcing to the world that you represent the council.'

Yang nodded. He looked at Stacey. He'd had an idea earlier and he wondered if actually now would be the right time to air it.

'So we've covered our borough, don't you think? Shall we head off and see how the other half lives north of the river and see some of their decorations?'

Stacey sighed. 'If we must. Where should we go?'

'We could go to the other end of the spectrum and

catch a bus to Oxford Street and Regent Street. See their displays.'

'I suppose. I bet the last time I went into the centre of London to see the lights I was a kid.'

'How come?'

'What's the point? I can't afford Regent Street prices.'

'But the lights are free. Have you never brought Grace?'

'I do not need Grace within a square mile of Hamleys. It could ruin both our Christmases.'

They hopped on a bus, changed at Lambeth and caught the number 159, saying nothing as it wound its way to Westminster Bridge. The bells of Big Ben rang out loud and proud as the bus whizzed over the bridge and past the enormous Christmas tree standing erect and sparkling with lights outside the Houses of Parliament. It was at least three double-decker buses high, and possibly a double-decker bus wide. Compared to the sad little affair standing in the square at Bermondsey, this was big and bold and, quite frankly, magical. Stacey wondered who had paid for that particular tree. Was it the taxpayers? Was it a gift? Who knew? The key question, she guessed, was: was it worth it?

The bus turned right up Whitehall and past Downing Street, the most famous residential street in the country perhaps, and home to the prime minister. She glanced up the famous street and saw the Christmas tree at the top. A fine elegant tree bedecked with multicoloured lights. She wondered what the current prime minister thought of spending money on Christmas celebrations. She wondered if he thought it was worth it.

And then up to Trafalgar Square. Stacey couldn't remember the last time she had seen the centre of London in all its Christmas glory. An enormous tree stood in the very centre with what must have been thousands of white lights twinkling all over it. It was truly spectacular as hundreds of people swelled around it, the National Gallery providing an imposing and fitting backdrop. She watched mesmerised as a young couple wrapped their arms around each other and took selfies under the tree. They looked so happy. Wow – to be that blown away by a Christmas tree and the person you were with. Day-trippers groaned under the weight of bags, as they slid into pubs to have welcome drinks before getting their trains home. Workers were meeting and kissing before heading off to the joys of Leicester Square, to the cinema or to find food. Tourists were laughing, giggling, smiling, heading towards the Theatre District or perhaps Covent Garden to see some free street entertainment.

Stacey gazed out of the window. Oh, how she wished she was going to meet someone, gather with friends, socialise. She couldn't remember the last time she had done that. Everyone looked as if they were enjoying themselves in the warm glow of the festive period. She hadn't felt the warm glow of anything for a very long time.

'Are you hungry?' asked Yang as they approached Piccadilly Circus.

'Always,' said Stacey.

'Right, come on, let's get off.' Yang leaped up and pressed the bell to indicate to the bus driver to stop at the next stop.

'What are you doing?' Stacey hissed. 'I can't afford to eat around here unless it's a slice of pizza that's been in a window for a week.'

'Don't fret. I know just the place for excellent free food. Follow me,' Yang grinned as he stepped off the bus and dived into the throng.

They pushed their way through Leicester Square. A huge crowd had gathered around a bunch of young male acrobats, exciting the onlookers in to a frenzy. Yang and Stacey had to squeeze their way past, shouting, 'Excuse me!' and 'Thank you!'

They passed the incredibly long line outside the Lego store. Excitable children were jumping up and down to keep warm, whilst equally excitable dads gazed eagerly through the window at the marvels inside, no doubt wondering whether they could ask Santa for some Lego this year. Grace loved Lego. Particularly the Harry Potter stuff. Stacey had been keeping an eye on eBay to see if anyone wanted to sell a second-hand set in the lead-up to Christmas.

Suddenly Yang turned right into a quieter road and Stacey spied the cheerful lanterns at the top of the street. She realised they were heading to Chinatown. They turned another corner and there they were. In another magical place. Not Christmas themed this time, but overhead the rows and rows of bright red and gold Chinese lanterns lit up the faces of the people milling underneath, peering at menus, trying to decide which one of the copious number of eateries they were going to pick.

It was clear, however, that Yang knew exactly where he was going. He pushed forward through the crowd before heading to the left side of the street. He paused and looked behind him to make sure that Stacey was still there, then opened the door to The Happy House.

The warmth hit them and Stacey's glasses immediately steamed up. As she took them off to demist them with a corner of her jumper she was engulfed in the arms of a woman around half her height.

'Welcome, welcome,' the woman cried. 'Welcome so much.'

Stacey tried to put her glasses back on to see this explosion of energy, but the woman wasn't having any of it.

'Please sit, sit here. Best seat in the house. Sit here now.'

Stacey found herself sitting in the window opposite Yang, who was taking his coat off as if this was all quite normal. She felt as if she'd been kidnapped by the world's nicest kidnappers. She looked up at her captor. She was small, under five foot, but round, curvy, with an abundance of jet-black curly hair and eyes that lasered into Stacey. She felt as if she were being pinned to the seat by them.

'Yang?' she asked, willing him to perform at least some kind of perfunctory introduction.

'What?' he replied.

'Erm, maybe an introduction?'

'Well, this is a Chinese restaurant,' he said.

'Of course, but . . .' She tipped her head towards the woman still piercing her with her gaze.

'Oh, yeah. Mum, Stacey. Stacey, Mum,' said Yang.

'Oh,' said Stacey. 'Wow. I had no idea. Erm. Hello.'

Yang's mum leaned forward to kiss her on both cheeks.

'I am so happy to see you,' she said.

'Mum, Stacey is just a colleague from work, OK? Nothing special.'

'Thanks,' said Stacey.

'Oh, I didn't mean . . .' jumped in Yang, looking horrified.

'Well, she looks special to me,' grinned Yang's mum. 'Very special indeed.'

'I'm so sorry,' said Yang, looking uncomfortable suddenly. 'Maybe this was a bad idea. Really, really bad idea. What was I thinking? Erm, Stacey, look, I'm sorry for anything inappropriate my mother says to you. She says stuff that's embarrassing. Like way worse than me. Erm, and she will say stuff that is embarrassing because she thinks I should be living in the suburbs with two kids by now and so she gets overexcited if she even sees me within two feet of a woman. She'll think you're my girlfriend and for the next year will not stop asking about you. I'm so sorry to put you in this situation. I mean, as if you and me would ever . . .'

'Oh, no, Mrs Chen,' said Stacey, slowly and clearly, 'I'm not interested in your son romantically AT ALL. Believe me.' She turned back to Yang. 'Will that help?' she asked him.

'Yes, that's very clear,' he replied quietly.

'I'll bring food,' said Mrs Chen, still grinning. 'No need to decide, no need to pay, no need for anything. I will bring you the best in the house.'

'No, honestly. Really, you shouldn't. I mean just a stir-fry would be great really, but please let me pay.'

'No,' Mrs Chen said firmly, putting her hand on Stacey's shoulder. 'You just sit here with my son. I will bring you everything you need.'

Stacey realised she really had been kidnapped, in this tiny little Chinese restaurant on the edge of Soho.

By the end of the meal Stacey couldn't remember the last time she'd felt quite so content. She'd been fed dish after dish of the most wonderful food. It just kept coming and she just kept eating. She couldn't help herself. It had been so long since someone else had cooked for her, so long since she'd sat in a restaurant and enjoyed the delights of food just arriving at the table. She'd forgotten the magic of that.

And then Yang's mum had sat and grilled her, but in a nice way. On a low heat until she felt all warm and fuzzy rather than burnt and crisp. She asked her question after question about her life, as if she was interested, as if Stacey was important. She couldn't remember the last time someone had spoken to her like that. She'd soon spilled the beans on her life with her daughter and how challenging that was alongside work, and how her family were no help whatsoever. She could have sworn Mrs Chen had tears in her eyes when Stacey said her mother only really spoke to her on her birthday and at Christmas, and then it was to ask her for money, because she thought she was loaded because she had a good job with the council.

'But you are still their daughter,' stated Mrs Chen, putting her hand over Stacey's. 'You need looking after, too.'

'I am,' said Stacey, now fighting back her own tears as she saw the look of concern in Yang's mother's eyes. Her own mother had never looked at her like that. Not even when she told her she was pregnant and didn't know what to do. She'd told her she was an idiot and should get herself down the abortion clinic.

Yang had long since disappeared and Mrs Chen had taken his seat. She had no idea why he had brought her here. She presumed it was because he was hungry and wanted to blag a free meal off his parents. What a lucky man Yang truly was. He wandered through life without really trying, had no responsibilities to speak of and a mother who was there to look after him at the drop of a hat. He truly led a charmed life.

Stacey didn't want to leave. She sat and drank coffee as a raft of waiters served hungry customers steaming plates of food. By now, Mrs Chen was buzzing around, ordering waiters this way and that, making sure they were on top of their game, service-wise. Yang eventually appeared from what Stacey assumed was the kitchen and went over to speak to his mum, who glanced at Stacey and then hurried back into the kitchen herself.

'I really need to go,' said Stacey. 'After School Club finishes in half an hour.'

'Right,' said Yang, looking awkward.

'I need to thank your mum, though. She's been so kind to me.'

'Well, she loves to talk,' sighed Yang. 'I'm sorry if she was too much.'

'You have no idea how lucky you are to have her,' said Stacey.

'I guess, when she gets off my back. You know, she can be such a nag, seriously.'

'Because she cares,' said Stacey. 'That's why.'

'Sure it is,' agreed Yang, looking distracted.

'Thank you, though,' said Stacey. 'For bringing me here. I mean I never go out for a meal, ever. And not without Grace. So this was amazing. Truly.'

Yang nodded. 'Nothing really. Stacey, I . . . I . . . wanted to ask you . . . well, wanted to say, that you know if you ever really need a babysitter, I could do it. I mean I'm not some crazy child-obsessed weirdo or anything. Don't worry about that. I mean . . . God, that came out wrong . . . I mean, I look after my nieces and nephews all the time so, like I say, if you're stuck for a babysitter then let me know. That's all. Just wanted to tell you that. Because I do get it, you know, that it's hard being female. I mean, being a single parent.'

Stacey felt her mouth open. Had Yang actually just said that?

'Would you really?' she asked.

'Yes,' he nodded.

Stacey couldn't believe what she was hearing. She looked at Yang. *Could* she ask him to babysit? He clearly came from a good family so she had no doubt he could take care of Grace OK. And she really was desperate to get out, and she knew exactly who she'd go out with, given half the chance.

'Well, actually,' she said, 'this dad outside school keeps asking me out and I'd really like to, but I haven't been able to say yes as I can never get a babysitter. Would you take care of Grace whilst I went on a date with him?'

She watched as Yang swallowed. 'Yes, I can do that,' he said in an unusually high-pitched voice.

'Seriously?'

Yang nodded.

'Can I text him now to see when he's free?' she asked.

'OK,' he replied, looking away.

Stacey got her phone out, her fingers almost stumbling over the keypad she was so excited. She looked up and grinned when she'd finished. 'I'll let you know when he replies,' she said.

'Cool,' nodded Yang.

Stacey reached to put her coat on just as Mrs Chen came dashing out.

'For your daughter,' she said, pushing a paper bag into Stacey's hands. 'She might like them.'

Stacey looked down, unable to believe her eyes. Could this woman get any more lovely?

'They are just fortune cookies,' said Mrs Chen. 'That's all.'

This time Stacey really did have tears in her eyes. She couldn't remember the last time someone had shown kindness to her tricky, slightly naughty, hyperactive daughter.

'Thank you,' she said, welling up.

'You visit again?' asked Mrs Chen.

Stacey nodded and embraced her.

'I'll get you to the bus stop,' said Yang, guiding her out of the door.

They walked in silence along the crowded streets.

'Well, here we are then,' said Yang, eventually. 'This is your bus stop.'

'Thanks, Yang,' Stacey said, giving him a warm smile. 'Thanks for dinner and everything. It was really nice,' she added awkwardly. She felt her phone ping in her pocket. She took it out. Her eyes lit up. 'Brilliant,' she said, looking up and grinning at Yang. 'Will says he can do this Friday. Is that OK?'

Yang nodded silently.

'You are the best,' she said. 'I can't believe I'm actually going on a date. Oh, Yang, thank you. This means the world.' She stepped forward and hugged him. She couldn't help herself. This had been such a good day when all she had expected was an afternoon walking the dreary streets of Bermondsey. She was actually going to go on a date for the first time in for ever. Maybe finally her life was going to take a turn for the better. She grinned at Yang and leaped onto the bus, giving him a cheery wave as she sat down.

He nodded back and walked away. Hands deep in his pockets. Head down.

Chapter 7

At exactly the same time as Stacey was waving at Yang from the bus, Jerry was donning his chorister's robes at the church of St Martin-in-the-Fields, which sits on the very corner of Trafalgar Square. Stacey and Yang had in fact gone straight past him, and had they looked across Charing Cross Road they would have seen him with his head low, marching down the street. However, if they had seen him, he wouldn't have told them where he was going. He'd only confided in Stacey so far that he sang in a church choir. He didn't particularly know why he hadn't shared news of this major source of joy in his life with everyone else. Hard to say. Was it that he thought they would laugh at him? Give him that classic British side eye when he announced he did something that they really didn't understand? Or was it the fact that he sang in a church choir? He had lived in the UK for many years and he was yet to understand how the British really viewed religion. He came from Missouri, where religion was a major part of community life, a thing that gathered people, brought families together, and yet he didn't get that sense here. British religious beliefs were something to be followed quietly, without fuss or drama. The first thing Jerry had done when he'd arrived was to go to church as he knew that was where he would meet people, and he had hoped that would be where he could sing. And he knew if he could sing then he would have at least some corner of happiness in his life.

It was no coincidence that he wound up in the choir at St Martin-in-the-Fields. It wasn't his local church, but it was the top of his list. Why? Because it appears in one of his favourite London-based films, *Notting Hill*. He liked to tell the folks back home that he sang in a choir on a movie set. It also blew him away that the church he sang in was over three hundred years old. Three hundred years old! One could argue that it was older than the United States itself. It was finished before the Founding Fathers signed the Declaration of Independence, for goodness' sake. This was old on a scale not available in his home country. In St Martin-in-the-Fields he felt part of history, part of something so solid and enduring that he could never be cut adrift.

And Jerry had to sing. Singing was therapy for him, the only thing that took him off into another world and made all his troubles go away. Singing was his lifeline. Of course, listening to singing could also do that for him. He was obsessed with musical theatre. Another factor that had kept him living within five miles of the very epicentre of musical theatre for the world. Just walking down Shaftesbury Avenue made his heart leap, and whenever he felt low or alone he would take himself down to the avenue of sparkle and shine and slide into the box office of one of the many musicals available and pray for a last-minute return ticket at a cut price. *Hamilton* was his all-time favourite – it blew him away – but *Six* was a close second. The tale of the six wives of Henry VIII was like a drug. It gave him a high like no other, every time he saw it.

But tonight was choir practice, so he didn't need to go and find his drug of choice. A shot in the arm of Anne Boleyn dressed like a Spice Girl singing about having her head cut off? No need for that. Tonight was especially exciting, given the choir were preparing for the carol concert – always a highlight, and so very British. He knew he would go home happy tonight.

'Hey, Jerry,' said Carol as she walked into the vestry. Jerry had already bagged the corner spot for them, slightly away from the rest of the twenty-two strong choir, who were getting their robes on. There they were shielded by a tall cupboard and so could gossip about their day and share strictly forbidden sweets. Carol, at sixty-two, was one of the oldest members of the choir and delighted in breaking the rules and winding up the choir master.

'Carol,' nodded Jerry.

'Good day?' she asked.

'Acceptable,' he replied. 'You?'

'Excellent,' she replied. 'Christmas cards written. Thankfully a few old codgers died this year so my list has dwindled slightly.'

'Every cloud, hey, Carol?'

'Every cloud, Jerry. You send Christmas cards, do you? It must be close to last posting dates for your folks back in Missouri.'

'Yep, all done. Then just the phone call on the day covers Christmas generally in the McKinley family.'

'Mm,' nodded Carol. 'You seen that man of yours this week?'

'For fuck's sake, Carol – sorry, God,' said Jerry, crossing himself and looking skyward. 'I told you, he's not my man – he's not anything – he's just. He's just . . .'

'Fucking you around?' she asked innocently.

'You cannot say that in a place of worship, Carol.'

'We should speak the truth, dear boy, in a place of worship and I for one feel that you are being fucked around. I will sing "O Little Town of Bethlehem" extra loudly later to compensate.'

'He's not fucking me around. We meet for coffee, we chat, he's made no advances whatsoever, so how can he be fucking me around? He just wants to be friends, clearly. He doesn't fancy me. He could be straight, for all I know.'

Carol arched her eyebrows. 'Straight men don't go for coffee and a chat. Straight men don't seek friendship. They just don't. He's gay, he fancies you, but he's fucking you around.'

'But why would he do that?' asked Jerry. 'Come on, you wise old beast. Why? If he is gay and fancies me then why doesn't he just ask me out or give me something?'

Carol looked Jerry up and down.

'Maybe he's waiting for you to grow a beard.'

'I didn't have a beard when I met him.'

'Maybe a moustache.'

'I didn't have a moustache, either.'

'Maybe he's waiting for a shift in personality. Maybe he's waiting for you to make the first move.'

'Screw you!' said Jerry. 'You know I'm incapable of first moves.'

'But you may have no choice, young Jerry. The path of true love never did run smooth. You may have to make the first move.'

'Who said anything about it being the path of true love?'

'Your face did. Every time I mention his name.'

'Does it really?' exclaimed Jerry, his hands flying to his face.

'Of course it does. I can spot the lovesick a mile off. You absolutely need to sort some treatment for that and I reckon your only chance of survival is to make the first move.'

'No. Can't do it. No way, Jose.'

'Big chicken.'

'If he wants me, he'll tell me. I just have to be patient. Anyway, Christmas is coming. Romance is in the air, right? Now is the perfect time for him to step forward.'

'Mm,' said Carol, offering him a jelly baby. 'Leave me the orange ones,' she warned. 'You could buy him a Christmas gift?' she suggested. 'You know, if that doesn't scream "take me over the frothy milk machine" I don't know what does.'

'And what would I buy, exactly? I mean, don't talk to me about Christmas gifts. We've just been landed with Secret Santa at work, but we're not supposed to spend any money. Do an act of kindness instead. I was kind of up for it until I knew who I'd picked. It's stressing me out thinking about that, never mind buying a gift for a man who may or may not fancy me.'

'Maybe you just need to think of what you would like from whoever picked you. I often do that. See something I'd like, then buy it for someone else. It kind of weirdly works.'

'Well, clearly all I want for Christmas is my tall dark handsome coffee-shop man, but the chances of me getting him are less than zero, as we have just discussed.'

Carol stared at Jerry and then said clearly and succinctly, 'Then let us pray.' She took both of Jerry's hands in hers, still clutching her bag of jelly babies, and then closed her eyes.

'Dear Lord,' she said. 'Please deliver to our dear brother Jerry the love of his life this Christmas in the form of hot guy in the coffee shop. May he come forth with love and kindness to Jerry and may he accept this gift graciously. We both promise to kick the ass of "O Come, All Ye Faithful" and even "Ding Dong Merrily on High" – arguably the worst carol of all time – at the carol concert, if you will just offer this kindness by then. I'm giving you a deadline, by the way, as I find that these things can drag on. The carol concert is next week, in case you don't have it on your calendar. We do, of course, expect you to attend. Dearly beloved, thank you and good night. Amen.'

'Amen to that,' said Jerry solemnly.

'Well, we've done all we can,' said Carol, opening her eyes and popping a jelly baby into her mouth. She reached into her coat, pulled out a hip flask and took a swig before handing it to Jerry.

'Really?' he asked. 'We're doing this now, are we?'

''Tis the season to be merry,' she said and winked, then slapped her hand to her forehead. 'I know what you should do,' she said. 'It's obvious, isn't it? I often find when you have these little conversations with God that he finds a way of giving you the answer to your prayers.'

'Really?' said Jerry. 'I've never found that.'

'Invite him to the carol concert,' said Carol.

'No way,' said Jerry.

'Come on!' said Carol. 'It's perfect. He gets to see you in a long dress by candlelight. If he's not going to fall in love with you then, he never will.'

'Why on earth would he agree to come and watch me sing carols?'

'Because he wants to fall in love with you, of course. It's the perfect way to find out what his intentions are. If he comes, that is the biggest God-damn sign above his head that he fancies you in the history of the universe. No man on this planet accepts an invite to a carol concert for the sake of friendship. That is pure love. You ask him next time you see him. Promise me. Then this matter is resolved.'

Jerry stared at her for a moment.

'OK, Carol. I will. But just because it's Christmas and . . . and, well, I am desperate.'

'No kidding,' replied Carol.

'Can you help me with the Secret Santa thing as well?'

'No way,' replied Carol. 'Doing a favour for a colleague at work? Are you kidding me? What a totally ridiculous idea that is.'

Chapter 8

Diane hadn't meant to call in at the theatre. Her intention had been to pop into town to see if she could nail down Chloe's Christmas presents before she arrived back from uni. Repeated requests to Leon to ask him to go to Selfridges in between performances had fallen on deaf ears and so now here she was, at eight o'clock at night, stomping down Oxford Street in a fury because it was so damn busy.

Selfridges was absolutely heaving. You would have thought it was the January sales. Diane squashed her way through, also managing to pick up a pair of leather gloves for Leon's dad and an elaborate jewellery box for Leon's niece. Two more to knock off the never-ending list. The list that Leon had shown no interest in whatsoever. Indeed, had he ever shown any interest at all in helping with Christmas preparations? Why, for the twentieth year running of their marriage, was she the one buying her husband's family Christmas presents? Why did he always get all the joy of Christmas and she got all the pain? Just because he was directing a bloody pantomime shouldn't mean he got out of all the domestic requirements of Christmas, should it? He got to celebrate Christmas every bloody day in that theatre whilst she sweated it out in the council house, counting beans. Why was she facing the Oxford Street crush whilst he was enjoying watching families enjoy the true spirit of Christmas? She forced her way out of the rotating door and took a deep breath, large yellow card bags knocking around her ankles.

She should go home. She'd had enough of this mayhem.

But she found she didn't want to. Home meant another Marks and Spencer microwave meal in front of the telly, watching TV ads of families planning the perfect Christmas. She didn't want to be alone – she particularly didn't want to be alone watching how Christmas should be, whilst she wondered if Leon was going to arrive at nine-thirty, straight from the theatre, or after midnight, straight from the pub.

And so she made an unusual decision. She'd go to his theatre and catch the last forty-five minutes of the show. Go and do something Christmassy, and then maybe she and her husband could walk down Regent Street and admire the lights together. Then catch supper together, in town, the two of them. And actually talk to each other rather than merely pass on messages via the hall table. Perhaps that would ease her frustration. Perhaps that would put some much-needed Christmas magic into their marriage. Yes, that would be good. Worth a try, at least.

The minute she stepped into the theatre she suspected she had made a mistake. The usher eyed her with suspicion until she explained she was Leon's wife and asked if she could just watch from the back.

'Oh, no,' said the elderly man. 'We can't have that. There's a box empty. You must have that.' He directed her up a set of stairs and through a tiny door that led to a private box to the left of the stage.

Diane hadn't been to the theatre very often since she gave up treading the boards herself. It still hurt, if she was honest. After all, she hadn't really had much choice. She got married, got pregnant and then quickly realised that for some reason no one wants to see a pregnant Roxie Hart in *Chicago* or Glinda in *Wicked* or Maria in *West Side Story*. And even when you don't look pregnant, nurseries aren't open in the evenings for childcare, and when your husband also works in the precarious business of theatre then someone has to find a nice stable job that pays the bills. And that was Diane. She got a job at the council because they let her retrain as an accountant and she'd been there ever since, forgoing the worry of stage fright for the worry of how much needs to be spent on toilet rolls in care homes in a year. It had been hard leaving the profession she loved and she feared going back would only make her long for it more.

She was right.

She didn't look at the stage to start with. Just gazed out at the audience. All completely rapt. Watching, laughing, having a great time. That's what she used to do, she thought. She used to give people a good time.

She realised she'd forgotten how to have a good time herself, never mind give other people a good time.

The audience burst into spontaneous laughter and she turned to the stage to see what was causing such mirth. The pantomime dame was in a kitchen scene involving custard pies. Diane could totally see why Leon cast him, despite his drink problem. His comedy timing was impeccable and his physical comedy couldn't help but make her laugh out loud, even though just five minutes earlier she had felt as miserable as sin. He was good, really good. She sat transfixed until Snow White arrived on the scene. She certainly looked the part: dark wig, pale skin. And she was a pretty good actress – convincing and funny. Diane was pulling for her and that was half the battle.

But then she started to sing.

She wasn't a bad singer – she was good, in fact – just, given all the physical stuff she was doing on stage, she hadn't got her breathing right. She was getting to the end of phrases and holding her breath, which made it sound like she was overreaching. It was possibly barely perceptible to the audience, but Diane knew if she could correct her breathing her voice would come across much stronger.

Diane sat through the rest of the performance until the closing number, when the whole audience were on their feet singing along. The performers each took a bow and received a standing ovation from the very appreciative audience. What a job. Fancy getting a standing ovation every day just for doing your job. Diane couldn't even get a cup of coffee and barely got a thank you from her boss. Ever. A round of applause? You have got to be kidding me. Even when she had discovered, after meticulously checking, that they had a twenty grand underspend in refuse collection, which had totally saved her boss's bacon. Did anyone say thank you? Did she get a standing ovation for that? Nothing. Zilch. Zip. He hadn't even given her the top grade in her annual review. She'd saved his bacon and he'd moaned that she needed to be a more positive role model in the office. Positive role model when you cannot even get a decent cup of coffee in your place of work.

The audience were filing out now, excitedly chattering about how marvellous everyone had been and how they had had the best time. That was work satisfaction right there in the words of a young girl who brushed past Diane in the lobby.

'I love Snow White,' she said. 'She was totally amazing.'

Diane pushed through the crowd to get to the stage door, phoning Leon as she did so in the hope that he would pick up and let her backstage.

'Are you OK?' he asked when he picked up.

'I'm here,' she said.

'Where?'

'At the theatre!'

'My theatre?'

'Well, it's not really yours, is it, but yes.'

'What are you doing here?'

'I was shopping on Oxford Street so I thought I'd pop in. Shall we go find some dinner?'

'Yes, yes, of course. I just need to have a word with Shelley, but come to the stage door. I'll meet you there.'

Diane pushed her way through the throngs outside deciding where to go and made her way to the back-stage door round the side of the building down a narrow alleyway. A few families were loitering, clutching programmes and Sharpies. Maybe waiting for the soap star or the lad who got to the semi-final of *Britain's Got Talent*, juggling ten clubs whilst balancing on a stool on one leg. She stood hovering, waiting for Leon to appear, which he soon did, waving cheerily towards her and beckoning her in.

Backstage was bedlam. And so utterly thrilling that Diane could hardly believe it. People were dashing around everywhere, shouting at each other, laughing, screaming, wiping off make-up literally as they went through the door. Oh, and the smell. The smell of backstage that she hadn't smelled in something like twenty years. Dust, must, hairspray, carpentry, oil, sweat, such a curious mixture of intense creativity. She was right back there twenty years ago, except in the thick of it. Right in amongst it rather than the observer that she was today.

'I just need to run through the penultimate number with Shelley and Baz. Something's not working,' said Leon. 'Can you give me twenty minutes?'

'Sure,' said Diane, transfixed, drinking it all in. 'It's her breathing,' she added.

'What is?'

'The problem with the number. It's her breathing. She's got the phrasing and the breathing wrong.'

Leon stared at her.

'Of course it is,' he said. 'Why hadn't I spotted that? You come with me.' He grabbed her hand and led her up a narrow set of stairs.

'So I bought Elspeth a jewellery box,' Diane began as they went down a narrow corridor against a tide of chorus actors fleeing the building. 'And that bag Chloe wanted. Oh, and I got your dad some gloves. I'll show them to you later. See what you think.' They approached another set of stairs and before she knew it, there she was, centre stage, holding her husband's hand, still clutching numerous large yellow bags and wearing her coat and scarf. The lights momentarily blinded her so she shaded her eyes to see that they were not alone. Snow White and the pantomime dame were hovering. Baz was tapping his foot impatiently whilst Snow White was nervously chewing her fingernail.

'I'm so sorry,' said Snow White to Leon. '"Finding Myself" just didn't land, did it? I'm not sure what happened.'

'No, Shell,' said Leon. 'You don't nail it, no. But may I introduce my wife,' he went on. 'She was, she was . . . on the stage, weren't you, love, many moons ago. She was brilliant, utterly brilliant. And she watched your number and said it's your breathing and your phrasing. That's what you said, wasn't it, Diane?'

'Well, yes,' said Diane, feeling very put on the spot. 'I mean, you are close, really close.'

'I could have told you that,' muttered Baz, still tapping his foot.

'Just an opinion,' said Diane. 'You might just want to rethink where you're taking your breaths, that's all. Worth a try.'

'Show her,' said Leon.

'What?' replied Diane.

'Just show her what you mean. You sing it.'

'Don't be stupid,' said Diane. 'I don't even know the song.'

'You can still read music, can't you?' said Leon, stepping forward to the edge of the stage. 'Pass me the sheet music for "Finding Myself", Steve,' he asked the conductor. 'Then let's just go from the opening bars, shall we?' He walked back towards Diane. 'Here,' he said, holding out the sheet. 'It's basically a rip-off of "Somewhere Over the Rainbow", right? Show Shelley how you would sing it.'

'No,' she said. 'I can't.'

'For goodness' sake, sing the freaking song,' said Baz, 'and then we can all get out of here.'

'I'll speak it,' said Diane as she reluctantly took the sheet music from her husband. 'I'm not singing.' The orchestra took up the opening bars. She cleared her throat and spoke through the lyrics, exaggerating her pauses, indicating where she thought Shelley should breathe.

She looked nervously up at her husband, who encouraged her to carry on. The lyrics and the music were simple and repetitive but required some contrast between the high and low notes where Diane felt Snow White had gone wrong. She dropped her shoulders, relaxed as she approached the key change in the final third of the song and, as she stood there, still wearing her coat, her shopping bags at her feet, she wished now she had just sung the notes. Just to see what it felt like. But she feared she would either have humiliated herself, or worse, really enjoyed herself, settling back into singing like putting on an old comfortable coat, wondering why she had ever stopped wearing it.

There was a split second of silence when she had finished. Her eyes were closed. She was in the moment. She was twenty-five again, on a West End stage. Just being there made her feel more alive than she had done in a very long time.

She heard a faint ripple of applause. She opened her eyes and saw Leon grinning and clapping, as was Snow White.

'That's brilliant, Di. Makes total sense. Now, can you mark that sheet up with where you were breathing, for Shelley, and how you were phrasing? Talk her through it.'

Leon handed her a pen, then turned his back on her. 'Baz, thanks for hanging around,' he said. 'Now come and show me the problem with your dressing room. I'll be back in a minute, Di,' he added, and disappeared off with his pantomime dame.

'How did you know to do it like that?' said Shelley, blinking at her. 'I totally get it. Do you still perform?'

'No,' said Diane. 'Haven't done for years.'

'How come?' asked Snow White.

She looked at Shelley. 'It's a young woman's game,' she told her. She swallowed. 'So make the most of it. You never know when it might end.'

'Did you love it?' asked Snow White.

84

Diane glanced up at the empty auditorium, then down at the orchestra pit where the musicians were packing up their instruments. Then she looked at the young girl standing in front of her with her entire life ahead of her.

'It was the love of my life,' she declared.

Leon was gone half an hour, leaving Diane to sit on the edge of the stage, legs dangling, watching the cleaners go up and down the stalls with bin bags and litter pickers. The band had packed up and gone, dashing off to meet musicians from other performances in the bars and restaurants that stayed open for the backstage theatre crowd. Diane swung her legs, gazing up at the rows and rows of seats, now empty and quiet. The view was the most beautiful she could imagine in the whole wide world. A theatre auditorium, alive with possibility, alive with potential emotion and feeling, despite the fact it was virtually empty. She thought of the council office. The atmosphere was the very opposite of a theatre auditorium. Dead, dull; no one really wanted to be there. It held no potential for anything apart from, perhaps, misery. She sighed. What had happened to her life? How had she traded the electric atmosphere of the theatre for the sombre ambiance of a council office?

She heard footsteps behind her and looked up to see Leon approaching.

'Sorry about that,' he said, taking a seat beside her. 'Baz needs his weekly moan in order to keep him functioning. Today it was the cold tap in his dressing room. Not cold enough, apparently.'

'Poor Baz,' she said, although she didn't mean it. Baz, who, as a middle-aged man, still got to work in the theatre impersonating a parody of a middle-aged woman as a pantomime dame. Oh, the irony that that part always went to men!

'Listen,' said Leon. 'I'm absolutely pooped. It's been a hell of a day. We've had the press in and I ended up doing some interviews for local radio in between shows. No time to myself at all. Do you mind if we jump on the tube and grab a takeaway in front of the telly?'

Diane stared back at him. 'Can I show you the gloves I got for your dad for Christmas?' she asked, reaching into the yellow bag beside her.

'No, honestly,' said Leon. 'I'm sure they're great. Just wrap them and give them to him.' She looked back. He was texting on his phone, laughing.

'What's funny?' she asked.

'It's the guys from the band. They're trying to get me to join them at the Rose and Crown. They keep sending me pictures of them in the Gents playing the ukulele.'

'We can go and join them,' said Diane. 'Really, we don't have to go and eat.'

'No, it's fine,' he said, shaking his head. 'It'll be a session and I don't need it. I just want to go home.'

'Why don't we grab a bite near here, then go home?' said Diane. 'We never eat out in town any more.'

'Diane, they're all either overhyped tourist traps round here or have a zero hygiene rating. I cannot afford to get food poisoning at this time of year. The entire production will fall apart. Tell you what, let's get a cab home, treat ourselves and I'll order a Deliveroo. I've been dreaming about a Big Mac all day.' He stood up and began walking to the back of the stage. She heaved herself up and dusted herself off. She took one last look at the auditorium and followed him out to flag down a cab and go home and eat a cheap burger whilst Leon ignored her and caught up on the current box set he was watching in his free time whilst he could have been being an actual fucking husband!

Chapter 9

It was the one-week anniversary of Jolene starting work at the council and she decided to mark it by going in early to put Christmas decorations up. She just thought the place needed a festive touch and that everyone could do with cheering up a bit. So far they all seemed so miserable. And they shouldn't be. Christmas was coming.

She'd had to put a chair on Barney's desk to reach the ceiling and hang the massive dangling foil concoctions. She had nearly fallen off at one point, which would have been a catastrophe. Death by falling off a highly dangerous office furniture tower whilst trying to attach Christmas decorations. But if you are going to die, not a bad way to go, she decided.

Barney had been the first to arrive, thankfully after she had finished decorating. He behaved as though he hadn't noticed either the decorations or that Jolene existed. He sat at his desk, put down his coffee and switched on his computer without saying a word to Jolene, who was still sitting at the meeting table in the corner. Jolene got the very distinct impression that

Barney didn't want her to be there. He barely spoke to her, and whenever she spoke she noticed he crossed his arms and sighed as though every single thing that came out of her mouth was a frustration to him. She had been racking her brains as to what she could do to get him on her side, even thinking that her decorating the office might work, as he'd mentioned that his late wife loved Christmas. But clearly not. He stared fixedly at his computer screen, deliberately ignoring her and her decorations.

Jerry, however, could not ignore them. He arrived next and the look of dismay on his face could have curdled milk.

'Where have these come from?' he asked. 'Is this the post department having a laugh or what? They're utterly hideous.'

'Oh, er, I put them up,' said Jolene. 'I thought it might get everyone in the mood,' she said hesitantly.

'Get everyone in *a* mood, more likely,' he muttered, setting down his free newspaper.

Yang merely raised his eyebrows when he walked in, then got his headphones out and attached himself to his music.

Stacey dashed in half an hour late, as usual. Panting something about having to go and see the headmistress at Grace's school because Grace was insisting on wearing her donkey tail in all her lessons and was being very disruptive.

'What the hell happened?' she suddenly said, looking up at the ceiling. 'Did a herd of unicorns throw up on our ceiling?'

'It was Jolene,' said Jerry, 'trying to cheer the place up.'

'Yes, that's all,' said Jolene, wondering why that was such a crime.

'Aaaah, of course it was,' said Stacey.

'I brought reindeer biscuits for the team meeting,' said Jolene hopefully. Why was it so hard to be nice to these people? And why were they all always so miserable? No one could be cross about reindeer biscuits, could they? And why did they all seem to hate everything to do with Christmas so much? She didn't understand. She'd hoped that the Secret Santa Project would get everyone in a festive mood, but it didn't appear to be working.

Then Diane came striding in with a face like thunder. She looked more than angry, she looked livid. A couple of strides behind her followed Kev, the man from HR.

'Look, Diane,' he said, running into her office, 'this is not really—'

'Sit down,' she commanded.

'But—'

'Sit down,' she repeated before she stuck her head out of the door and shouted into the office, 'Team meeting – now!'

Jolene looked around her, petrified, wondering what on earth was going on. Jerry stood and picked up a pen and notebook, and Jolene followed suit. She followed him into Diane's office. Stacey soon joined them, arching her eyebrows at Jerry. Then Barney ambled in, sat down heavily in a seat and crossed his arms defensively.

Diane looked around her.

'Jolene, fetch Yang,' she instructed. Jolene high-tailed out of the office and jumped up and down in front of Yang, who was nodding his head to whatever was streaming through his headphones.

'"Dance of the Sugar Plum Fairy",' he offered as he took one of his headphones off.

'Diane needs you in her office, now. Urgent meeting.'

'Oh, sorry,' he said. 'I'll be right there. Just need the loo.'

Jolene shook her head rapidly. 'Not sure she'll want to wait. The HR guy is in there.'

'Not good,' he muttered, putting his headphones on the table and heading towards Diane's office. He took the last remaining chair, rendering Jolene seatless.

'Drag in a chair,' Diane instructed.

Jolene turned and grabbed the nearest one, which happened to be Barney's.

'Not my chair,' he bellowed. 'That's my chair.'

'Sorry, sorry, so sorry,' muttered Jolene, pulling it out of the office again. She grabbed her own seat, which was very uncomfortable, and finally sat down to join the others.

'Right,' said Diane. 'I have just come out of a briefing meeting with HR and rather than me pass on the news I thought it only fair that HR should come and do their own dirty work.'

'Really, Diane,' said Kev, looking extremely flustered, 'we provided you with all the tools. Line managers are meant to be briefing their teams, not the HR Department.'

'Why?' asked Diane.

'Er, because that's your job,' said Kev. 'I'm sure it's in your terms and conditions. I can look it up for you, if you want, and if you have an issue perhaps we can set up a meeting between you and your line manager to discuss your concerns over your job role.'

'My concern over my job role is that I didn't realise that I had to do all the shitty stuff. Deliver news and decisions that I was not a part of. To be dictated to. I hadn't clocked that. I didn't realise that I worked for a dictatorship.'

Jolene looked nervously around the table. Everyone was leaning well back, not wanting to get caught in the crossfire.

'Are you aware of our counselling number?' Kev asked Diane. 'Stress in the workplace is very common and not something you should suffer alone.'

'The only thing giving me stress is the cock-eyed way people make decisions in this place and then expect the rest of us to just lie down and take it. Now, Kev, please will you deliver the message directly to my team?'

Kev looked around nervously. He took what looked like a PowerPoint presentation out of a plastic sleeve and turned over the first page. Diane slammed her hand over the paper.

'These guys don't need the bullshit preamble about efficiencies and effective working. Just cut to the chase, Kev.'

Kev looked round the room.

'We need to reduce head-count across the board,'

said Kev. He swallowed. 'Diane has been asked to lose one body from this department.'

There was silence round the table.

'I knew this would happen,' said Stacey, instantly looking close to tears.

'I'm not going anywhere,' said Barney, folding his arms even tighter than they were before.

'We're overstretched as it is!' complained Jerry.

Yang bowed his head.

Jolene scanned the room. Diane looked livid still. Jerry, Stacey and Yang looked pretty defeated. Barney looked defiant. She swallowed. This was her worst nightmare. There was really only one answer, though, and she knew it.

'It should be me,' she said, her voice breaking as she spoke. 'I was last in. I'll just go now, shall I?' She got up from her chair, fighting back the tears.

'Sit down,' commanded Diane.

Jolene sat down. No one was going to argue with that command.

'You're safe,' Diane said to her. 'You're part of the graduate training scheme so you don't come out of my budget. You're not part of my head-count. It has to be someone else.'

Jolene stared back at her.

'But that doesn't seem fair,' she said.

Diane sniffed. 'Welcome to the real world, honey,' she said. 'Life isn't fair.'

'But, but . . . that feels like I'm taking someone else's job,' Jolene continued, 'and you're all way more qualified than me, and have been here so much longer.

That can't be right, can it?' She looked at Kevin. 'Can it, Kevin?' she asked him.

'Yes, why don't you explain it to her?' said Diane, folding her arms in much the same was as Barney had done. Everyone turned to look at Kev.

'Well, it's, er, about budgets, you see, and your wages in the first year of you being a graduate trainee are paid out of a different budget, which has already been committed, not the budget for this department. We're asking all departments to make salary savings.'

'What you will learn, Jolene,' said Diane, 'is that, for the most part, the world of work is unfair. You will experience many times in your working life unfair activity and there is nothing you can do about it. People will decide things that affect your work without consulting you. You will not be congratulated for your humungous efforts but will be chastised and punished for the smallest error. As you get older your acquired skills and maturity over many years will not be valued. Instead you'll be sidelined for your age, whilst younger models will be brought in to make the same mistakes that you've already learned from. You will experience many different changes of leadership and structure, all of which will emulate identical philosophies of times gone by, but will be deemed as the brave new world until they crash and burn and you are forced to go back and do it the old way. Your life choices will not be respected, and you'll be expected to put work before illness or children or major life events, such as watching your child win a medal at sports day or play a donkey in their one and only Nativity play. Work will ask you to miss moments that should be lifetime memories for the sake of attendance at a meeting that you have absolutely no influence over, and that shouldn't be happening in the first place. The world of work is not fair, Jolene. End of.'

There was silence around the table.

'On behalf of the HR department, I'd like to point out that we do everything we can to make work a fair environment,' said Kev. 'And most importantly provide a safe place for people to come and tell us of any unfair practices.'

'So if I walk into your office after this meeting and tell you of this outrageously unfair practice, then you are going to sort it out, are you?' asked Barney. 'If I come and tell you that I can't lose this job because I'm too old to get another job and . . . and I've worked for the council for thirty years and that means nothing and that doesn't seem fair, you're going to listen, are you?'

Jolene looked at him, amazed. That was the most she had ever heard him say.

'Yeah,' nodded Stacey. 'What if I come down there and say you promised me flexitime as those are the only hours I can do because I'm a single mum and my whole life depends on it, and I work above and beyond every day, and catch up at home at the weekend because I so need this job. What are you going to say to that?'

'Look,' said Kev, holding up his hands. He looked at Diane, clearly wanting her to help him out, but she was equally clearly having none of it. 'I'm sure you all have a million reasons why you need your jobs, but tough decisions have to be made. We need to save money. Now, I'm really sorry, but I have to be in a health-and-safety forum in the other building in five minutes so I have to go.' He got up and straightened his jacket. 'Please can I signpost once again the counselling helpline that HR set up—'

'Get stuffed, Kev,' said Diane.

Kev nodded and backed out.

'I'm sorry, guys,' said Diane. 'I had no idea this was coming. This morning was the first time I heard about any people cuts. I'll be going to see the council leader about this to make my case that we can't afford to lose anyone, but it seems that it's across the board so I don't hold out much hope.'

Jolene looked up forlornly at her Christmas decorations hanging from the ceiling next door and thought about the reindeer biscuits under her desk that she had planned to distribute at the team meeting. She didn't think any of them would be in the mood for them now. The world of work wasn't working out at all how she had wanted it to.

She glanced over at the person to whom she had been assigned Secret Santa. She absolutely knew that the thing they would most want for Christmas was to keep their job. That would truly make their Christmas. She wondered if there was anything at all she could do to make sure that happened.

Suddenly a woman with grey hair burst into the office.

'The mayor has been waiting,' she announced, glaring at Diane.

'What for?' replied Diane.

'The Children's Christmas Party meeting,' replied the woman. 'It was due to start five minutes ago. He's left for the day now; says he'll see you in his office at nine sharp on Monday morning.'

'Bloody hell,' said Diane. 'He still thinks he's going to throw a party when we're cutting jobs? Where does he think he's getting the money from?'

The woman shrugged. 'I think that's what he wants you to find the answer to, and he wants you to make it happen. Everyone else has refused to help him. He's determined to do something. I put the meeting in your diary yesterday.'

'That's the last thing I need,' said Diane. 'We really have too much on.'

'I'll go,' said Jolene, shooting up her hand.

Diane stared at her.

'I really don't think—' began Jerry.

'No, I think that's a good idea,' interrupted Diane. 'Thank you, Jolene. You go to the meeting. He'll be nice to you. Just listen to what the mayor has to say about this Children's Christmas Party. Take notes, but tell him that I said we have no money. That's all you need to do.'

'Great, brilliant,' replied Jolene, getting up. 'I'll start working on it now.' She pushed past the mayor's secretary, who had arrived to share the news.

'Not sure that's a good idea,' muttered Jerry.

'Not sure any of us are in the right frame of mind to be discussing Christmas parties,' replied Diane. 'And Jolene needs something to do. Deflecting the mayor would be really useful. What's the worst that can happen?'

'I think we'll find out,' replied Jerry.

Diane looked at him. 'Brief her, will you?' she asked. 'Tell her to make sure he knows there is no money, whatever he's got in mind.'

'Will do, boss,' said Jerry. 'Will do.'

'And I'm sorry about the head-count announcement,' added Diane, looking round the table at Jerry, Yang, Stacey, and Barney. 'I really didn't see it coming. I've no idea what I'm going to do.' She put her head in her hands.

'You'll work it out,' said Jerry. 'You always do.'

Chapter 10

On the dot of five o'clock that evening Barney reached forward to switch his computer off as he always did.

Five minutes earlier Jolene had already tidied up her makeshift desk and closed her laptop down. Barney got up to take his coat from the rack by the door, buttoned it up and turned to leave without saying a word. Just as he did every night. Jolene shouted a hasty farewell as she scampered out the door after him, determined not to let him out of her sight.

Outside on the pavement, he pulled a knitted hat out of his pocket and put it over his head before heading left. Cars streamed past on the road, their headlights illuminating a very gentle snowfall, otherwise invisible in the dark air. Jolene smiled. She hoped it would get heavier. A dusting of snow on the ground over the weekend would be lovely. She walked briskly until she was alongside Barney. She was on a mission.

'Hi, Barney,' she said. 'Didn't know you lived this way. Mind if I walk with you?'

Barney barely glanced at her, just continued straight ahead, his hands deep in the pockets of his wool coat.

Jolene didn't know what to say but she knew she needed to make conversation so she came out with the bog-standard opener for the entire duration of December.

'So, are you ready for Christmas, then?' she asked.

He said nothing.

'I'm getting there. My closest friends live all over the place so I'm in the process of making them stuff. You know, stuff you can post. I've been crocheting A LOT! I think they're going to really love what I've made. And as for family, well, they're easy. Dad is obsessed with Arsenal so I give him Arsenal-branded stuff every year. Then Mum, well, last year I made her a cardigan, which she really liked, but this year I'm thinking we might go and do something together. So, maybe a pottery class or something. Something we can both enjoy. I used to do pottery up at uni and I really miss it. What about you, Barney? Do you have many to buy for?'

'No,' he replied gruffly.

'Oh, right, good. That means it's not so hard, then. Pretty straightforward, not having too many.'

Barney stopped abruptly at the edge of a road to let some cars go by. Then he pressed ahead.

'I've already sent one present,' said Jolene. 'To my friend in the Cook Islands. Which I'd never heard of until we connected online. It's a small island in the Pacific, kind of not far from New Zealand. She says I can visit any time, but I've looked at flights and they are so expensive, and I've still got my student loan to pay off and all that, so I don't think it will be soon. Have you ever heard of the Cook Islands?'

'Yes,' said Barney as they headed through a gate into a park. It was very dark, with just a few lamps casting a dim light. The snow was getting slightly heavier now, to Jolene's delight. However, she suddenly felt ill at ease. Where were they? She had been so busy chatting that she hadn't noticed where they were going and now they were somewhere that was, quite frankly, a bit scary.

Barney stopped abruptly and faced her. 'Why are you following me?'

'I . . . I thought you might want some company on the way home.'

'Well, I don't,' he said, turning and heading further into the park. She glanced back to where they had come from. She didn't like the look of it. So dark. She didn't want to be alone here. This was a scenario a female in her position would be warned not to enter. She rushed to catch up with Barney.

'Can I just walk through with you the rest of the way. I . . . I don't really want to walk alone.'

'I'm not walking through,' said Barney.

'Oh,' said Jolene. 'Where are you going then?'

'Here,' he said. He strayed off the path and walked towards a clump of bushes. Oh my God, thought Jolene. What is he doing? What have I done?

She watched as Barney approached a bench just in front of the bushes, brushed some snowflakes off the seat, then sat down. He pulled his coat closer around him and bent his head. He sat absolutely still for what seemed like for ever. Jolene had no idea where she was now and no idea how to get out of the park. She had no choice but to go over and slowly lower herself beside him on the bench, trying to be invisible.

Barney stayed with his head bowed for some time as she sat as quietly as possible. Her eyes were getting used to the dark and she could now see that they were at one end of a large open space surrounded by trees. She could hear the hum of London in the background and the glow of the city rising above the trees. She felt herself relax slightly, feeling less threatened She could see her breath in the cold air and she watched as it twirled upwards, mingling with Barney's.

Eventually Barney raised his head and looked across the field.

'I'm sorry,' said Jolene. 'I was scared to be alone and I didn't know where I was.'

'Then you shouldn't have followed me, should you?'

'I'm sorry,' she said again. She paused for a moment. 'Where are we?' she asked. 'It's kind of beautiful. I imagine it's lovely in the daylight.'

Barney sighed. 'It's Vauxhall Pleasure Gardens,' he said. 'Have you never been here before?'

'No,' said Jolene. 'Didn't even know it was here. Never heard of a Pleasure Gardens.'

Barney coughed.

'It opened in the mid-seventeenth century,' he began. 'There were hot-air balloons and tightrope walkers and fireworks and music, apparently.'

'Wow,' said Jolene, trying to imagine all that happening so long ago. 'Do they have entertainment here nowadays?'

'They sometimes have a big screen over the summer, showing films, I think.' He paused and swallowed. 'They used to have an ice rink, right over there,' he said, pointing.

'Oh, I bet that was lovely,' said Jolene. 'I wonder why that stopped.'

Barney shook his head. 'It didn't pay, I guess. Like most things, if it doesn't make money it disappears.'

They sat in silence for a few more minutes.

'So,' she said eventually. 'You come here often, do you?'

Barney leaned back on the bench and folded his arms closely round his chest.

'Nosy, aren't you?' he said.

'I'm just trying to make conversation,' she said. 'My mum says I ask too many questions, but I'm just interested. I like talking to people. I'll go, if you want to be alone, though.'

Barney didn't reply for a moment. Then he said, 'I met my wife on our first date here. I bought her an ice cream from the kiosk over there. I pushed my daughter round in a pram every Sunday morning whilst my wife went to church. I taught my daughter how to ride a bike over on that pathway and we came here to take photographs the day she got married. And every Christmas Eve we would come ice skating. Family tradition, just as it was going dark. Then we'd go to the Nelson for a drink and fish and chips on the way home, then church at midnight to sing a couple of carols.'

Barney's voice cracked ever so slightly towards the end.

'It's a very special place, then,' said Jolene.

Barney nodded.

He shifted in his seat to one side. He took his phone out of his pocket and shone its torch at the back of the bench. There was a plaque. Jolene leaned forward to read.

IN LOVING MEMORY OF LINDA CALLOW
(1959–2020)

HERE WHERE GOOD TIMES HAPPENED

Jolene couldn't quite make sense of what she was reading. Then, of course, it struck her. How could she have been so stupid?

'Was Linda your wife?' she asked.

'Of course she bloody was!' exclaimed Barney. 'Do you think that I'd come and freeze my nuts off for anyone other than my wife?'

'Sorry, sorry, it's just that I'm prone to getting things wrong and misinterpreting things, so I ask questions to help make sure I've got it right.'

Barney leaned back against the bench and covered up the plaque as though she had offended his wife by merely asking the question.

They fell into silence again. Jolene gazed across the black field.

'She was young,' she stated.

'Correct,' clipped Barney. 'Too bloody young.'

'Was it cancer?' asked Jolene.

He didn't answer for a moment and she was worried that again she had asked the wrong question.

'Covid,' replied Barney. 'Bloody Covid.'

'I'm so sorry,' said Jolene.

'Whilst Boris was fannying around with what to do about bloody Christmas I wasn't allowed to say goodbye to Linda in hospital. She died alone on 1 December.'

'Oh God,' gasped Jolene again. 'I'm so sorry.'

'She loved Christmas,' he continued. 'She'd have the tree up on 1 December. We'd each have an Advent calendar; bloody carols would be playing constantly in the house. Constantly. She loved carols.'

He bowed his head.

Jolene froze in fear, worried that she had made him cry.

'Her Advent calendar is still on the mantelpiece,' he said. 'She'd planned ahead and looked it out in good time. Then she went into hospital. Every day since she died I come downstairs, hoping that it was all a nightmare and I'll see she's actually opened the doors. But she hasn't. They're all still shut.'

Jolene wiped away a tear. That was the saddest thing she had ever heard.

'So forgive me for not getting all excited about Christmas and your decorations and your biscuits and your Secret bloody Santa Project. Christmas simply does not bring joy into my life. Quite the opposite. Christmas means remembering what I've lost, and the time I was separated from my wife when she needed me most, and the fact that I never got to tell her the things I wanted to. I never even got to say goodbye.'

'I'm so sorry, I didn't mean to upset you,' said Jolene.

'Well, you did,' said Barney. 'You young people are all the same. All you can think about is yourselves and having a grand old time and doing exactly what you want to do. To hell with what anyone else is feeling or doing. You reckon you're the first people on this earth with your oh-so-clever ideas about how we should all be doing things. Let me tell you, Jolene, I have worked for the council for thirty years and you are not going to last five minutes. I've seen it time after time. You come in all bright eyed and bushy tailed, full of energy, and then the minute the going gets tough you're out of there. You just can't hack it. No stamina, no resilience in your generation whatsoever. You'll be gone by Christmas, mark my words. You'll never cope.'

Barney got up and walked away.

Jolene waited, then followed him at a distance until they were out of the park. Then she went home, trying to work out how on earth she was going to show him that she wasn't like the other people who arrived at the council and gave up. She'd stick at it. She knew she would. She was also frantically trying to work out what on earth she was going to get for Barney for his Secret Santa that would bring him any Christmas joy whatsoever.

Chapter 11

It had taken Yang two buses to get to Stacey's flat. He'd given himself an hour, worrying he was going to be late, cursing himself the whole way there. How had he got himself into this situation? He'd only offered to babysit for Stacey because he hoped to get on her good side, but then she'd used his offer to accept a date with a single dad from outside school! Oh, the irony! He could only hope the date went really badly. Then it might have been all worth it.

He eventually got off the bus with his guitar slung over his shoulder and a bag full of Chinese food clutched in his hand. His mother had insisted on him bringing it the minute she learned that he was heading over to Stacey's.

'I don't need to take food,' said Yang to his mother. 'It's not a date. She's going *on* a date and I'm staying at home and looking after her daughter.'

'No harm in it, though, is there? The date might go badly and Stacey will come back hungry and there you will be, ready to console her with Kung Pao Chicken.'

Yang realised what a horrible mistake he'd made the minute Stacey opened the door to her flat.

She looked utterly amazing. Like, next level. Her dark hair was in an updo and she was wearing a dark green fitted knee-length dress with high heels. Yang's jaw literally dropped. However, attached to her right leg was a small child, wailing. Stacey looked frazzled and close to tears.

'Hi, Yang,' she said. 'Come in.' She shuffled to let him past with Grace still attached to her leg. He walked down the narrow hall and into a small lounge. Stacey trudged behind him, pulling Grace with her.

Stacey had a look of sheer desperation on her face.

'Erm, I'm not sure I'll be needing you after all,' she began, wiping a tear from the corner of her eye. 'Grace has been like this for the last hour. She doesn't want me to go out. I was just about to call Will to cancel.'

Good idea, thought Yang. Let's just stay in, the three of us, and eat Chinese food.

He looked at Stacey as another tear slipped down her face. She looked absolutely devastated. He gave a big sigh.

He turned to Grace. 'So, I'll take this Chinese food back with me then, shall I?' he asked her. 'It's a shame because I was looking forward to sharing some prawn crackers with you.'

'What are prawn crackers?' she asked. 'Crackers you put prawns on?'

'Have you never had prawn crackers?' asked Yang.

'No. I have cheese crackers and we take crackers to Nana's at Christmas, but me and Mum pull them all because Nana's usually asleep. Are prawn crackers like

Christmas crackers? Do you get a present with them. Is the prawn a present? Do you get free prawns with the crackers?'

Yang sat down on the sofa and put the white plastic bag on the coffee table in front of him. He opened the bag and looked inside, then looked back up at Grace.

'Why don't you come and try one with me?' He pulled out the paper bag of prawn crackers, took one out and put it in his mouth. 'The thing I really like about prawn crackers is that they crackle on your tongue, sort of like very quiet popping candy.'

'I love popping candy,' said Grace, letting go of her mother's leg and stepping forward to take a prawn cracker. 'But Mum won't let me eat it. She says it makes me crazy. Which is stupid.' She put the cracker in her mouth and smiled. 'You're right, it is like quiet popping candy,' she said. She looked up at her mum. 'Look, I'm not going crazy,' she said to her.

Stacey smiled a watery smile. 'No, you look remarkably not crazy,' she said. 'Why don't you go and get some plates for you and Yang, and if you ask him nicely he might let you try some other Chinese food.'

'Will I like Chinese food?' Grace asked him.

'Er, yes,' said Yang. 'Chinese food makes people happy so you're bound to like it.'

Grace skipped off through a door into what must be the kitchen.

Yang looked up at Stacey. There were tears in her eyes again. 'Thank you,' she said, putting her hands together in gratitude. 'That was . . . erm, amazing. You are so good with kids.'

Yang shrugged. 'As I said, years of practice with nephews and nieces. It's fine. You go. Enjoy, OK?'

'Thank you. I won't be late.'

Yang shrugged again.

Stacey nodded. 'Great. I really do appreciate this.'

Grace came back in, balancing two plates and a bottle of ketchup. 'Haven't you gone yet?' she said to her mum.

'I'm just going,' laughed Stacey.

'Don't let Isaac's dad touch you,' added Grace. 'Promise.'

Yang raised his eyebrows at Stacey.

'Understood,' replied Stacey, giving her daughter a small salute. She turned and fled. Yang heard the door bang behind her.

'Isaac's dad is an utter bastard,' said Grace as she laid out the two plates on the coffee table.

Yang decided it wasn't his place to correct her language.

'How do you know that?' he asked, getting cartons out of the bag.

'Isaacs's mum said so,' she replied. 'She says it most days when she picks up Isaac.'

'Right, well, maybe she just thinks that. Maybe he's actually all right.'

'No, Evie's mum said so, too.'

'How does she know?'

'I think she went out with him and it didn't go well.'

'OK . . .' said Yang. 'Do you like sweet and sour?'

'Well, I like sour sweets so I think yes.'

'Not really the same, but I tell you what, I'll put a little on the side and you can try it and tell me what you think.'

Grace nodded. She looked at Yang. 'I like you,' she said.

'Thank you,' replied Yang. 'I like you too.'

'Will you kiss my mummy?'

Yang spat his sweet and sour chicken out so it landed on the carpet.

'Mummy won't like that,' said Grace, jumping up and running into the kitchen. She came back out with a kitchen roll. 'You'd better clean it up or else she won't want to kiss you.'

He tore off a piece of kitchen roll and reached down to gather up the stray chicken.

'I don't think me and your mum will be kissing,' said Yang.

'Why not?'

'Well, because we're not in a relationship.'

'You could be. I'd like you to be my new daddy. As long as you keep bringing me prawn crackers.'

'Grace, me and your mum are work colleagues. That's it. In any case, she's out on a date, you know. Clearly she likes Isaac's dad, so he's more likely to become your new dad than me.'

'I don't want a bastard to be my new dad,' said Grace. 'I'd like you to be my new dad.'

Yang looked at Grace. Boy, was she a piece of work. No wonder Stacey was always frazzled.

'Can I show you my donkey costume in a bit?' she asked.

'Sure,' said Yang, relieved to get onto safer ground. 'I'd like that.'

'Would you?'

'Of course. Your mum has been talking about your donkey costume loads at work. So, you know, it would be good to actually see it.'

'Why have you brought a guitar?' she said, pointing at the guitar leaning against the sofa.

'Because I play and I thought I might be able to have a practice whilst I'm here.'

'Will you play for me?'

'Sure,' said Yang. 'Will you be critical?'

'I'll tell you if I like it or hate it. I'll tell you if it sucks.'

'Perfect,' said Yang.

Yang had taken Grace through his entire repertoire by the time Stacey came home. Her critique had been in depth for each song.

'Too slushy.'

'Yuck.'

'Average.'

'What does "clandestine" mean? Is it a made-up word?'

'The first bit was good, but then it went downhill.'

'Scrap it. It will never catch on.'

'Well, thank you very much, Simon Cowell,' said Yang after a while. 'Really useful feedback.'

'Is that it?'

'Thought you weren't enjoying my songs.'

'I'm not, but I think this is helpful for you.'

'Yes, it's really deflating my ego. Thanks so much for that.'

'You are welcome. Do you have a song about a donkey?'

112

'No.'

'Why not?'

'I don't have deep feelings for donkeys. Not deep enough to write a song about them.'

'I would if I could. I love them. Donkey love is the best kind of love.'

Yang smiled and struck a chord. Then he started to croon.

Donkey Love . . . is the best kind of love.
Donkey Love . . . is everlasting love.
Donkey Love . . . beats any kind of love.
Donkey Love . . . is all you need.

'I love it!' shrieked Grace. 'Why didn't you sing that one before, instead of all the rubbish ones?'

'I've just made it up. That's why.'

'What now?'

'Yes.'

'Sing it again, sing it again! It's my favourite song in the whole entire universe.'

Donkey Love . . . is the best kind of love.
Donkey Love . . . is everlasting love.
Donkey Love . . . beats any kind of love.
Donkey love . . . is all you need.

'It's sooo good,' Grace shrieked again, jumping up and down. 'You could be the next Taylor Swift with that song. I've got a ukulele. Will you teach me how to play it on that?'

By the time Stacey walked through the door with Isaac's dad, Grace had helped Yang add another verse, which seemed to be just a repeat of the key lyric 'Donkeys made Jesus so let's all adopt a donkey.'

'Are you still up?' said Stacey as she walked in.

'Mum, Mum, Mum, we wrote a song about donkeys!' shouted Grace as she hurled herself at her mother.

'Lovely,' said Stacey. 'But you really should be in bed.'

'We need to sing it for you NOW,' demanded Grace. 'Please, Mummy, please.'

'OK, OK,' said Stacey. 'Have you said hello to Isaac's dad?' She indicated the tall slim man standing behind her in designer jeans and purple cashmere sweater under a smart black three-quarter-length coat. He looked and smelled expensive. Yang hadn't liked the sound of Will and he definitely didn't like the look of him. Too good looking and too well dressed. Everything that Yang thought he wasn't.

'Hello, Isaac's dad,' said Grace, not even looking at him, but rushing over to stand beside Yang.

'Will, this is Yang,' said Stacey.

Will nodded at Yang and offered his hand to shake. 'Thanks for babysitting,' he said. 'If you fancy earning some more money, I'm always looking for someone to look after my boy when he stays with me.'

'Oh, no, this is just a favour,' said Yang. 'A one-off. I work with Stacey.'

'Oh, I see,' said Will. 'Well, never mind. The offer's there if you ever fancy it.' He held up a bottle of wine. 'Where are your glasses?' he asked Stacey.

'I'll get them,' she replied. 'You take a seat. I won't be a moment.'

Grace was virtually sitting on Yang's knee by now, openly staring at Will, who had sat himself down and was checking out the room.

'Did you have a good evening?' asked Yang.

'Shhhh,' whispered Grace through gritted teeth. 'Don't make him feel welcome. He's an utter bastard, remember.'

That got Will's attention.

'She's erm . . . seven,' said Yang, trying not to laugh.

'Isaac said you were a lively girl,' Will said, trying to smile.

Stacey sailed in with three wine glasses and put them down on the table.

'None for me, thanks,' said Yang. 'I really should go.'

'Please can we sing our donkey song first?' said Grace. 'You must hear it. It's by far Yang's best song.'

Stacey looked at Yang. 'I didn't know you were a singer.'

'Well, you know,' said Yang. 'Just a little.'

'He's amazing,' said Grace, 'the best singer in the whole world.'

'You didn't say that earlier,' Yang said to Grace.

'I did so. Tell him to sing, Mummy. You have to hear him sing.'

'Only if he wants to,' she replied. 'I'm sure he wants to get out of here.'

'You'll play our song, won't you?' said Grace. She nudged him. Yang picked up his guitar.

'You need to sing too,' he told Grace. 'Don't leave me hanging. After three. One, two, three.'

Donkey Love . . . is the best kind of love.
Donkey Love . . . is everlasting love.
Donkey Love . . . beats any kind of love.
Donkey Love . . . is all you need.

Grace and Yang sat and sang their song while Stacey smiled broadly and Will stroked the back of her leg. He barely looked at them as they sang their hearts out about donkeys. Yang decided that Grace was absolutely right. Will probably was an utter bastard.

As soon as he had struck the last chord, Yang got up ready to leave and started to pack his guitar away.

'It's the best song, isn't it?' Grace asked her mother.

'It's great, really is,' smiled Stacey. 'Sounds like you have had a good time.'

'I'd better go,' said Yang. 'Places to go, people to see and all that.

'It's been a very interesting night,' he said to Grace. He offered his hand to shake and she took it.

'It's been the best fun. I liked everything about it,' she stated. 'Don't bother with the black bean stuff, though, next time. Not great unless you smother it in ketchup.'

'I'll pass that on to my father,' he said. 'He's only been cooking that dish for forty years.'

'You'll come and babysit again, won't you?' Grace said.

Yang looked over at Stacey. She mouthed a sorry.

'We'll see,' he replied. 'Keep singing our donkey song.'

'I'm going to sing it at school on Monday,' she announced.

'Magic,' said Yang, edging past her to the door.

'Now go and brush your teeth,' said Stacey, 'whilst I say bye to Yang.

'You OK?' she asked Will, who had already knocked back a glass of wine.

He nodded and reached forward to pour another glass.

At the door, Stacey hugged Yang, to his surprise.

'Thank you so much,' she said. 'Can't tell you how grateful I am. Just . . . well . . . to go out and have adult company. It's just brilliant. I've had such a good night, I can't tell you. Will is great, isn't he?'

Yang glanced through the door to Will, who had kicked his shoes off and was pointing the remote control at the TV.

Yang nodded. 'It's been fun. With Grace, I mean. She's fun to be with. She made me laugh.'

'You don't have to say that,' she told him. 'She can be difficult.'

'I mean it. I see where she gets her bluntness from.'

Stacey smiled. 'I think I get it from her.'

'Sorry about the donkey song. I think you might be hearing it a lot.'

'I'm sure I will, but it's put a smile on her face so I will enjoy it. The first twenty times.'

'Well, enjoy the rest of your evening,' said Yang, nodding awkwardly.

'Thanks again,' smiled. Stacey. 'Really actually very good of you.' She looked confused. They smiled awkwardly at each other.

117

'Good. Well, I'll see you Monday,' said Yang.
'Will do. Bye then.'
'Say good night to Grace.'
'I will. Bye, Yang.'

Chapter 12

'Who are you?' demanded Cecil, the mayor, the following Monday morning when Jolene walked into his office.

Jolene stuck out her hand and grinned. 'I'm your Christmas party planner from Accounts. Diane sent me.'

Cecil looked confused. He eyed the elf jumper she had carefully chosen for today's meeting. It had a hat on it with a real bell. It was one of her favourites.

'Diane sent you?'

'Yes,' nodded Jolene. 'That's it. Diane, tall, absolutely stunning, with a heart of gold but slightly scary.'

'I know who Diane is.'

'Good, well, she sent me and I come with notepad in hand and I'm ready to hang off your every word.'

That seemed to do the trick. Cecil seemed to like the idea of someone hanging off his every word and so invited her into his wood-panelled office. It was large and spacious and, unlike every other office in the building, was not crammed with desks and filing cabinets.

Framed photos of mayors gone by lined the walls. Cecil took his green leather chair behind the desk and indicated for Jolene to take a seat in front of him.

She sat down with a slight jingle of her elf jumper and took off the top of her pen. She grinned. He grimaced back. They sat in silence.

'So what is your vision?' asked Jolene eventually.

'For what?'

'For the party.'

'Oh, yes, the party. What I need you to get for me . . . sorry, what is your name again?'

'Jolene.'

'Jolene?'

'Yes, Jolene.'

'As in Dolly Parton?'

'Yes, as in her song.'

'Right, Jolene, I need you to get a picture of me on the front of the *Gazette* with local children looking like I've made their Christmas.'

Jolene wrote down every word he said. She looked up.

'That doesn't sound like a party,' she said, confused. 'I thought that's what you wanted, not newspaper coverage.'

'It doesn't have to be a party exactly, just something so bloody amazing, such a spectacle, that the *Gazette* wants to plaster my face all over their front page.'

Jolene nodded. She bit her lip. She thought the mayor wanted to do something good, not just get his picture in the paper. She thought about the PowerPoint presentation she had prepared at home the night before.

She hadn't been told to put any ideas together by Diane, but she thought it would be helpful nonetheless. To try to take the burden of the mayor's request off Diane. Think of a solution and present that to the mayor so Diane wouldn't have to do any more thinking. However, she'd spent all night thinking about what might be magical for the kids. Not what would get the mayor in the paper.

The mayor was looking at her expectantly. She wriggled uncomfortably, which made the bell jingle on the front of her jumper.

'Well?' said Cecil. 'Speak!'

Jolene put her laptop on the mayor's desk with trembling hands. She wasn't sure her suggestion was going to be what the mayor wanted at all. But she had no choice. She had to say something. She pulled her chair closer to the desk, turned her computer round and opened it up so that the mayor could see.

'So,' she said, showing the mayor a picture of stars and the moon on the screen. 'I was thinking that the most important person to children at Christmas is . . .?'

'Me?' asked the mayor.

'I'm sure you're right up there, but I was actually thinking of Father Christmas and how all children love the idea of him travelling round the sky to deliver all the presents.'

'Yes, yes, of course, but why are you showing me pictures of stars? What have the stars got to do with it?'

'I was thinking that we could sort of have a party based on Father Christmas's journey through the sky to get to the children of Bermondsey from where he lives, and I was thinking: where is the best place to look at the sky and imagine Father Christmas travelling thousands of miles?'

'Greenwich Observatory?' said the mayor, shaking his head. 'What are you on about? What are we doing having a party in Greenwich? I don't want pictures of Greenwich in the *Gazette*. I want Bermondsey in the papers. Bloody Greenwich gets far too much coverage as it is. Just because they invented time there or some other nonsense.'

'No, I wasn't actually thinking of Greenwich. Well, I was thinking, if it's not too ambitious, what about the London Eye? We could take over some pods and look into the sky and see if we can see where Santa lives.'

'And where is that?' asked the mayor, raising his eyebrows.

'We could say he lives on the brightest star in the sky and see if we can see it. Then I was thinking that maybe we have Santa ready and waiting when they get off the capsules. Like he's travelled all across the sky to come to Bermondsey to see them especially.'

The mayor stared at Jolene. She thought perhaps she'd gone too far. She thought it was a magical idea, if she was honest. If someone had taken her on a journey through the sky and Father Christmas was waiting at the end, then that would have been pretty spectacular. She gave the mayor a nervous smile. He'd leaned back in his seat and was looking through narrowed eyes. She noticed a gravy stain on his tie. Bound to happen, she thought, given all the lunches he must be invited to as mayor.

She didn't know if she should proceed or give him time to process what she had said. She waited a while longer, then flicked onto the next screen.

There was a picture of several smiling elves. 'What would be amazing is if we could get elves to take them on the capsules,' she continued. 'They could be their elf guides through the skies, pointing out where Father Christmas lives and the route he might take. How magical would that be? And then they would disembark their capsule and the elves could escort them to Santa, who had landed behind County Hall and was waiting for them with presents.'

The mayor stared at her. 'Where do I come in? I don't want to be Santa. No one will know it's me.'

'Of course we'll have to get a "real" Santa for that role. Er, maybe you could be Chief Elf or – I know – what about Mayor of Lapland. You've come along to help Santa out, make sure he gets to Bermondsey safely for this very important party.'

'So I could just wear what I'm wearing?' said the mayor. 'Including my ceremonial chain.'

'Yes,' replied Jolene. 'I mean, we might add a touch of Lapland. A little snow on your shoulders, maybe?'

The mayor was nodding thoughtfully, which Jolene took as a good sign. Abruptly, he stood up. And for the first time offered his hand.

'Done,' he said, pumping her arm up and down.

'What's done?' she asked.

'Your party. I like it. I like it a lot. So just get it done. Off you go. I'll see you there.'

Jolene felt her jaw drop open. A mixture of shock

123

and delight. He liked it. She could not wait to tell Diane. She would be absolutely over the moon. She was sure.

'Brilliant, amazing,' she grinned. 'So glad you loved it.'

He paused. 'Oh, I didn't say I loved it. I'll only love it if you get me on the front page of the *Gazette* in front of Bermondsey's own London Eye with an elf and a small child . . . and Father Christmas, I suppose. You got that?'

Jolene nodded. 'Got it,' she said. 'You can count on Accounts.' She threw her head back and laughed. 'Wow, that's funny,' she said.

'You can go now,' said the mayor, glancing at his watch. 'Just tell me what time you want me and which of the press are coming.'

Jerry did not throw his head back and laugh when Jolene debriefed him and Diane later that day on her meeting with the mayor.

'You told him what?' he said.

He had started to breathe heavily and looked nervously towards Diane, who was sitting with her eyebrows arched.

'Let me get this straight,' Jerry said to Jolene. 'You told the mayor he could have a trip on the London Eye with a load of children accompanied by elves.'

'Do you not think that's good enough?' Jolene asked Jerry, feeling worried. She really thought she'd done an excellent job. She'd come out of the mayor's office buzzing, practically doing cartwheels down the corridor.

124

But now Jerry was facing her and he did not look anywhere near as ecstatic as she was. She cast her mind back to Jerry's instructions before the meeting with the mayor. A Christmas party he'd said, for the children. That's what she had done and the mayor had been delighted. Jerry did not look delighted.

'What did I say before you went into the meeting?' he said to her.

'A Christmas party for the children,' she replied.

'What else?'

'Don't be put off by how much the mayor looks like the Fat Controller?' she replied.

'What was the most important thing I said to you?' he demanded.

Jolene really had no idea.

'I don't know,' said Jolene. 'Was it to make it really Christmassy?'

'No,' said Jerry. 'That wasn't it. I said very clearly, I thought, that you were to be very clear with the mayor that there was no money to spend. That whatever he wanted, it had to be cheap. And what you appeared to have agreed to is the hiring of the London's biggest tourist attraction, the hiring of real-life elves and Father Christmas.'

Jolene blinked back at him.

She nodded. 'And I promised the mayor his picture on the front of the *Gazette*.'

'Of course you did,' sighed Diane.

'Surely people will offer to do all that for free, if it's for the children?' Jolene said.

'Do you think?' asked Jerry.

125

Jolene bit her lip. Actually she did think, but that didn't look like the answer Jerry was looking for.

'Elves!' he went on. 'Elves? You going to get elves for free, are you, at Christmas? You going to get elves full stop? Where on earth do you think you are going to rustle up elves at this time of year? Do you not realise how busy they are? It's Christmas, for goodness' sake!'

Jolene had to admit that finding elves at any time of year quite frankly might be a stretch.

'I'm sorry, Diane,' said Jerry, turning to the boss. 'I thought I'd been clear.'

Diane was tapping her pen on the table rapidly.

'I'm sorry,' said Jolene, looking at Diane. 'I didn't mean to bring disrepute to the Accounts team.'

'Shall I go back to the mayor and tell him it's all been a big mistake and we can't possibly do this for him?' Jerry asked Diane. 'I mean, what's he doing asking this department to do this anyway? Why hasn't he got one of his own team sorting this out?'

'Because he's got no money left in his budget and, stupidly, I've helped him out in the past,' sighed Diane. 'I found him some spare once in the Facilities budget that I keep back for emergencies. But there is no spare any more. Everything is cut back to the very bone.'

'I'm so sorry,' said Jolene. 'I just thought he wanted to do something nice for the children and I got carried away. And . . . and . . . I wanted to show you that I could help. Do something for you because I don't think I'm doing anything useful at all. And the one thing I can do is organise a party. I was social sec of our college. We had the best parties, everyone said so.'

'This is a bit different from a disco in a college bar,' stated Jerry.

Jolene shook her head. 'I would never just organise a disco in a college bar. We always had a theme; we took socials to a new level. I convinced the dean to let us bring an entire travelling circus onto campus to teach us all circus skills as part of freshers week.'

'Really,' said Jerry sarcastically.

'Why don't you just let me have a go?' pleaded Jolene. 'Please, just let me try. I mean, as he admits, he doesn't actually want a party, all he wants is a photo opportunity. Let me see what I can do? It's not like you've asked me to do anything else. I'm so bored. Please let me do this.'

Diane continued to tap her pen for a moment. 'I might be able to get you some elves,' she said eventually.

'Are you feeling all right?' Jerry asked her.

'Fine,' said Diane.

'Then tell us of these mythical elves that you know of,' said Jerry.

'You know some elves?' asked Jolene in awe. She thought she might be sick, she was so excited. Her boss knew elves!

'Well, my husband, he's directing *Snow White and the Seven Elves* in the West End and—'

'What are the chances?' said Jerry, wide eyed. 'I mean, what *are* the chances.'

'And he has real elves in the show?' asked Jolene in absolute awe.

'No, of course not. They're not real elves, they're little people; you know dwarfs.'

127

'So you could get hold of seven dwarfs/elves for the party?' Jolene asked in awe.

'I think there might be as many as nine, including understudies,' replied Diane.

'Would you ask them?' asked Jolene, her hands clasped together in prayer. 'Please would you ask them?'

Diane blinked back at her. 'I can ask my husband to ask them. They might do it as a publicity thing for the pantomime, as well, if we said there would be press there.'

Jolene got up out of her chair and hugged Diane. 'I knew it. I knew we would be able to find some elves somewhere. Sometimes you just have to dream big, then somehow the stars align and your prayers are answered.'

'Hang on a minute,' said Jerry. 'You still need to hire the London Eye and get a Santa Claus.'

'And what about the children? What did the mayor say about that?' Diane asked Jolene.

'Oh!' said Jolene. 'He never said. Will he be getting the children?'

'Definitely not,' said Diane. 'He'll expect us to just rustle some up out of nowhere. That will be the last thing on his mind.'

'What about Stacey's daughter's class?' said Jolene. 'Like an end-of-Nativity party for them. Can we invite them?'

'I don't see why not,' said Diane. 'It would certainly solve one problem.'

'I think we're all forgetting something here,' said Jerry, looking flustered. 'The cornerstone of Jolene's what-shouldn't-be-epic party plan is the London Eye. And that's never going to happen.'

'The mayor said the London Eye is within the Bermondsey Council,' said Jolene. 'So would that help? Would the people who run the London Eye want to help the council once in a while – especially if it's for the children?'

Diane stared at Jolene for a moment.

'Perhaps you and me should pay them a little visit,' said Diane to Jolene. 'Maybe it is worth asking them.'

'Really?' said Jolene. 'I don't want to put you out at all. I could go on my own.'

'Barbara, the GM, is a bit of a tough cookie. We'll both go. You go and get on to her office and set a meeting up.'

'Thank you,' said Jolene, backing out of the office. 'You won't regret this, I promise. It's going to be great.'

Jerry stood up and closed the door behind her.

'Are you sure about this?' he asked Diane. 'I can have a word with the mayor's PA and probably make this all go away.'

Diane shook her head, peering through the glass door at Jolene, already on the phone.

'She's showing enthusiasm,' she said. 'She wants to make stuff happen and we have done nothing but dampen her down. We should be encouraging people like Jolene, not crushing them.'

'If you say so,' said Jerry. 'Erm, whilst I've got you on your own, can I just ask you something?'

'Sure.'

'Everyone would like to know what the timetable is for making a decision about the new structure.'

'I need to make my recommendation before Christmas,' Diane said, 'unless I can think of another option, but I have no idea what. I'm sorry. It really sucks, I know. I'm very aware I'm going to ruin someone's Christmas.'

Jerry sighed. 'Well, my Christmas won't be up to much anyway. Another microwave meal in front of the television for me, so you know . . .' he shrugged.

Diane smiled at him. She suddenly felt bad that it was possible that Jerry was the person she spent most time with in her life and yet she really knew so little about him. 'I'm sorry to hear that,' she said. 'No one special on the scene to share the day with, then?'

'No such luck,' said Jerry.

'About time you found a man, isn't it? You been on Tinder or Grindr or whatever it is people do these days?'

'Not my scene,' said Jerry. 'I just loiter around coffee shops, hoping to get noticed.'

'Oh, and how's that working out for you?'

Jerry felt himself inexplicably blush.

'Come on, spill,' said Diane. 'So far it's been a tough day. Please make it better with some bona fide romance news.'

'Oh, it's nothing really. Nothing. I mean, it's going to come to nothing, but I've been talking to a guy. Just at the coffee shop. I go there on my way home to delay the inevitable empty-flat nightmare. Anyway, he's always in there. And we got chatting. And now he saves me a seat and we chat every day and, well, that's it really.'

130

'That's it? He saves you a seat every day?'

'Yeah. That's it.'

'Wow. And you like him?'

'Oh yes. I don't know. We just connect somehow. I've never known anything like it. He makes me feel like I'm the only person in the room. We've never even touched and yet I have never felt so close to someone.'

Diane swallowed. It sounded wonderful. How she wished she felt like that with Leon.

'So have you never asked him out or anything?' she asked.

'Well, I have sort of asked him out now. Been bullied into it, really, by my friend from choir.'

'You go to choir?'

'Yeah.'

'How did I not know this?'

'You never asked.'

'What kind of choir?'

'A church choir.'

'Wow. So you like to sing?'

'Yeah. It's kind of my escape. Sounds silly, I know.'

'Not at all,' replied Diane, looking at him in surprised awe. 'Not at all.'

'Anyway, Carol from choir told me to ask him to this candlelight carol concert thing we're doing. She thought if he came that would prove he's definitely gay and definitely likes me.'

Diane looked at him for a moment. 'You're not even sure he's gay?'

'I think he is; I just think he's holding something back. I don't know. He doesn't really talk about himself at all. He says he has a complicated life. And that's all he says. I wonder if he's in a relationship, or married, even.'

'Well,' said Diane, 'there's nothing as complicated as marriage, I can tell you.'

'I'd sure like to try complicated one day,' said Jerry wistfully.

'And did he pass the test? Did he say yes to the concert?'

'He said he'd try,' replied Jerry. 'Said he'd do his best.'

Diane looked at Jerry. 'Sounds like he has complicated commitments.'

'I know. But I will live in hope.' Jerry got up out of his chair, clearly wishing to close the subject. 'Anyway, I'll let everyone know that we'll have news before Christmas on proposed head-count reduction. Thanks for telling me.'

'I wish it was more positive news,' said Diane, watching him leave, thinking how much Jerry deserved someone and how sad it was that he might be alone at Christmas. She really needed to make sure she made the most of Chloe being with her – and Leon, of course.

Jerry filled Stacey in on the bus on the way home that night.

'I suppose it's better to know as soon as possible,' she said. 'Means I can hit the ground running in the new year, looking for a new job.'

'If it is you,' said Jerry. 'I have no idea which way she's going to go, and don't forget there will be a consultation period and they'll have to look to see if they can place whoever it is in another job in the local government.'

'I know,' said Stacey. 'But it's hassle, isn't it? And I need flexitime. Just as I thought my life was looking up and I had less to worry about, there's always something that puts a spanner in the works.'

'Oh my God,' breathed Jerry. 'I forgot to ask you about your date. How did it go? You need to tell me all about it.'

'I went on a date,' stated Stacey, her frown replaced by a smile. 'For the first time in what – eight years!'

'Insane,' said Jerry. 'Makes me want to weep for you. So how was it?'

'Great, good. I mean, it ticked all the boxes of a great date. We met at a restaurant. A nice restaurant. Only adults, no children, no highchairs, no colouring-in sheets, no kids' menu, no dodging pushchairs, no chicken nuggets, no soft play area, no chips squidged into the carpet, no rows and rows of ketchup. They had tablecloths, Jerry. I didn't know restaurants did tablecloths any more. Velvet chairs that would have been destroyed by ketchup-smeared hands. But they didn't seem to care. No worrying about dirt or grubby fingers or breakage issues. It was an amazing place.'

'You have been a long time in the child wilderness,' said Jerry. 'You poor, poor thing. What did you eat?'

'This was a revelation. I had something I wanted. Just me. Not something I ordered in case Grace decided she didn't like what she'd ordered. Unbelievable.'

'And how was the guy – you know, the man – the person who took you there? The other factor to this date.'

'He was great,' said Stacey. 'We chatted, we talked about his work. I tell you, he has a really good job in the city. Like seriously good. He travels a lot and he seems to be at conferences all the time. We talked about the breakdown of his marriage and how hard it's been on him, we talked about how difficult his ex-wife has made his life. It was great. Proper grown-up chat. You know: adult stuff. He made me feel like an adult.'

'Mm,' said Jerry, thinking that it didn't seem as though they had talked much about Stacey's life, but he didn't want to burst her bubble by mentioning it.

'Did he pay?' asked Jerry. Always a make or break on a first date, he thought. Although the etiquette was a bit trickier when you were gay. It seemed very clear cut that the man always paid on a male/female first date.

'He did!' said Stacey. 'He said he'd pay as long as we went back to mine for coffee. Which was very kind of him.'

'So . . . er . . . did you . . .?' asked Jerry.

'Did we what?'

'Kiss.'

'Well, we tried,' said Stacey. 'Sort of. Grace kept appearing to sing us the donkey song so eventually we had to give up. Will said next time we'd go back to his. No idea how I make that work, though.'

'Donkey song?' Jerry asked.

Stacey laughed. 'Oh, it's the cutest thing, really. She wrote it with Yang. She's totally fallen for him. Having said that, he was amazing. I never would have thought it. Grace was literally screaming, hanging onto my leg, before he arrived. Begging me not to go out. Then he came with food from his parents' restaurant, got her eating prawn crackers, and she couldn't have cared less where I went. Then when I came back, they'd written a song together about a donkey! She now talks about Yang all the time and sings the song all the time. It's driving me mad.'

'Wow,' said Jerry, impressed. 'Yang sounds like your regular Mary Poppins. I still cannot believe he offered to babysit for you. Just out of the blue like that?'

'I know,' said Stacey. 'I didn't pause to ask why. Just snapped his hand off, as you can imagine. Grace is absolutely desperate for him to babysit again and I can't seem to make her understand it was a one-off. That he was just being kind.'

'But what are you going to do about a babysitter if you want to keep on seeing Will?'

Stacey shrugged. 'He's coming over for dinner at some point soon. He seems happy to come to our flat. Especially if I'm feeding him, he says,' Stacey laughed.

I bet he is, thought Jerry.

'It was just so nice to be out,' sighed Stacey. 'And with a man who's solvent and ticks so many boxes. Oh, and guess what. He mentioned they have a very swanky office party at the Tower of London. Oh my God. What I would do to go to that. Can you imagine? It would literally be like all my Christmases

135

had come at once. Much better than our Christmas Coffee!'

'So did he invite you?' asked Jerry.

'Not yet,' said Stacey. 'But I'm working on him. No idea what I'd do about a babysitter, though. Anyway, your turn. Update me on your Christmas kiss plans with coffee-shop man.'

'Well,' said Jerry. 'I'm full of Christmas hope for this evening at the carol concert. In my head I'll be standing at the front of the church in my robes and we'll start with a rousing chorus of "O Come, All Ye Faithful" and I won't have spotted him. But then, just as we get to the last verse, the door at the back will creak open and it will be him, and our eyes will meet across a crowded church and it'll feel like a choir of angels is singing and the lights will glow behind his beautiful head, and it will seem as though the Angel Gabriel has arrived, and he'll give me a small wave and then find a seat. Then every so often – and definitely during "Silent Night" – we'll catch each other's eye and grin shyly, you know, like this.'

Jerry took off his glasses and grinned in a very weird way.

'Delightful,' said Stacey. 'That's a weird sex face, if ever I saw one.'

'Good, I've been practising,' said Jerry. 'Then afterwards, in the crypt, with the mince pies and mulled wine, he'll approach me and say that's the most beautiful music he has ever heard and then he'll snog my face off.'

'In church!' exclaimed Stacey.

'No, not really. That would be nice but I suspect it's a fantasy too far. Actually, what will happen is he'll walk over and ask if I have plans, and I'll say no, even though there's a choir drinks reception in the pub opposite, and then we'll skip off to some lovely little bar he knows and he'll tell me he's been in love with me since the first time he met me and thank goodness for Christmas so he can finally share his true feelings. Then "Last Christmas" by Wham! will come on the sound system and we'll fall into each other's arms and share a Christmas kiss. And we'll all live happily ever after.'

'Amen,' said Stacey.

'Amen to that!' agreed Jerry.

'Maybe we'll both get our Christmas kiss this year,' said Stacey.

'Wow,' replied Jerry. 'Wouldn't that be something?'

'Wouldn't it just,' said Stacey.

Chapter 13

'Yoo-hoo,' shouted Diane as she barged her way indoors. 'I'm home!'

No one replied. There were boxes, bags and suitcases strewn all along the length of the hall. She was sure Chloe hadn't taken this much stuff with her when she'd started university a few short months ago. What had she been doing, going to car-boot sales every weekend? Was that an old slide projector balancing on the hall table, knocking the carefully placed baubles out of the way? Where on earth had she bought that?

Leon had begrudgingly agreed to fetch his daughter when he realised he could use it as an excuse to pop into the Theatre Royal in Brighton and meet up with the director there for a chat. He'd left early that morning to miss the traffic, giving Diane time to put the final touches to the tree in the bay window in the lounge. She'd wrapped lights around it and left them on all day. She knew it was a waste of electricity but she wanted the house to look festive to welcome her daughter back home. She stuck her head round the door. The tree looked fantastic but Leon and Chloe were nowhere to be seen.

She went back into the hall and took her coat off before smoothing her dress down. They must both be in the kitchen, she thought, enticed by the smell of the stew she had put in the slow cooker that morning. Diane had decided Chloe would need comfort food after ten weeks without her mother's cooking. Stew and dumplings was one of Chloe's favourites. She couldn't wait to sit down at the kitchen table with her and hear all about her first term at university whilst they ate good food and drank red wine. Now she could actually feel as if it might be the start of Christmas.

She pushed the kitchen door open and there indeed was Chloe, drinking tea at the table with her feet resting on the knee of an unknown boy, a man, a stranger, in her house, when all she wanted to do was totally monopolise her daughter.

'Mum,' said Chloe, leaping up out of her chair and flinging her arms around her. 'Oh, Mum, so good to see you.'

'And you,' replied Diane, closing her eyes and breathing in her daughter's embrace.

'This is Bertie,' said Chloe, pulling away and indicating the stranger at the table. 'Say hi, Bertie.'

'Hi,' grinned Bertie, giving her a little wave.

'We gave him a lift to London. His parents are up in Derbyshire so he's getting the train up north in a few days. Dad said it would be OK if he stayed here until then.'

Diane felt stunned. Bertie looked perfectly nice as she watched her daughter curl her arms around his shoulders, but she knew that Bertie would inevitably be getting all of Chloe's attention when she wanted some of Chloe's attention now that she was home.

'Of course,' said Diane, heading for the kettle so they couldn't see her face. 'That would be fine, no problem.'

It was a massive fucking problem.

'Cup of tea?' she asked brightly.

'We've just had one,' said Chloe, 'but you sit down. I'll make you one. You've been at work all day.'

'What do you do?' asked Bertie. 'If you don't mind me asking.'

Yes I do mind you asking, thought Diane. I hate you asking because I hate what I'm about to say.

'I work for the council,' she said. 'In the accounts team.'

'Oh, must be very interesting work,' replied Bertie.

No, it's fucking hideous, thought Diane. 'What do you do?' she asked Bertie.

'Oh, Mum,' said Chloe. 'He's a student of course. Second year media studies.'

Diane nodded. 'Media studies?' she said.

He nodded. 'I want to be a TV producer,' he added.

Of course you do, thought Diane, in awe of his youthful optimism. She could do with a bit of that.

'There you go, Mum,' said Chloe, putting a mug of tea in front of her and sitting down.

Diane had a million and one questions she wanted to ask her daughter but not really in front of this stranger. It would sound like the third degree and she didn't want to come across like that. She sipped her tea and looked round awkwardly.

'So how have you been, Mum?' asked Chloe.

For fuck's sake, thought Diane. I don't want to tell my daughter in front of Bertie that my life pretty much sucks at the moment. That work is utter shit, that I've got to make someone redundant and that home life sucks too because my husband is never here and when he is, he's always distracted to the point that I think he might be having an affair, and I feel like a terrible person because I haven't rung my mother in at least three weeks and I haven't bought nearly enough Christmas presents and we will have to go to a real-life supermarket in Christmas week, and it's all going to be an absolute disaster.

'I've been fine, thank you,' she said tightly. 'Fine.'

'Oh, Dad says to tell you that he'll be back around nine.'

'Nine!' exclaimed Diane. 'What do you mean, nine? There are no performances on a Monday.'

Chloe shrugged. 'He just said he had to go somewhere and to tell you that he'd be back around nine.'

Diane looked at the slow cooker bubbling away in the corner of the room and the bottle of red wine she'd got ready. Her wonderfully cosy family dinner, the first in ten weeks, had just gone up in smoke.

'Right,' she muttered. She looked up at Bertie. 'Well, at least you can have his stew.'

He looked immediately uncomfortable.

'Is it your special stew?' asked Chloe.

'Yes,' said Diane. 'I made it specially.'

'That's lovely, Mum, but Bertie is a vegetarian.'

Diane nodded. Of course he was. She couldn't help it: her brain immediately went to the fridge to work out what vegetarian options there might be. Cheese toastie or boiled egg were all she could muster up, given she hadn't bothered with a supermarket delivery in a long time.

'You don't need to feed me,' Bertie grinned. 'Honestly. I'll grab something when we go out.'

'You're going out?'

'Yeah,' said Chloe. 'Sara and Jess are already back. We're meeting them down the pub at seven.'

'Right,' nodded Diane. 'Of course. No problem.'

It was a problem, of course, of epic proportions. She'd been excited all day about finally having a shred of family life back that evening. The three of them around the kitchen table, sharing their lives over the last ten weeks, laughing, smiling, hugging. For Christ's sake, this evening had even made her excited about Christmas for the first time this season. Having the three of them together for Christmas had given her a shred of festive joy and now it was in ruins.

She looked up. Chloe had her feet on Bertie's knee again and he was gently stroking her leg whilst she stroked the back of his neck. This looked serious. Having said that, she was pretty much like this with her sixth-form college boyfriend, and that had all ended very abruptly after they'd been interrailing.

'So I've mentioned it to Dad,' said Chloe, 'but I've been invited up to Bertie's for Christmas. All his family will be there and I'll only be gone Christmas Eve to the day after Boxing Day, and Dad said he's working every day apart from Christmas Day. He said Christmas Day is always a bit of a wipe-out anyway, so he'd prefer a quiet one and we could do Christmas another day, couldn't we?'

Diane stared at Chloe. She would have liked to say she couldn't believe what she was hearing, but she could. Of course her daughter wanted to be with this exciting new man for Christmas and not her miserable boring mother and father. Quite frankly, if Diane had a choice she wouldn't spend Christmas here either.

She looked at Chloe, who was so flushed with youth and love it was scary. She looked so unbelievably happy.

'Of course,' said Diane. 'That's fine. Now I'll just nip upstairs and get changed. Excuse me a minute.'

Diane left the room. A tear trickled down her cheek. She dashed upstairs and locked herself in the ensuite, putting the toilet lid down and sinking onto it, then putting her head in her hands. She couldn't bear it. She couldn't bear the thought of Christmas, not without her daughter there to bring some sense of joy of being together. Some sense of ceremony that they would play out. The happy family all back together for Christmas. What would even be the point of getting up on Christmas Day if Chloe wasn't here? She could see the day looming in front of her. Leon would lie in until lunchtime, feigning exhaustion from his very difficult and distracting job in the theatre. Traditional Christmas lunch would be pointless. Leon didn't like turkey; she didn't like Brussels sprouts – and since she would be the one expected to cook it then why should she or would she? Why on earth would she bother? She'd have to get herself a cheese toasty and open the fizz on her own at 1p.m., then settle in front of the telly until Leon finally appeared in his dressing gown, having apologised for not getting her a Christmas present because of his terribly difficult and distracting job in the theatre. He'd ask when lunch was and she wouldn't know what to say to him she'd be so angry at the assumption that she would still be cooking his dinner despite the fact that Chloe was not there. Then he'd go to the kitchen, grab some crisps and the bottle of whisky, and ask if he could put *The Railway Children* on. His favourite movie to watch at Christmas and one that made her want to slit her wrists.

It would be the most depressing day she would ever spend. All she'd wanted was a day with her family, and all she was going to get was a day with her husband taking her for granted as he always did.

Still, she thought, trying to gather herself. She pulled off some toilet roll and blew her nose. Good job she hadn't ordered a big Christmas delivery from the supermarket. Sounded like she might be able to get Christmas dinner from the local petrol station. A sandwich meal deal for two!

Chapter 14

'You,' said Carol to Jerry, when he'd put on his cassock and checked his hair in the mirror, 'look utterly adorable.'

Jerry looked back at her. 'Not sure the word adorable is entirely correct to describe a grown man dressed as a choir boy!'

'Well, you do. All innocent and gorgeous,' she said, pinching his cheek.

'Again, possibly inappropriate, Carol,' he told her.

'Would it be inappropriate to offer you a wee nip of the old Dutch courage?' asked Carol, pulling a hip flask from under her cassock.

'Entirely and utterly essential,' he replied, holding the flask to his lips and taking a deep gulp. 'I'm not sure my heart rate can cope with the tension that I'm currently feeling.'

'Has he been in touch at all since you invited him?'

'He sent an emoji of a candle an hour ago.'

'Right. Does that mean anything? Is it a euphemism, you know, like an aubergine?'

'How do you know about aubergines?' asked Jerry.

'They talked about it on *This Morning* some time ago.'

'OK. Well, no, I don't think a candle means anything. But I guess it could mean he's holding a candle for me?'

'Oooo, good one. Like it. But does that mean he's coming?'

'I have absolutely no idea.'

'This is soooo exciting,' announced Carol. 'Not since I went to the Plasterers' Ball in 1965 and was hoping that Ray Entwhistle would be there have I felt this excited.'

'Was he there?' asked Jerry.

'No,' said Carol. 'His bus never turned up. But that night Jack asked me to do the Viennese Waltz and, well, he was a tremendous dancer – and lover, as it turned out.'

'Too much information, Carol.'

'Not really. I did marry him.'

'Wow,' said Jerry. 'I wonder what would have happened if Ray had turned up then. You might never have danced with your future red-hot lover and husband.'

'I know! Last time I heard, Ray did time for aggravated burglary, so thank God for a shoddy bus service in 1965 is all I can say.'

Jerry shook his head. 'That blows my mind,' he said. 'Your life could have been entirely different had that bus showed up. And who knows where my life might end up if this guy turns up tonight?'

'The absolute joy of life,' said Carol, jumping up and down. 'The anticipation is nearly killing me. I cannot contain myself. You will introduce me, won't you, if he does come? I'm dying to see what all the fuss is about.'

'Of course,' said Jerry. 'After all, this was all your idea. I'd still be just having coffee with him on a near-daily basis by now.'

'Instead of waiting for him to turn up to church to see you in a white dress. It couldn't be more romantic.'

'Right, everyone, gather round,' came the booming voice of the choirmaster as he clapped his hands. 'We'll have a very quick warm-up and then it's show time. Places, please.'

The candle-lit church looked stunning as the twenty-two-strong choir, each chorister holding a lit candle, filed out of the vestry. Jerry concentrated hard on not setting fire to the very long hair of the girl in front of him whilst he strained to scan the congregation to see if he could catch sight of coffee-shop man. He also had to sing his harmonies to 'Silent Night', and doing three things at once was taxing him. The choir walked all the way down a side aisle to the back of the church before turning into the central aisle to parade towards the altar. It was a calm and beautiful moment. The candles flickered as the voices of the choir filled the air. Fairy lights twinkled on a Christmas tree and spotlights lit the wooden Nativity scene displayed on a table near the front of the church. The air was truly magical. Whatever you thought of religion, this was a special moment. People united through song in the most stunning environment as they had done for hundreds of years. No one could fail to be moved by it.

Jerry already had goose bumps, but he felt as if his heart had leaped into his mouth as he passed a man on the end of a pew who wore a red scarf much the same as the one that the coffee-shop man wore.

He glided slowly past him as he sung, '. . . all is calm, all is bright . . .'

He thought his heart was going to burst out of his chest. He couldn't help but look over. And just as he did, so did the man, and it was him. The coffee-shop man had turned up. Had turned up to watch Jerry sing carols in a candle-lit church. He couldn't quite believe it. They exchanged a grin before Jerry realised he'd nearly bumped into the girl in front of him. He slowed down, but he couldn't wipe the massive smile off his face. They continued to glide forward, then fanned out at the top of the aisle to take their places at the front of the church and face the congregation for the first time.

'So?' hissed Carol as she settled next to him.

'He's here,' he hissed back.

'Thank the Lord,' said Carol. 'Our prayers have been truly answered.'

'Amen,' said Jerry.

The rest of the concert went by in a haze as Jerry sang his heart out, filled with love and joy and happy ever after. He belted out 'Once in Royal David's City', followed by 'O Little Town of Bethlehem' before calming down somewhat when they got to 'Away in a Manger'.

However, the magic of the occasion nearly did bring him to tears. He didn't have a clear view of coffee-shop man as his sightline was obstructed by a very tall man in front of him, but he could see the red scarf for most of the time to reassure him his man was there. He simply couldn't wait to finish the concert so he could rip off his cassock and run into his arms.

'You go,' said Carol, in the vestry when they had finished. 'Go get him. Go snog him, go do something with him – I don't know what – but you go and keep the Christmas dream alive.'

'Will do,' he said, beaming at her. 'And thank you,' he added, clutching her arms. 'Thank you for praying for me. I can't thank you enough.'

'Merry Christmas, one and all,' laughed Carol. 'Now go.'

Jerry had chosen his outfit under his cassock carefully. He'd picked a Scandinavian-style jumper: red and white, with deer prancing in horizontal rows. He felt it showed his fun festive side without being gross or tacky. That was the image he wanted to portray to coffee-shop man, who always looked smartly dressed.

He approached the throng around the mulled wine station at the back of the church, holding his breath. It suddenly hit him that he might not wait, he might just leave, not having understood that the invitation to carols extended to the essential mulled wine and mince pies afterwards. He scanned the crowd, his heart thumping. What if he had left? What would that mean? He had no idea.

Someone had put a Christmas CD on and Cliff

Richard was belting out 'Mistletoe and Wine'. What a killer combo, thought Jerry, weaving through the crowd. The words hinted at such opportunity for joy and romance.

Then he saw a flash of red on the periphery of the crowd and made a beeline for it. But he felt the head chorister grab his hand en route.

'Great performance tonight, Jerry,' he said. 'Real energy. So glad you're with us.'

Jerry beamed back, pulling his hand away. 'Thank you,' he said. 'I'm so very glad too. Sorry, but there's someone I need to catch up with.'

He turned and literally bumped into coffee-shop man, who had clearly been making his way towards him.

'Gosh, sorry,' said Jerry. 'I was just coming to find you.'

'No problem. I got you a mulled wine, although I wasn't sure if it's your drink of choice.'

'It's not anyone's drink of choice really, is it? I mean, who really wants hot wine? Stroke of genius, branding it as a Christmas drink. The only way to shift it, I imagine.'

'Bit like your Eggnog Latte?' said coffee-shop man.

'Oh, no, I like Eggnog Latte; I'd drink Eggnog Latte all year if I could.'

'Well, you're weird.'

'I guess I am,' grinned Jerry. 'Most definitely. And proud of it. I mean, we couldn't get weirder than this, really, could we? A first date in a candle-lit church surrounded by geriatrics drinking lukewarm wine.'

The minute he said it he regretted it. Why had he said 'first date'? It wasn't a first date, was it? So why had he said it? In his head, of course, it was a first date. But he didn't need to say that out loud. And the look on coffee-shop man's face told him that it had been the wrong thing to say. His face had fallen and a serious tone had taken over.

'Look,' he said, 'shall we take a pew?'

Nice, thought Jerry. Nice to hear someone using the term when there was actually a pew to take.

'Sure,' he said, leading the way back to the front of the church to a pew overlooking the wooden Nativity scene. He shuffled along and sat down before turning toward coffee-shop man and raising his cardboard cup.

'Merry Christmas,' said Jerry.

'Merry Christmas,' said the man, before taking a sip. Jerry watched as he lowered his cup and looked down into it as if contemplating what he was about to say. Jerry's heart sank. The signs weren't good. His body language indicated that he was struggling for words. Not a good sign at all.

'Look,' said the man, looking up now into his eyes. Jerry felt himself about to pray, yet again. 'Look, I'm so glad I came tonight . . .'

There's a 'but' coming, thought Jerry. I can hear it. Please, God, not the 'but'.

'But I don't know where you think this is going, but . . .'

OMG, not one, but two 'but's.

'I mean, I really, really like you and I wish with all my heart this was a first date, I really do, but . . .'

Jesus, a third 'but'.

'I came here to tell you that I can't see you for a while. I mean, I know we're not seeing each other but . . .'

Four 'but's. The more buts, the more difficult the conversation, reckoned Jerry.

'What I mean is, I love our chats at the coffee shop, I really do, but I just need some time to sort myself out. I'm just not in the right place at the moment to start anything more. I'm so sorry.'

He looked down into his now empty cup.

Jerry nodded. What did that mean, he thought. Not in the right place. Already had a boyfriend? About to go to jail? About to sign up to some major reality TV show? Moving to Guatemala? What did he mean, not in the right place? He was here, sitting next to him, having turned up to watch him sing. How could that mean he wasn't in the right place?

'Can I ask you what place you are in, exactly?' asked Jerry. Praying it was the reality TV option, not the already has a boyfriend option.

He shook his head. 'It's very complicated,' he said. 'I'm . . . I'm . . .'

Go on, thought Jerry. Just spit it out.

'I'm just in a difficult place right now and until I can work that out, then, well, I'm no use to anyone, quite frankly.'

'A difficult place' could mean anything. Jerry bit his lip to try to fight back the disappointed tears.

'Will you always be in a difficult place?' he asked.

The man shook his head. 'I hope not,' he said. 'I really

152

mean that.' He looked up at the sky-high roof of the church. 'Coming here, wanting to come here, has made me realise that I have to face up to it. I have to sort my life out, but there's a lot I need to sort out, so much.' He gave a massive sigh as though the weight of the world was on his shoulders. All Jerry wanted to do was put his arms around him and tell him it was all going to be OK, but he wasn't sure that was the right thing.

'I'm sorry,' the man said, turning to face Jerry again. 'So sorry. I didn't mean to lead you on or anything, I really didn't, but I just needed to come and see you. I'm sorry to have caught you up in it all, but . . .'

And another 'but' . . .

'. . . I think I'd better go.' He stood. 'You were wonderful, by the way. Great voice. Great performance. Thanks for inviting me and, well, I hope you have a Merry Christmas.'

Jerry swallowed and looked away. He couldn't watch him leave. He looked firmly forward, staring at the wooden Virgin Mary before he brushed a single tear away.

He wasn't sure how long he'd sat there before he sensed someone making their way down the pew to sit with him.

'I am not liking this scene,' said Carol. 'You sitting at the front of the church alone. Why aren't you already in Soho snogging his face off or something?'

'You have such a stereotypical view of gay men,' sighed Jerry.

'Tell me if that's not what you'd like to be doing right now?'

153

Another tear slipped down Jerry's cheek and he lay his head on Carol's shoulder.

'The Christmas fairy tale turned into a nightmare, huh?' she asked.

'I made some stupid joke about first dates and then he sat me down and said he was in a difficult place. That he couldn't start anything right now. He had stuff to sort out and that it would be better if we didn't even meet in the coffee shop for a while.'

'A difficult place?'

'That's what he said.'

'Being anywhere near me after I've eaten Brussels sprouts is a difficult place. Did he explain his difficult place?'

'Not really. I mean he seemed pretty depressed about it. I can only assume he's involved with someone else, but then why come here at all? I mean, why not get himself out of the relationship if it makes him miserable? I don't really understand. I don't know what to think. Maybe there is a glimmer of hope – that he can get himself out of this difficult space he speaks of – but it is hard to tell when he didn't really explain.'

'Relationships are so complicated,' said Carol. 'You can never really understand other people's fully. And I have to say, getting out of a relationship is one of the hardest most complicated things you ever have to do. He perhaps just doesn't know how to do it.'

'Maybe,' replied Jerry. 'But it doesn't help me, does it? I don't think I've ever been happier than whilst I was up there singing Christmas carols and thinking about what was going to happen, and now I think I've never been sadder. Bloody Christmas.'

'Mm,' sighed Carol, kissing the top of his head. 'Merry bloody Christmas.'

Chapter 15

Diane was sitting in darkness in the lounge apart from the fairy lights flickering on the tree. She was nursing a glass of whisky, rolling it round and round in the cut-glass crystal, a wedding present from Leon's aunt and uncle, occasionally taking a sip.

There had been an awkward dinner with Chloe and Bertie. Not that they were awkward, but she certainly felt like she was intruding on a couple's meal. She didn't know her place without Leon there to balance things. She was a third wheel, a gooseberry, a pity guest. Chloe laughed and giggled and occasionally invited her into their world, but Diane had struggled to engage as she considered the imploding of all her Christmas wishes. Which were simple, after all. To spend time with her family.

They'd offered to clear away but Diane had shooed them off, telling them to go and meet their friends. She slowly loaded the dishwasher to the background noise of Radio Four until the kitchen was spick and span, all was in place and yet nothing at all was where it should be.

She'd then poured herself a large glass of whisky and proceeded to the lounge, putting on a vinyl LP of Bing Crosby on Leon's vintage record player, which sat in the corner.

It was an hour and a half before she heard a key in the lock. She wasn't sure what she had been thinking about. It was as though her mind was suspended, frozen, awaiting a seismic shift that would unlock it again.

'Hello,' she heard Leon call. She couldn't even respond. She heard him traipse to the kitchen, switch lights on, bang cupboard doors, open the fridge, the tinkling of ice in a glass and then finally footsteps back down the hall and into the lounge.

'Oh good God, woman,' he said, jumping when he turned a table light on to reveal her sitting there. 'What are you doing in the dark?'

She turned to look at him slowly. 'Perhaps it's where I've always been,' she replied.

'What do you mean?' he said, sitting beside her on the sofa.

'In the dark.'

She felt him swallow and take a fortifying glug of his drink.

'Where've you been?' she asked, biting her lip to stop the tears, watching the lights twinkle incongruously cheerfully in the mirror opposite them.

'Sorry,' he said. 'I had to do something.' He took another glug.

'What did you have to do?'

'Oh, just a work thing. You know how it is. Nothing really.'

Diane paused. 'No, I don't know how it is. How is it, Leon?'

'How's what?'

'How is it that you can clearly turn up for someone else but you cannot turn up for me or your daughter on the first night she's home from college? How is that, Leon?'

He shifted on his seat. 'I'm sorry.'

'I made a meal, I bought a tree, I decorated it before I went to work. I bought your favourite wine – not mine, not Chloe's, yours. You see, I mistakenly thought this would be a special night. The three of us together after ten weeks. But no. You had to do something. Something so casual, so insignificant that it was really nothing.'

'I didn't realise that tonight was going to be such a big deal,' he said. 'You never said.'

'First night our daughter's home from uni. And you're not working. It's not rocket science, Leon. Surely it's obvious that tonight was going to be a big deal. Why should I have to tell you that?'

'You're right. You shouldn't have to tell me. Sorry.'

'And you told her it was OK to go to her boyfriend's for Christmas. Have you any idea how much I've been looking forward to spending Christmas with her?'

Leon shook his head. 'I'm so sorry. I didn't think. I've just been a bit distracted.'

Diane let out a deep sigh. 'You're always distracted. Always. And do you want to know what I think you're distracted by?'

'What?' asked Leon, looking alarmed.

'You,' she replied. 'Always you. You are so focused on whatever is going on in your life that you fail to notice anything that's going on in mine – or anyone else's, for that matter. It's all about you, Leon. It's always all about you. You couldn't give a shit about what I'm doing. And what really gets to me is that you couldn't give a shit about what I'm doing for you.'

'That's not true,' said Leon. 'I really appreciate everything you do for me.'

'Bollocks!' shrieked Diane. 'I showed you all the Christmas presents I'd bought for your family the other day and you couldn't care less. No thanks, no nothing.'

'I thought you liked shopping.'

Diane thought she might scream. 'I hate Christmas shopping. Everyone hates Christmas shopping.'

'I didn't realise,' said Leon.

'You never do. Because you pay absolutely zero attention to me.'

Leon looked down. She thought he might be crying. Good, she was glad.

'I just facilitate your life,' she said. 'That's all I am to you. I do everything so that you can focus on you.' She felt herself close to tears now.

'I'm sorry,' he murmured.

'Do you have any idea how jealous I am of you?' she said.

'Jealous?' he said, looking up.

'Jealous,' she repeated. The tears were flowing down her cheeks now. 'You get to go to the theatre every day to work. You get to do something that you love, every single day.'

'I know I'm very lucky,' he nodded.

'I used to have that,' said Diane, her voice trembling.

Leon didn't say anything. Tears were pouring down his face now, too.

'I'm sorry,' he said again. 'I feel like I've really screwed your life up. I don't know what to do to make it better.'

Diane wasn't sure either. This was the most honest conversation they had had in for ever. She didn't know what the answer was, but she knew that getting her innermost feelings out was at least making her feel better.

Diane considered her next question carefully. 'Are you seeing somebody?' she asked.

There was a slight pause. So small and yet so significant.

'What do you mean?' he asked.

'I mean, are you seeing somebody? Are you having an affair? Do I really need to spell it out?'

Leon said nothing.

'Is it Amy?' she asked.

'No,' he said immediately. 'No, not Amy. No.'

Diane turned to look at him. 'But it is someone?' She watched as his mouth slightly dropped but no sound came out, no words of denial. Just shock that she'd asked the question he didn't want to be asked.

'Look, it's so not what you think,' he said. 'Really it isn't.'

'Isn't it?' asked Diane. 'Tell me. I'll decide that for myself, shall I?'

He turned to face her and took her hands in his. 'I have had feelings for someone, but I can absolutely

160

tell you that I've done nothing about it. Absolutely nothing at all. Until tonight . . .'

Diane closed her eyes; she could not bear to look at him.

'Tonight . . . I told them that nothing could happen between us. That's where I was.'

She opened her eyes. He was looking at her sincerely.

'I told them that we shouldn't see each other again. That's what I went to do.'

'Why tonight?' she asked.

'Things had come to a head. It was about to go further and I had to do something about it.'

'You left me and our daughter to go and tell someone you couldn't have an affair with them?'

'I didn't realise. I didn't think. I don't know what I was thinking. I don't know what to think any more.' He looked scared and confused.

'Sounds like you cared more about letting this person down than being with us.'

'I was trying to do the right thing,' pleaded Leon. 'I'm trying to do the right thing. That's all I'm trying to do. I'm here now, aren't I, with you?'

Diane swallowed.

'Are you?' asked Diane. 'Are you really? I don't think you've been here for some time.'

They were looking each other in the eye. Leon was breathing very heavily; Diane was holding her breath.

'No,' he said eventually. 'No, I haven't.'

'What are we doing?' asked Diane.

'I don't know,' said Leon. 'I really don't. I feel terrible. Awful. I just don't know what I want. I really don't.'

Diane looked at him. His expression implied he was expecting some kind of sympathy for his predicament. She wanted to strangle him with the red scarf he was still wearing around his neck.

Chapter 16

Diane walked into her office and slammed down her files. Everyone jumped out of their skins. It had been a quiet morning so far – everybody had very much kept themselves to themselves – but there was something of an atmosphere. Jolene had hardly dared say a word to anyone. Stacey was running late due to an issue with the school over Grace's continued insistence on wearing her donkey costume for all her classes, but everyone else looked as though they were attending a funeral.

'Team meeting, now!' shouted Diane from her office.

Everyone glanced at each other before getting up and dragging themselves into her office.

'Right,' declared Diane. 'Who's up for cancelling Christmas next year?'

Jolene's eyes shot wide open. Diane's eyes were blazing. She had a strand of hair out of place, which wasn't like her. What on earth had happened?

'Definitely me,' muttered Jerry. 'Can't be cancelled soon enough, if you ask me. Most massive waste of time and effort ever!'

Jolene glanced over to him. He had been exceptionally quiet all morning. He'd kept disappearing and when he was at his desk just stared into space, which was weird as he was normally very focused on his work.

'Are you OK?' asked Jolene.

Jerry turned his full gaze towards her and for the first time she noticed his eyes were rimmed red, as though he had spent a large chunk of time crying recently.

'No,' he said eventually. 'I'm not all right and the sooner this Christmas palaver is over, the better, if you ask me.' He turned to look at Diane. 'Where do I sign? I'm all in for cancelling Christmas.'

'Well, I've been thinking,' said Diane. 'I can't face the thought of having to make one of you redundant because of this stupid head-count reduction we're being forced to do so I was wondering if there's anywhere else we could cut costs.'

'We've been through everything,' said Jerry.

'But what about the Cost of Christmas report you are working on, Yang?' said Diane. 'What have been your findings so far?'

'Well, we've pretty much gathered all the costs and they do stack up to a large amount,' he replied. 'You also said we needed to try and work out what return we're getting from this investment. Are we getting value for money? But the benefits of Christmas are so intangible.'

'I think that's the key,' stated Diane. 'If we can prove that the expenditure on Christmas is not value for money then we can firmly recommend that Christmas should be part of the cost-cutting exercise. If we can do that then we might save some jobs.'

'I see what you're saying,' said Jerry, nodding. 'If it's a case of choosing between Christmas or employment then maybe we should think very hard about what goes into that report.'

'That's it,' said Diane.

'But . . . but, you can't cancel Christmas.' Jolene had to pipe up; she couldn't believe what she was hearing. 'It makes everyone so happy.'

Jerry turned to her. 'No, it doesn't,' he retorted. 'All Christmas *ever* does is entice you into this weird sense of hope that your life is going to be dramatically happier just because it's Christmas, that you're going to have this warm fuzzy feeling the whole time, and this perfect person is going to appear and love you and kiss you under the mistletoe, and it never bloody happens!' He slammed his hand on the table.

Jolene jumped.

'Christmas is the worst let-down ever known to man,' declared Jerry.

He was so violent in his opinion, Jolene thought she might cry.

'Wow,' said Yang, 'I mean, I don't celebrate Christmas, but surely it's not that bad. Did you have a bad evening?' he asked.

Jerry just shook his head.

Diane leaned over and clutched his arm. 'I had a crappy night too,' she said. 'Amongst other disasters, my daughter came home from uni and declared she

165

wouldn't be spending Christmas with us. She's spending it with her new boyfriend's family.'

'Oh, gosh,' said Jerry. 'I'm so sorry. That's tough. You see: Christmas is advertised as the best time to spend with those you love. And when that doesn't happen – well – the disappointment it creates is unreal!'

Jolene watched as Jerry's eyes filled up. Whatever had happened had been devastating.

'This will be my fourth Christmas without Linda,' said Barney quietly.

All eyes turned to Barney. Jolene swallowed. Ever since their night in the park when Barney had painted such a picture of his love for his wife and his wonderful Christmases as a family, he had totally shunned her. It was as if he was embarrassed that he had let her glimpse his sorrow and his loss. She was also still desperately trying to show him that she could be an asset to the team since he had basically told her that her entire generation were work-shy good-for-nothings. Unfortunately, the only thing she had been given to do was the mayor's event and she wasn't sure if Barney even approved of that.

Barney was staring back at them, a look of grim determination on his face. 'You have no idea how bad Christmas can be,' he said. 'No idea. Christmas with only the memories of the people you love is the worst feeling in the world. All Christmas does is remind you of what you've lost. You just know you'll never have a merry Christmas ever again.'

He didn't cry, he didn't shed a tear, just stared down at the table.

166

Jerry was the first to speak.

'I'm so sorry,' he said quietly. 'I'd forgotten Christmas must be impossible for you, Barney. I'm an idiot. I mean, I'm upset about Christmas because someone didn't ask me out, for goodness' sake. What am I thinking?'

Barney looked at Jerry, and Jolene held her breath. She thought Barney might say something to Jerry he may regret. She's noticed that Barney was always very quiet when Jerry talked about his love life. He was of a generation that might not be used to homosexuality being openly discussed and she wasn't sure what his views were.

'You only get upset when you really care about something,' said Barney. 'That's what Linda used to say, anyway.' He was looking straight at Jerry.

'But if you can't have the thing you care about, then that really hurts,' replied Jerry.

Barney shrugged. 'Maybe you just haven't tried hard enough.' He paused. 'I had to try really hard to get Linda.'

'What did you do?' asked Jerry and Yang in unison. They looked at each other, embarrassed.

'You don't want to know,' said Barney, with a shrug.

'We do,' urged Jerry and Yang in unison again.

'Well,' he said, shuffling in his seat. 'If you're really that interested: I got a job at the ice rink where she used to go skating. I knew the minute I saw her I wanted to marry her, but I couldn't skate so I got a job giving out boots. Just at the weekend. I made myself talk to her a bit more every week. I asked her the Saturday before Christmas if she was coming to

167

the Christmas Eve session. She said yes and I said I'll see you on the ice then and she said – and I'll never forget her saying this – she said, yes, that would be really nice.' He swallowed.

'Wow,' murmured Jolene.

'I couldn't skate,' he continued, 'so she took my hand on Christmas Eve and guided me round and never let go.'

'Wow,' said Jerry, wiping a tear from his eye. 'Now that is a great Christmas story.'

'Six weeks I worked at the rink before Christmas Eve,' he said. 'Sometimes you just have to get yourself in the right place to get the girl, or guy, or whatever you want.' He glanced pointedly at Jerry and then at Yang.

Diane gave a big sigh. 'Thanks for sharing that, Barney. But we had really better get back to trying to save everyone's job?' She turned to face Yang. 'Tell me exactly where we're at with Christmas costs, Yang.'

Yang was still staring at Barney.

'Yang,' said Diane again.

'Sorry, what was that?'

'What stage are you at with the Cost of Christmas report?'

'Oh, sorry. So Stacey and I have gathered everything we could think of from all the separate budgets. The thing is, it's never been put together before. Of course, there are all the actual decorations, which sit in one budget, but then the electricity sits in another. Then there are the electricians and the maintenance guys, which sit somewhere entirely different. Then, of

168

course, storage costs have never been attributed to Christmas at all and that's a huge chunk of money. What I've also done is some forecasts of where these costs might go over the next five years, considering inflation and replacements, which I've tracked back from previous years, as well as rising energy costs. I would expect the cost of Christmas to have risen by twenty-two per cent in the next five years. Which interestingly is in line with what experts believe will happen to household spending on Christmas over the same period. Typically, family households spend 156 per cent of their monthly income on Christmas,' said Yang.

'Wow,' said Diane. 'It's the most stressful time of the year by a long way and yet it's costing me more than my summer holiday. Christmas is just a money pit. So it sounds like the costs are stacking up nicely. Now we just need to show that we're not getting the required value from that expenditure. Any ideas, anyone?'

'We did discuss doing a survey,' said Yang. 'Of the public in the area. We can draw up a questionnaire that gives us data on whether the public think they get value for money from what the council spends on Christmas. That should give us something.'

'Good idea,' agreed Diane.

'I could do that,' said Jolene. 'I designed loads of surveys at uni. I've got a programme that you can plug the data straight into.'

'OK,' nodded Diane. 'You work with Yang on designing a questionnaire, Jolene. We should do it soon.

Whilst all the expenditure is on full display. Can you get yourselves organised for Friday? We don't have much time.'

'Definitely,' said Jolene. 'I can knock one up after this, Yang, and show it to you.'

'Great,' nodded Yang.

'Then who's up for going out into the field, asking the questions?' asked Diane.

'I will,' Jolene immediately volunteered. Jerry and Yang quickly followed.

'Do I have to?' asked Barney.

'I think your knowledge of the area would be really helpful,' said Diane. 'Why don't you go out with Jolene, seeing as she's not so familiar.'

'Really?' he asked, looking disappointed.

'I'll do all the hard work,' said Jolene. 'Ask all the questions, set it all up. All you need to do is tell me where to go.' This could be her chance to show Barney what she was made of.

'I think you two could make a good team,' said Diane.

Barney grunted and gave Diane a funny look. 'If you say so.'

'Right, good,' said Diane. 'That's settled. Let's see where we get to. See how much the public would really miss Christmas if we cancelled it. Now, anything else?'

Jolene raised her hand.

'It's all right, you don't have to put your hand up, Jolene.'

'I'm just checking you're OK for our meeting tomorrow at the London Eye, regarding the mayor's party,' she said to Diane.

Diane nodded. 'I hadn't forgotten. I need you to be very clear on what we're asking for, Jolene.'

Jolene nodded enthusiastically. 'I won't let you down. And . . . and can I just check if we're still doing the Secret Santa Project?' asked Jolene. 'That isn't cancelled, is it?'

Diane looked at Jolene. 'No, Jolene, I guess not.'

'Good,' replied Jolene. 'I've had an idea for mine, actually,' she continued. 'Especially after today's chat. Oops, I've said too much,' she said, clamping her hand over her mouth. 'Sorry.'

'I've still no idea,' said Jerry, miserably. 'I just don't know what this person wants.'

'Talk to them,' said Jolene. 'That's how I got my idea.'

'Sure,' said Jerry, looking unconvinced. 'I'll try.'

'The thing is,' said Diane, 'we haven't got time, have we? Well, I haven't. I've no idea how I'm going to sort mine out.'

'But we make time to shop, we make time to clean, we make time to cook, we make time to wrap all the stuff we've bought,' said Jolene. 'Maybe we should redirect some of that time to thinking about what would really make someone's Christmas.'

Diane stared back at Jolene. She wished Leon was using some of the time he wasn't having to use desperately trying to deliver the perfect family Christmas to working out what would make her Christmas. But then again she had no idea what on earth would make her Christmas this year either.

Chapter 17

Jolene had decided that she would wear her elf jumper again today for the meeting with the General Manager of the London Eye – the one with the hat stitched to it and with a real bell. She thought it would be fitting.

Diane, however, gave her a frosty glare when they met outside the enormous wheel on the edge of the River Thames. The wind was howling down the South Bank and Diane was wearing a smart long black overcoat and did not look too chuffed to be going to a meeting with someone dressed for a Christmas party.

'Shall we go?' said Diane. She looked Jolene up and down and then sighed. 'Let's get this over with, shall we? Have you brought your PowerPoint presentation?'

Jolene jumped round, revealing a bright yellow rucksack on her back. 'In the bag,' she said. 'In the bag.'

'Right, let's go,' said Diane. 'I'll do the introductions and then you hit her with it, OK, Jolene?'

'Absolutely,' said Jolene, grinning. What a cool meeting this was going to be, she thought. A meeting with the General Manager of the London Eye alongside super boss Diane. She was actually starting to enjoy her job.

She wasn't loving it so much about twenty minutes later, when Barbara Vasey looked totally uninterested whilst Jolene took her through her presentation. She looked to Diane for help, but she was just staring out of the window. Jolene could feel the event slipping through her fingers. She completed her run-through of the magical journey that the children of Chilwell Primary School would go on, courtesy of the London Eye, but she could sense by the look on Barbara's face that perhaps she didn't see it as quite so magical.

'It sounds totally wonderful,' said Barbara, leaning forward, 'and really there's nothing we would like to do better than—'

'It really is a great opportunity,' said Diane, turning her gaze onto Barbara.

'I know it is, but—' said Barbara.

'I mean, we probably should be charging you for this really, but I guess if you cover your costs then that's OK?'

'Charging us?'

'Such a brilliant new product idea, isn't it, that Jolene here has brought to you?'

'I'm not sure—'

'I mean, if my daughter was younger then it would be something I would have had to do for her. I would imagine every child would want to go on an elf-escorted journey to see Santa Claus, using the one and only

London Eye as their magical transport. It would be the best way to see Santa in the whole of the city. Think about how much you could charge for that? I wonder that you haven't thought of it before, and here we are, bringing it to you complete with publicity thrown in. What a way to launch a new product. By giving exclusive preview trips to the children of Bermondsey.'

Jolene watched as Barbara stared at Diane.

'I mean, I think the publicity could be great for you,' continued Diane, 'and it really is good that we keep relations between the council and yourselves on a positive note, seeing as your planning permission will be up for renewal in a few years' time.'

Barbara remained silent. Jolene sensed that she should also remain silent. She wasn't sure entirely what was happening but she felt a shift in the atmosphere of the room. Barbara was now fully engaged. Not distracted by her phone or her computer on her desk. She looked at Jolene, which she took as her cue.

'It's for the children,' said Jolene, 'and what could be better than putting a smile on children's faces at Christmas?'

Barbara leaned back. 'You can have two capsules at 5.30 p.m. the Thursday before Christmas. That's it. You need to be off the premises by 7 p.m. My press officer will be in touch and she'll be given free rein to invite whatever press she deems fit for photos of all participants. Consent forms to be issued for us to be able to use photographs of the event on our website and in our brochure. Understood?'

Jolene was about to reply with a massive yes before Diane cut in. 'Totally understood.' She rested her hand gently on Jolene's arm, warning her not to speak. 'Right, we've used up enough of your time,' said Diane, getting up. She held out her hand to Barbara. 'A pleasure doing business with you.'

'Likewise,' nodded Barbara.

'Just make sure you stick to the times I've stated,' said Barbara. 'I don't want to be paying a chunk of overtime.'

'Of course,' replied Jolene. 'Oh my goodness, you are both the most amazing people I have ever met,' she said, jumping up and down and attempting to hug them both at the same time. 'A-Ma-Zing – that's what you are.'

'Time to go,' said Diane. 'Come on, Jolene, we've taken up too much of Brenda's time already.'

'It's Barbara,' said Barbara.

'Yes, yes, of course,' said Diane, ushering Jolene out of the office. 'Come on, let's go. Bye, Barbara.'

'Bye, amazing lady,' Jolene shouted behind her. 'I love you!'

They were back out on the street by the time Diane and Jolene next spoke, the gigantic frame of the London Eye, behind them, effortlessly sending count-less people into the sky.

'I knew we could do it,' said Jolene. 'Just knew it. You were brilliant in there. I have no idea what you were talking about but you were amazing.'

Diane faced Jolene with the same grim look on her face as she'd had on before the meeting.

'Sometimes, Jolene,' she said, 'when you want something from someone, you just have to work out what's in it for them.'

Jolene thought about Diane's words.

'Understood,' she said. 'I'll make a note of that. Brilliant. Just the elves and Father Christmas to sort out now.'

Diane looked at Jolene and then at her watch. Why not, she thought. Might as well see if they can do something about those elves right now, whilst they were out and about. She took her phone out of her pocket and called Leon. He didn't pick up. She looked at her watch again. The matinée was due to start in a couple of hours. He should be at the theatre. They could probably catch him there, and if she took Jolene with her then that would hopefully avoid any awkward conversation.

'Let's go see about those elves right now, shall we?' she said, striding along the South Bank back towards the tube.

Diane's heart was pounding at a terrific pace as she approached the theatre. It was lunchtime but she knew there was only one place to find Leon, and if they were going to secure the elves they may as well do it now whilst she wasn't taking no for an answer. Maybe there were a few questions she should be asking Leon whilst she was here as well. They had avoided each other ever since the standoff in the lounge. Since then, he'd been lying in each morning before she went out and coming home ever later. Her mind felt like a lead weight on her shoulders, his words haunting her, spinning round and round in her head until she felt physically sick.

She couldn't get out of her mind how it had felt the moment he'd told her that he had turned down an affair. The most surreal, bizarre moment she had ever felt in her entire life. She was trying desperately to come to terms with the fact that the moment – the very split second – he told her he had rejected the opportunity to go with someone else, her heart had sunk. Yes, sunk, until her brain had kicked in and told her stupid heart not to be so ridiculous and react in a sane, rational way like a normal wife. She should be beside herself with relief that he had put a stop to it, shouldn't she? Happy that he'd probably had sex offered to him on a plate and he had turned it down despite the fact she could not remember the last time they had had sex. This was a golden opportunity to reassess their marriage, make a new start, put the spark back in, as it were. This was their second chance to make each other happy.

And yet she could not shake off that split second of disappointment that he hadn't said yes to whoever the woman was who had offered herself to him. That he hadn't taken that route, giving her the perfect exit from her marriage. Guilt free, decision-making free. Oh, yes, my husband had an affair and so I had to leave him – of course I did.

Her husband having an affair would put an end to the long-standing narrative in her head in which she constantly wrangled with herself as to whether she was happy or not. Her husband having an affair would answer that question. She would no longer have to lie in bed in the middle of the night, wondering what had happened to her life, wondering why she woke up miserable. It would knock out the massive unanswered question, which was whether she was happy in her marriage.

She wasn't unhappy, she thought, but neither did it give her happiness. Her heart didn't sing when Leon walked in the room, but then she put that down to nearly twenty years of marriage. Domesticity and the need to pay bills and raise a daughter and decide who cleaned the toilets and who did the washing up and who organised his sister's kids' birthday presents. All the logistical stuff was sure to knock the stuffing out of any marriage, and yet everyone had that, right? Everyone had stuff to manage between them, and yet they stuck with it, got some kind of joy out of it, to make it all worthwhile.

But try as she might, she couldn't find that joy. They never saw each other, for a start. Leon's work hours totally contradicted hers and he showed no desire to make any changes to rectify that. As such, their brief exchanges were crammed with logistics planning and the passing on of messages. No time for pleasantries or just chat. Not at midnight when he finally rolled in after a performance.

As for intimacy – well, it was a relief to her that as menopause set in and her libido took a holiday, so had his. He'd not reached out to her as he fumbled into bed in the middle of the night in a very long time.

It suited her down to the ground, but it did nothing to help their flagging relationship, just deepened the divide between them until they became literally just like ships that passed in the night.

Until Monday night. When they had had the most direct conversation in years. When more honesty had passed between them than in an entire decade. When he'd admitted to being tempted by an affair but he had turned it down. Much, as it turned out, to her disappointment.

She headed through the doors of the theatre with Jolene, in her elf jumper, trailing behind her. She'd promised Jolene some elves and she would have to deliver now, by hook or by crook. Focus on that. Sort her failing marriage out later.

'This is, like, the best day of my life,' said Jolene, looking round in wonder at the ornate entrance hall to the theatre. 'But can I ask what we're doing here?'

'We're here to get your elves,' said Diane.

Jolene looked at her in wide-eyed astonishment. 'Are you kidding me?'

'Hopefully not,' said Diane, pushing through the doors to the back of the stalls. She hoped she would catch Leon unawares as they prepped for the matinée performance.

She looked down the auditorium and could see the back of Leon's head alongside two others in an otherwise empty auditorium. She strutted down the aisle as Snow White and her 'elves' did a number on stage: the one Shelley had been struggling with when Diane last came to the theatre.

'Diane,' said Leon, standing up. Diane didn't stop as she continued to the front of the stage and sat herself down on the front row next to Leon and a man she didn't know. Jolene sat down beside her.

'Still the most exciting day of my life,' she whispered to Diane.

'What are you doing?' Leon leaned over and asked.

'No worries,' said Diane. 'We won't get in the way. I just need to ask you to have a word with your elves.'

'About what?' asked Leon.

'A party,' said Jolene helpfully.

'Who's that,' mouthed Leon to Diane.

'Jolene.'

'Jolene?'

'Jolene.'

'Joleeeeeene,' grinned Jolene.

'What party?' asked Leon.

'Well,' said Diane, 'it's not really about a party. I'm actually here to do you a big favour as well as you helping me out, for a change.'

Leon looked sheepish. 'Go on,' he said.

'So you said you were struggling to sell tickets for the show after Christmas.'

'They're a bit sluggish,' said Leon.

'Then I might have a PR opportunity for you.'

'Oh, yes?'

'We're organising a party for the mayor, who wants a photo op with the local kids. Anyway, we're going to take them on a ride on the London Eye to see Santa Claus, and Jolene here had this idea that it would be great to have elves as their escorts. Brilliant photo op for your show. The press officer for the Eye is already on it. They've seen the potential for a new experience, but we could use it to promote your show too.'

Jolene leaned round and waved at Leon. Diane slapped her hand down.

'Why are you doing this?' asked Leon.

'It's a long story. Jolene promised the mayor elves, and so I thought you could help. You owe me, after all.'

'When do you need them?'

'Next Thursday at 5.30 p.m. for an hour tops. You should have plenty of time to get back to the theatre.'

Leon stared at her. The number that Snow White and the seven elves had been doing on the stage came to an end and everyone looked expectantly at Leon.

Leon stood up.

'OK,' he said, addressing his cast. 'First things first. This is my wife, Diane. She does a really important job for the council.' He glanced back at her. She pulled a face. 'Anyway, she's organising a party on the London Eye. Who wants to go? You need to be in costume and happy to have your photo taken by the press.'

'Oh, yeah,' said one of the cast. 'I'll do anything for the press.' He struck a model pose, making everyone laugh.

'Is it free?' asked one of the elves near the front of the stage.

'Yes,' replied Leon. 'You'll need to chat to some kids but I'm sure you'll see eye-to-eye on that one.'

'Aaah, very funny, boss,' said the elf, chuckling. 'Count me in. We can all do that, can't we?' he asked his fellow actors.

They all seemed to agree.

'Right – good,' he said, turning back to Diane. 'I think you have your elves.'

'Thank you,' nodded Diane, getting up to leave. 'Her breathing still isn't right,' she said, nodding at Snow White, waiting patiently in the middle of the stage. 'It's better, but the last few bars still need work.'

Leon looked at her and nodded. She brushed past him and he caught her arm.

'Show her,' he said.

'What?'

'Get on that stage and show her how it's done.' He looked up at the stage. 'My wife is here again, Shelley,' he called. 'Don't you think it would be useful to hear her sing it? She agrees it's better, but the last few bars need work.'

'Oh, would she? That would be amazing,' said Snow White. 'Honestly.'

'No,' said Diane, shaking her head. 'No, I have to get on. We need to go back to the office.'

'Please, Diane,' asked Leon.

Diane looked back at him and couldn't help herself. It just came out. 'Why should I do anything for you?'

The air was so loaded between them it was unreal. She wondered what it was going to take to clear it. It wouldn't happen here, of course, not in front of the cast of *Snow White and the Seven Elves*. Heaven knew, the person Leon rejected could be in the room. She looked round for Amy, the assistant director.

'Don't do it for me,' he said. 'Do it for you. And do

it for a young woman starting out in the business who is asking for your help.'

'You can sing?' gasped Jolene, unable to contain herself. 'I never knew that.'

'She used to be a West End performer,' Leon told her. 'One of the best. Come on, Diane. Please sing,' he said, taking her hand and leading her towards the steps at the side of the stage.

Before she knew it, Snow White was handing her her scarlet cloak, which Diane took and wrapped around her shoulders. Leon handed her the sheet music and she took a deep breath, looking out at the empty auditorium. She glanced back at the real Snow White and said, 'Come, hold my hand. I'll squeeze your hand when I take a breath. Might help?'

Shelley stepped forward gratefully and they both took centre stage.

The music struck up from the orchestra and Diane glanced down at the notes on the page, although she knew she didn't really need them. Jolene was beaming up at her, already enraptured. She'd better not disappoint, she decided. Maybe she should try to enjoy it. Make the most of it. Because it sure as hell was never going to happen again.

The first couple of notes were a bit shaky. She stumbled and asked the orchestra to stop and start again.

If in doubt, belt it out, she told herself. She drew another deep breath and indeed belted it out this time, singing from deep in her chest, all her training coming back to her. She soon found herself getting lost in the moment, the notes flying to her lips and coming out into the air in a most pleasing fashion. She dropped Shelley's hand and started to deploy her arms and her whole body, reinforcing the depth of feeling in the notes. She felt the adrenalin flow through her body and she went to another place, her happy place, which she had not been to in a very long time. Lost in the music, lost in the feeling of the sound flowing through her body. Lost in her sole focus of trying to convey the emotion of the words through song.

The key change went exceptionally well. It could have been tricky and tripped her up, but she dealt with it and felt herself building to the inevitable crescendo of the song that musical theatre was so adept at. She took a step forward to the front of the stage, trying to connect further with her minuscule audience. Make them believe in her, Snow White, who had found her love and family in the party of elves and yet still felt alone. She sang of her longing to find true love for herself, something that was hers. Entirely hers. Diane knew she was singing a song that was about longing for a prince to come and rescue her. Except Diane wasn't singing about being rescued by a man in her own mind. With all her heart she was singing about something – anything – that might rescue her from her dissatisfaction with her life. She didn't know what it was but she knew she needed to be rescued.

The last line of the song was 'Bring me my love.'

She took a deep breath and belted out the line with all the emotion of a middle-aged woman who needed love in her life and she had no idea where she was going to find it.

She raised her hands in the air on the last note and closed her eyes putting all her power into it. The note ran out, the orchestra stopped and there was silence.

Then there was a standing ovation.

She opened her eyes to see her tiny audience grinning from ear to ear and clapping their hearts out.

Next minute, Jolene was up on stage beside her, hugging her and jumping up and down.

'Amazing, amazing, amazing, amazing!' she shouted at the top of her voice.

'Thank you,' blushed Diane.

She looked over and Leon was clapping his hands with the rest of them. Looking proud, she thought. That felt kind of nice.

'Tremendous,' said Leon. 'You've not lost it at all.'

'Thank you,' said Diane, feeling quite emotional. She was still really stuck in the song, still in the moment.

'I'd forgotten how good you were,' continued Leon.

He'd forgotten a lot of things about the way she used to be, she thought. They locked eyes.

'It's a long time ago,' she replied.

He nodded. 'It reminded me of when you were in *Cabaret*. You weren't the star but you should have been. You stopped the show, literally. She stopped the show,' he told the mini audience. 'You should have got a lead at some point,' Leon told her. 'You really should.'

'Maybe I would have done if I hadn't given up,' she replied.

Their eyes locked again.

Leon blinked first.

'I'm sorry,' he said.

She didn't say anything. She couldn't.

Leon turned to Jolene. 'Did I see you filming it?' he asked her.

Jolene nodded vigorously, sending her hat bell chiming away.

'Sure did,' said Jolene. 'Can't wait to show everyone at the office.'

'No,' said Diane, 'I think that really I—'

'Could I have a copy?' asked Leon. 'I, er . . . it will be useful for us to watch for Shelley's breathing. Is that OK?' He looked at Diane.

'Sure,' she shrugged. 'Do what you like.'

'Thanks,' he said. 'And I'll make sure I get all the elves to you.'

'Thanks,' she shrugged. She took off the Snow White robe and handed it back to Shelley with a big sigh. She walked off the stage and headed straight down the side aisle, Jolene running to catch up with her.

'I cannot believe how good you were,' said Jolene. 'Honestly, amazing. Why did you give up? Did you stop enjoying it?'

Diane stopped in her tracks and stared at Jolene.

'Stop enjoying it?' she gasped. 'Never. It was the love of my life.' She remembered she'd said that before, quite recently, but she couldn't remember who to. Must be something to do with middle-age, all this yearning for times gone by. She took one last look at the stage then turned back to Jolene. 'Now, let's go back to my real job, shall we? I need to decide whether to cancel next Christmas for the whole of Bermondsey.'

Chapter 18

Stacey was out of breath by the time she picked Grace up after school. She'd done a mad dash to Aldi to get food for that night's dinner with Will. She'd even splashed out on some after-dinner mints. She had no idea why, but they were cheap and in the middle aisle and she just couldn't resist. There had also been a cheap box of Christmas decorations knocked down in price as it was now mid-December and for the first time in a very long time she actually felt inclined to decorate the flat. Now that Will was on the scene it felt as though Christmas didn't hold the doom and gloom it normally did. She might have a fighting chance of enjoying this Christmas. As long as she kept her job, of course. She decided for this evening, however, that she would put that to the back of her mind.

She needed a quick getaway from school so that she could get back to the flat and begin cooking. However, Grace's teacher had other ideas.

'Miss Bentley,' said the slightly terrifying Miss Shepherd. 'Can I have a quick word?'

'If it's quick,' said Stacey. 'I do have to get home.'

'Well, I'll get straight to the point. You need to ask your daughter to stop singing her donkey song throughout the Nativity play rehearsals. It's very disruptive. Now, I have explained this to Grace but she insists on carrying on.'

Grace looked up at her mum. 'They won't put it in the play,' she said. 'I told them I wrote it and it's about a donkey so it fits, but they won't put it in. So I think if I keep singing it all the time then eventually they'll get to love it and then put it in the play.'

'We already have many songs in the Nativity, Grace,' said Miss Shepherd. 'You can sing those all you like.'

'But none of them are as good as "Donkey Love". And I wrote it with my friend Yang. Surely you want a song in the play, written by one of your pupils? Rather than other people we've never ever heard of?'

Stacey looked at Miss Shepherd. She thought her daughter had a point.

'But it wouldn't be very fair to give you a solo, would it?' said Miss Shepherd.

'Toby has a solo because he always gets a solo because he's very good at singing and it impresses all the parents. Evie has a solo because her dad is a governor and Amir has a solo because you need to show that you're kind and fair to all races and religions. Now, I would like a solo because I wrote "Donkey Love".'

Stacey had to smile. Grace had totally nailed Miss Shepherd. Miss Shepherd looked at Stacey pleadingly but Stacey wasn't in the mood for saying the right thing to suck up to the teacher. She was tired of her daughter being dismissed as naughty and troublesome when actually she was spirited and super-bright and probably had ADHD.

'We haven't really got room for any more soloists,' Miss Shepherd said.

'Why don't you let Grace sing her song at the end?' asked Stacey. 'Like a farewell song?'

Stacey really couldn't think of anything worse for all the parents than being serenaded by her daughter wailing 'Donkey Love', but it might just make Grace's Christmas and so she was willing to offer it up.

Stacey watched Miss Shepherd's face fall. It was not the closing number to her magical Nativity play that she was looking for.

'Oh, yes! That's a brilliant idea,' said Grace. 'Brilliant. I'll be like the encore. Is that what they call it?'

'That's right,' said Stacey, grabbing Grace's hand. 'All sorted then. Now we'd better go. Things to do. Places to be. Goodbye, Miss Shepherd. See you at the Nativity.'

'Wow, Mum,' said Grace as they walked away. 'You were awesome.'

For the first time in ages, Stacey felt awesome.

Not so much two hours later. Sweat was dripping off her nose as she laboured over a hot stove. She'd decided to do a roast chicken, seeing as they had company, and she and Grace never had a Sunday roast as cooking for two seemed like too much effort.

She'd forgotten how much effort it was.

Peeling potatoes and carrots and parsnips and making stuffing and gravy and trying to juggle all that in her single oven with just four gas rings on the top. This was hard work after a full day at the office. What with that and trying to make sure that Will was happy as he sat in the lounge enjoying a beer whilst Grace insisted on watching cartoons. Stacey had tried to persuade Grace to help her with dinner, but Grace had refused, saying she had important television to watch. Stacey apologised to Will, who smiled and asked if there was another beer.

Eventually Stacey put the beautifully crisp chicken on the tiny kitchen table and announced that dinner was served. Grace ran in and plonked herself on the middle chair, forcing Will into a chair that had him virtually sitting in the kitchen doorway.

'Sorry, it's a bit tight in here,' said Stacey.

'It's really only big enough for two,' said Grace, looking pointedly at Will.

'It's fine,' said Will. 'Cosy. This looks amazing, by the way. I never cook for myself like this.'

'We don't normally eat like this,' Grace told Will. 'It's just because you're here. Normally it's beans on toast in front of *Pointless*.'

'Not every night,' said Stacey.

'You're right,' said Grace. 'Sometimes we're late and have to watch *The One Show*.'

'So,' said Stacey, clapping her hands together. 'Dig in. Don't let it go cold.'

'Great,' said Will, picking up his fork and helping himself to a chicken leg.

190

'You should ask if me or Mum want a leg first, shouldn't he, Mum?'

'No,' said Stacey, 'he's a guest.'

'But that's not what you say when we're the guests. You tell me to wait for everyone else to pick.'

Stacey sighed. 'Why don't you tell Will about your solo in the Nativity play?'

'I'm singing "Donkey Love" at the Nativity,' she told him. 'It's going to be epic.'

'"Donkey Love"?' asked Will.

'Yes. The one that I wrote with Yang. We played it to you when you came back the other night.'

'Really,' said Will, raising his eyebrows at Stacey. 'That song. Wow. Well, I very much look forward to hearing that.'

'Mum told Miss Shepherd to let me be the farewell song at the end. Mum was amazing. Miss Shepherd really had no choice.'

'Very impressive,' said Will, looking admiringly at Stacey. 'There aren't many people who get away with telling Miss Shepherd what to do. I'll have to take you with me next time she hauls me in over some bee in her bonnet about Isaac.'

'You must tell Yang,' said Grace to her mum. 'Can you ask him to come? He should come and see our song played in front of all those people.'

'I'm not sure he'd want to or be able to,' replied Stacey.

'Of course he would want to,' said Grace.

Will was shaking his head. 'Look,' he said to Grace, 'he's a young guy, he's got other priorities. He'll be out with his girlfriend or the lads or something.'

'He hasn't got a girlfriend,' said Grace. 'I think he likes you, Mummy.'

Will laughed. Stacey looked shocked. 'Did he say that?' she asked.

'No,' replied Grace. 'But I think he does and I think he would be a very good boyfriend.'

Will was still laughing. 'I don't really think your mum is in the market for a boyfriend, are you?' he asked her, with a grin.

'I guess not,' she replied, smiling back at him.

Grace turned to Will. 'Yang will come if Mum asks him. I know he will.'

Stacey looked at Will. He shrugged as if to say he'd tried to help but failed. Stacey knew there was no way Yang was going to watch Grace sing a song about donkeys, even if he had written it. And all that nonsense about him fancying her. That was just wishful thinking by Grace. Now all that was going to happen was that the Nativity play and her performance would be ruined by the fact that Yang wasn't there. Christ, who would be a parent!

'I'm going to eat this in front of *Danger Mouse*,' said Grace, picking up her plate and making her way sulkily out of the kitchen.

'We have a guest,' protested Stacey.

'It's OK,' said Will. 'Let her watch her programme. Any more gravy?'

'Er, yeah,' said Stacey, reaching round behind her to get the saucepan off the hob. She topped up the gravy jug with a heavy heart. She'd been really looking forward to a proper sit-down meal like a normal family

192

for once. Clearly Grace didn't have the same aspirations as she sat sulkily in front of the TV and turned *Danger Mouse* up to loud.

Two hours later and the evening was looking up. Stacey and Will were entwined on the sofa, halfway down a bottle of wine and watching a new drama on the TV. Grace had gone to bed and Stacey felt all warm and fuzzy. She and Will had kissed long and deep during one of the ad breaks and it felt fantastic. This is what it must feel like to be in a happy relationship, she thought. Eating together, drinking together, cuddling together, kissing together, watching the telly together. This is what most normal people of her age had, and she wanted it. She wanted more of it. It was the most contented she had felt in a long time. She looked up at the tinsel, hastily erected over the top of the mirror before Will arrived. Maybe there was something to look forward to about Christmas after all. Maybe, just maybe they might end up spending Christmas with Will and she could finally tell her mum that she had other plans for Christmas lunch. What a great Christmas that would make it.

It got to ten o'clock and she couldn't help but yawn. It had been a hell of a day. Full day at work, shopping for dinner, picking up Grace, cooking a meal. And she still had the washing up to do. It really was time for bed. But Will looked so settled with his leg draped over the sofa arm and his arm draped round her shoulders, she didn't want to bring an end to a lovely evening just yet. She'd already told him that he couldn't stay over as she had a very early start and she wasn't sure Grace was ready for overnight guests just yet. She looked up at him and leaned in for a long slow kiss. Wow – that made her feel alive for the first time in a very long time.

'I've been meaning to ask you something,' he said when their lips finally parted.

Stacey sat up. This sounded good; this sounded exciting.

'Go ahead,' she grinned.

'Would you like to come to my works Christmas ball, you know, the one I mentioned that's at the Tower of London? Because, well, I was going to go with my mate Jacko, but he's taking his new girlfriend so would you come? I don't want to be a Billy No-mates. The thing is, it's a really posh do so everyone dresses up. I'll be in a tuxedo, so you need a special dress . . .' He tailed off as he saw a tear drop down her cheek. 'Why are you crying?'

'You had me at Christmas ball,' she said. 'Oh, and tuxedo. You must look really hot in a tuxedo.'

'Well, you know,' he said. 'I do scrub up all right. So you'll come?'

'Try and stop me,' said Stacey. She leaned forward to hug him. 'Thank you,' she said. 'You've just made my Christmas.'

'It's just a party,' replied Will.

'To you, maybe. But I've not been out to a party in the last hundred years. I feel like I'm Cinderella who has actually got invited to the ball.'

'OK,' said Will. 'As I said, the women really go for it dress-wise . . . have you got anything?'

194

'Tell me exactly,' she asked. 'What type of thing? I don't want to get it wrong.'

'Well,' said Will. 'I don't know . . . like what you might see on the red carpet. That type.'

Stacey nodded. 'I haven't got anything like that, but I might just know a fairy godmother who could help me out in that department.'

'Great,' said Will. 'And you can always come back to mine afterwards?' he said, raising his eyebrows.

'Oh, blimey,' said Stacey, slapping her forehead. 'I need a babysitter. When is it?'

'Next Wednesday,' replied Will.

'Christ, that doesn't give me much time.'

'What about Yang?' asked Will.

'Yang?' said Stacey. 'He only did it last time as a favour.'

'Won't he do it again? I'm sure if you asked him nicely? I mean, he really likes you, according to Grace,' he said with a smile on his face.

'Shut up,' she said, punching him on the arm. 'She's just being stupid. Anyway, I can't ask him. Honestly. It's not fair. I'll just have to work something out. Pray for a Christmas miracle.'

Chapter 19

Later that week Jerry and Yang spent a morning pounding the High Street, doing mini questionnaires with the great British public, hoping to gather data that might support the plan to cancel Christmas in the borough. They had asked every question that they thought would give them insight into how the expenditure on Christmas was viewed by residents in the area and were now back at the office trying to work out what it all meant.

'In summary, then,' said Jerry as they scanned down a spreadsheet, 'sixty-two per cent of our respondents said they thought the Christmas lights of Bermondsey High Street offered poor value for money and fifty-nine per cent thought that the money spent on Christmas decorations would be better spent elsewhere. Also, interestingly, ninety-two per cent thought that our Christmas decorations were the worst they'd seen south of the river. Sixty-two per cent went to the lights switch-on and seventy-eight per cent of those thought the choice of celebrity was poor and that we'd be better off without a celebrity.'

'And the big indicators are no better,' added Yang. 'Seventy-five per cent said they thought the investment in Christmas in the area offered poor value for taxpayers' money. And, probably most crucially, sixty-eight per cent ranked traffic-calming measures as well as public toilets and refuse collection as a higher priority for council spending than Christmas.'

'So, in conclusion, I think it's safe to say that Bermondsey Council does not deliver on Christmas to its residents and we therefore propose to cancel it next year,' said Jerry.

Yang raised his eyebrows. 'Looks that way,' he agreed.

Jerry sighed. 'I know we're doing this to show we can make cuts in other places apart from head-count, but something about this doesn't feel quite right.'

Yang shrugged. 'It's hard for me, when I don't have an affinity for Christmas. Not sure what the right answer is. Does feel a bit weird, though. It sounds right on paper and logical to stop spending money on it, but it's a head decision, not a heart decision. Not sure that's the right way to treat Christmas.'

Jerry nodded. 'I know I was saying how much I hated it the other day, but maybe if it wasn't there, maybe if we stopped doing stuff for Christmas, then I'd miss it. I don't know. All depends on your circumstances, I suppose. Christmas can either make or break you. I mean, take Stacey, for example. Now she has a man on the scene, she's suddenly excited about Christmas. She's so grateful to you for the babysitting, by the way. She's asked me before, when she's been desperate, but me and kids are like oil and water. There ain't no mixing happening. I repel them and they repel me. Quite literally. You, however, I hear were a massive hit.'

Yang smiled. 'Grace is great. Honestly. You just need to keep her busy.'

'A regular Mary Poppins, Stacey said. And you made Stacey's Christmas wish come true. You gave her a boyfriend. Would have been great if you'd got her in the Secret Santa Project.'

Yang looked around furtively. 'I did, actually,' he said.

'What! Really? Is that why you offered to babysit. Now I get it. Now it makes sense.'

'Er, no, actually. I wanted to help, that's all. It seemed like she was really struggling, like she needed a night out, so I just offered. No big deal. I'll have to try and think of something else for her Secret Santa.'

'Oh, that's an easy one,' said Jerry. 'Slam dunk. I know exactly what will make her Christmas.'

'What?' asked Yang.

'The guy, Will, who she went out with the other night?'

'I met him briefly.'

'Well, he's invited her to his work Christmas party in the Tower of London. For Stacey this is like Cinderella being invited to the ball. Can you imagine going where kings and queens partied centuries ago? Unbelievable. Anyway, she's beside herself with excitement, but guess what she needs?'

'A babysitter,' said Yang, looking crestfallen.

'Exactly,' said Jerry. 'It's a gift of a Secret Santa present. Absolutely guaranteed to make her Christmas.'

'I guess that's what I should do then. Let her go to the ball with Will,' said Yang slowly.

'Absolutely,' replied Jerry. 'It's going to blow her mind. Do it soon, though; she's getting desperate. Wow, you're so lucky. I still have absolutely no idea what to do about mine.'

'Do you have any idea who's got you?' asked Yang.

'No,' said Jerry, shaking his head. 'Can't say I've noticed anyone making enquiries, put it like that. Mind you, it's impossible for my Christmas to be made now. Literally all I wanted for Christmas was this guy I met in a coffee shop, who I thought was interested, but that's gone. Done. Over. My Christmas is already ruined, so good luck to whoever has me, in that case; it's an impossible task.'

'Sorry to hear that,' said Yang.

Jerry paused. Yang looked so down in the mouth. 'How about you?' he asked Yang. 'Could someone make your Christmas?'

Yang looked at him startled before he shook his head. 'No,' he said. 'No one special.'

'Come on,' said Jerry. 'Spill the beans. I know that look. There is someone, isn't there?'

Yang stared back at him. 'There is someone,' he said eventually. 'But I'm certain I'm the very last person she would want in her Christmas stocking.'

'Oh, Yang,' said Jerry. 'Really? You've been struck with the most awful state to be in, like me. The state of unrequited love.'

'I guess so,' he replied.

'How long?' asked Jerry.

Yang shook his head. 'Maybe a couple of years?'

'Wow. That's a long time. And you're sure she won't . . .'

'No, it's never going to happen. Never in a million years.'

'I'm so sorry for your loss,' said Jerry, putting his arm around Yang. 'Not worth a shot, though, because it's Christmas? I mean, that was what I did. Well, my friend Carol made me, to be honest, but she was right. At least we moved forward, even if it was in the wrong direction.'

'What did you do?' asked Yang.

'Basically put myself in a position where it was blatantly obvious what I felt. I wouldn't have done it if it hadn't been for Carol but I'm glad I did. When you have strong feelings for someone then I guess it has to come out at some point. Otherwise you're just stuck.'

'I'm not sure I can do that,' said Yang. 'Could make life impossible even to try.'

'Think about it,' said Jerry. 'You never know, it could work out brilliantly or at the very least you begin the process of attempting to move your affections to someone else. Not that I'm anywhere near that,' he said with a sigh. 'I really should take my own advice.'

Yang shook his head. 'Not sure she even likes me. I'm absolutely certain she doesn't see me in that way at all and I know I'm so not her type. So, you know, it really is hopeless.'

Poor Yang, thought Jerry. He really did look totally dejected.

'What is her type, do you think?' asked Jerry.

'Suave, sophisticated, well dressed, great job, your basic nightmare.'

Jerry looked at the outfit Yang was wearing today. He had on a baseball shirt and jeans. His dress sense really was all over the shop. Today he was dressed like an eighteen-year-old who worked in McDonald's. How Jerry would love to give him a makeover. Might just improve his chances with whoever this mystery woman was.

'Hopefully whoever has your Secret Santa will come up with some ingenious plan to get you out of this funk,' said Jerry, patting his shoulder.

'Now that would be a Christmas miracle, for sure,' said Yang. He sighed and looked back at the computer screen. 'Right, shall we get these numbers into a PowerPoint for Diane?'

'Let's do it,' replied Jerry.

Meanwhile Barney and Jolene were still out and about, trying to gather their evidence of the value of Christmas, much to Barney's distress. He thought he should have been left to man the office. He was a sixty-three-year-old man, for goodness' sake. What was he doing on the High Street in December, in the freezing rain, babysitting Jolene? Showing her where the borough started and finished. To be fair, she had kept her word and was doing all the questioning of the general public whilst he sheltered under shop awnings out of the weather. And she was doing it with a smile on her face, which was more than he could have managed, particularly given that the questions were stupid and pointless. She'd stood there and done at least twenty questionnaires whilst he'd stood and watched, insisting he kept dry. He had to respect that.

He dug his hands deep in his pockets as Jolene approached him, having just spoken to a woman with a pushchair. She had that stupid elf jumper on again. What was she wearing that for? They were only here because of her, anyway, he reminded himself. If the council stopped recruiting young people for just five minutes then they wouldn't be needing to get rid of the oldies like him on such a regular basis. When Jolene offered to leave, Diane should have snapped her hand off, in Barney's opinion. Last in, first out had always been a fine idea, as far as he was concerned. Still, this idea of cutting Christmas wasn't a bad one. If it kept him in a job then he was all up for it.

As Jolene brushed the rain off her umbrella he suddenly had a thought as to where they should go next to get suitable opinions for Jolene's survey.

'Shall we head to the café over there?' he said. 'I bet there will be plenty of people in there that will talk to us about Christmas. And we can get out of this horrendous weather and drink a cup of tea.'

'Great idea,' said Jolene. 'They'll be relaxed in there too. Tell us what they really think.'

As they entered the café, Barney looked around. There was a chap in the corner he knew. Perfect.

'Hello, Sid,' said Barney. 'Mind if we join you? This is Jolene. I've no idea why she's dressed like that but I recommend you don't ask.'

'How do, love?' replied Sid. 'You take a seat.'

'Thanks,' said Jolene. 'I'm dressed like this because it's nearly Christmas.'

Barney held his hand up. 'Sid's not interested,' he said.

'Oh, OK, no problem,' said Jolene, grinning.

'Mind if we ask you a few questions?' continued Barney, ignoring her. 'We're on council business today and your opinion is valuable to us.' He said 'valuable to us' whilst holding his fingers up in quotation marks. Sid laughed.

'Bleeding hell, it's a long time since my opinion was valuable to anyone.'

'Not what Bella says,' said Barney.

'It's exactly what Bella says and you know it.'

'How is she?' asked Barney.

'Still missing Linda,' said Sid. 'She says pottery class isn't the same without her.'

Barney blinked, then coughed. 'Well, I'm not missing those wonky vases she used to bring back,' he said.

Sid laughed. 'You can have some of Bella's. We've got enough for a flower shop and enough wonky teacups for an entire café.'

'I'll pass,' said Barney. 'I couldn't understand how she never seemed to progress. Always wonky.'

'Oh, it's really hard,' said Jolene. 'Brilliant fun, but really difficult. Me and my mates tried it at uni. Had such a laugh. I really must try and sign up for a class

203

in London. I could do with finding some new friends.' She gave a deep sigh. It was the first time Barney had ever seen her frown. It didn't suit her.

'Right,' said Barney. 'Why don't I take the lead on this one?' He got a piece of paper out of his pocket with the questions on that Jolene had given him.

'Actually,' said Jolene, 'would you mind if I filmed you, Sid? Could be useful. Get your expressions.'

'Film away,' said Sid. 'You gonna make me a star?'

'I'll do my best,' grinned Jolene.

'Right,' said Barney, putting his glasses on. 'First question. Do you think the Christmas lights on the High Street represent good value for taxpayers' money on a scale of one to five, with one being poor and five being excellent value for money.'

'Well,' said Sid. 'They're a bit shit really, aren't they?'

'Would you like to expand?' asked Barney.

'Of course. My opinion of the lights on the High Street is that they're a bit shit. Barely notice them, to be honest. I mean, they're barely worth having. And as for the tree – it's more of a branch really, isn't it? Bit of an excuse for a tree. I remember when it used to be enormous, like twenty foot high, when I was little.'

'Perhaps it just looked tall because you were little?' asked Jolene.

'No, no, love. It was enormous. And me ma would bring us all to look at it, she would. We'd come specially just to see the tree, then we'd walk down to the park. I bet you remember it, don't you, Barney? You'd go down the park and there would be ice skating and lights in the trees and it was . . . it was . . . magical. Really it was.'

'And you don't think it's magical now?' asked Jolene. 'I mean, it looks pretty good to me.'

'I'm old,' said Sid. 'Nothing about the present is magical any more. Not seen through old eyes. Being old stinks. Growing old means the magic is wiped out of your life. I have to rely on my memories to bring the magic.'

'So true,' nodded Barney.

'I tell you what we should be spending taxpayers' money on,' said Sid. 'They need to sort the bloody public toilets out and mend the potholes in the road and have cheaper parking. That's what they should be spending the money on. Not the pathetic excuse of the Christmas lights they put up now. Might as well not bother.'

Barney nodded in agreement.

'But,' said Jolene, peeping out from behind her phone, 'will anyone remember the better toilets or the smooth road or the reduced congestion? I mean, you make Christmas when you were young sound amazing. Do you not want your grandchildren to have those sorts of magical memories? Feeling part of the community, standing gazing at the tree, watching the lights getting switched on, or ice skating in the park.' She glanced at Barney. 'Would you not want your grandchildren to have the chance to fall in love with someone at the ice rink?'

Barney suddenly felt a tear spring to his eye. He could picture Linda on the ice so vividly, even now. Probably the best moment of his life.

'Don't you want the future generations to have the chance to make those memories?' continued Jolene. 'Aren't they the very things that make life worthwhile? We shouldn't be losing that. You just said that was all you had: your memories.'

Barney and Sid stared back at her. Then looked at each other.

'I suppose I can always go for a pee in McDonald's,' said Sid eventually. 'And I am partial to a sausage and egg McMuffin. Can I get you a cup of tea, young lady?' he asked Jolene.

'That would be lovely,' answered Jolene.

'I'll get them,' said Barney, getting up. 'She's worked really hard this morning.'

Jolene looked up at Barney in surprise.

'Then we need to tell you about the time we broke into the ice rink in the middle of the night and played ice hockey with a frozen turkey and some golf clubs. Remember that, Sid?'

Sid laughed. 'Remember it well, my man. Remember it well.'

Chapter 20

Somehow there were just ten days until Christmas. Diane couldn't quite believe it. It was team meeting time and there was a lot to get through to make sure they made it to Christmas in one piece.

'Right, Jolene,' said Diane, sitting down at the table. 'Let's start with you. Why don't you update everyone on where you're at with the mayor's event?'

Jolene looked round the table. 'Diane sang on the stage in the West End – it was totally and utterly amazing,' she said.

'I didn't mean that part,' said Diane.

'You did what?' said Yang.

'I'll explain in a minute,' said Diane. 'Tell them about the meeting with Barbara Vasey.'

'Well, she was a bit dismissive at first – in fact, I thought she wasn't listening to me at all – and then Diane said the magic words and, hey presto, we have two capsules on Thursday from 5.30 p.m.'

'Bloody hell,' said Jerry. 'What were the magic words?'

'Impending planning permission,' said Diane.

Jerry shook his head in awe. 'Genius, utter genius. That's why you're the boss.'

'Thank you,' nodded Diane.

'But you haven't heard the best of it yet,' said Jolene. 'We just strolled into this theatre on Shaftesbury Avenue and there were the elves – our elves – on stage, and Diane asked her husband, can I have your elves and he turns to the elves and says do you want to go to a party on the London Eye and have your photo taken, and they all jump up and down in excitement and said yes they would like to go to a party and have their picture in the paper, and then the man asked Diane, our boss, if she'll help with this song they're practising and so she gets up on stage and sings her heart out and I filmed it so we should set up a WhatsApp group called Diane's Singing, or something, and you should watch her because she is sooooooooo good.'

Everyone looked aghast at Diane.

Diane looked round defiantly. 'You all knew that's what I used to do, right? Before this.'

'No,' said Jerry. 'You know how much I love musical theatre and you never told me you used to be part of it. Never. I would have remembered it. I'm googling you,' he said, picking his phone up.

'Don't,' shouted Diane. 'It's all in the past. A very long time ago. And that is where it's staying.' She glared at Jolene, wishing she had told her that she was not to mention her singing under any circumstances.

'So,' said Diane, 'as Jolene says, we have the London Eye, and some elves. Jolene, all you need to find now is a Santa Claus.'

'I'll be Santa Claus,' said Barney.

Everyone turned to stare.

'Wow,' said Jolene. 'Thank you, that's amazing. You won't regret it.'

'Mm, maybe,' said Barney, shifting in his chair. 'Linda always used to get me to do it years ago for playgroup and for the school. Said I made a good Santa. Had the right girth.'

'Are you sure?' asked Jolene. 'I'd got my dad on standby, but he's as skinny as a rake so not quite got the figure for it. You would be so much better. But only do it if you want to. I mean, I don't want it to upset you if it reminds you of Linda.'

'As you said earlier,' said Barney, looking at Jolene, 'memories are really important. Especially the happy ones. I'm lucky enough to have many happy memories being Santa years ago. Why not make a few more?'

'Thanks, Barney,' said Jolene. 'That's amazing. Stacey kindly put me in touch with Grace's school,' she continued. 'The teacher was delighted. Said she was trying to think of a treat for them after the Nativity play and this is perfect. She did make one request, though. I think it came via Grace.'

'Oh God, what has she asked for?' asked Stacey.

'They want to come in their Nativity play costumes. In fact, I think Grace demanded that she come dressed as a donkey,' said Jolene with a smile.

Stacey shook her head. 'That girl,' she sighed. 'I'm going to the Nativity play later so I can check out the costumes, if you like. How would it look in the photo op, do you think?'

'I think it will look fantastic,' said Jolene. 'A full Nativity play cast, Father Christmas, some elves, and the mayor – bound to make the front page, don't you think? You cannot get more Christmassy than that. I told the teacher that was fine. Did I do right?' she asked Diane.

'Sounds like you have it all under control,' said Diane. 'Well done.'

'Can I ask a massive favour?' asked Jolene. 'I could really do with some help on the night. Just to make sure everyone is in place.'

'I was planning to come anyway,' said Diane. 'You'll need help controlling the mayor.'

'I'll be there to keep an eye on Grace, anyway,' said Stacey.

'I can come,' jumped in Yang. 'No problem. Just tell me what I need to do.'

'Father Christmas will be there, of course,' smiled Barney.

'Oh, I'll come too then,' said Jerry. 'Wouldn't want to miss out on a free trip on the London Eye, would I? And there are no choir rehearsals now that we've done the carol concert so I've nothing better to do.'

'Wait,' said Jolene, staring at Jerry. 'I didn't know you sang in a choir. That's really . . . interesting. Where do you sing?'

'St Martin-in-the-Fields,' replied Jerry. 'We just did a concert for five hundred people, actually.'

'Noted,' said Jolene, nodding. 'Very good to know.'

'Right,' said Diane, 'the mayor's event is under control. Now, how is project "Cancel Christmas", going?'

Jerry opened a file and handed copies of a spread-sheet around the table.

'So myself and Yang completed a total of forty-five surveys and the results are pretty conclusive, as you see. I think we need to do a few more to make it robust, but there wasn't one person who said that the Christmas expenditure represented value for money. I think we'd be well within our rights to suggest that Bermondsey Council does not deliver on Christmas to its residents and so we therefore should look to present it as a cost saving for next year.'

Diane swallowed and nodded. 'OK,' she said. 'So what did you conclude, Barney and Jolene, with your interviews?' she asked.

Barney said nothing, leaving Jolene to fill the void.

'Er, we did twenty-five interviews in total,' she began.

'Twenty-five!' exclaimed Stacey. 'Why did it take you so long?'

Jolene looked awkwardly at Barney. He still said nothing, despite the fact the reason was that Jolene had done the vast majority on her own. 'We were really listening,' she said. 'Listening to them talk about Christmas.'

'Jolene did most of the work,' interjected Barney. 'That's why we didn't do as many. She didn't want me to get wet in the rain, which was very good of her. But Jolene is right: we really listened. Listened to what they said about Christmas, not just the answers to the questions.'

'And what did you conclude?' asked Diane.

Barney looked at Jolene. She gave a small nod, indicating for him to go ahead.

'It had given them memories. Memories they treasured in a way that better public toilets and better roads never could,' he said, looking at Diane intently. Then he turned to Jolene. 'That's what they said wasn't it, Jolene? How special their memories were of Christmas.'

Jolene nodded rapidly. 'Yes, Barney,' she replied. 'That's exactly right. The lights, the tree, the ice rink when we used to do it. All of that was part of happy memories. Happy times. And yes, they want money spent on all the stuff that's falling apart, but maybe not at the expense of Christmas.'

Diane didn't know what to say. She'd thought cancelling Christmas was going to be the thing that got her out of making anyone redundant. Now it sounded as if it wouldn't be as straightforward a decision as she had thought.

'So it's a tough choice,' she said, looking round the table. Everyone was looking nervously back at her. Clearly all thinking the same thing. It wasn't going to be easy choosing between someone's job or taking away part of people's Christmas memories in the area.

'Well, we could probably do with a few more in-depth interviews,' said Diane, looking down and shuffling papers. 'And then . . . and then we shall see where we're at.'

'I'm sorry you're in this position,' said Jolene suddenly.

'What position?' asked Diane.

'Having to make this horrendous decision. And at Christmas too. I imagine it's very stressful. I hope whoever has picked you in the Secret Santa Project can work out how to bring you just a little bit of joy. I really do.'

'Thank you, Jolene,' replied Diane. 'I hope so too.'

'Er, can I ask a question about that?' said Yang. 'The Secret Santa Project, I mean.'

'Yep,' said Jolene.

'Well, does it have to be secret? I mean, I've been given a good idea but it can't be a secret. I kind of have to do it now, really.'

'Will it make someone's Christmas?' asked Jolene.

'I believe it will,' said Yang, looking at Jerry. He smiled and nodded back.

'Well, brilliant. Great. Yes, just get on with it.'

'What now?'

'Why not?'

'Er, OK. Well, Stacey, I got you. And, er, I believe you have been asked to a party and you need a babysitter, so can my Secret Santa be coming to look after Grace for you?'

Stacey sat there stunned. Then she leaped out of her seat, ran round the table and hugged Yang.

'How did you know? That is the absolute best gift anyone could give me. I couldn't ask you again – it didn't seem right – but a Secret Santa gift, amazing! It's in the Tower of London, can you believe that? The actual Tower of London. This is the best Christmas ever,' she said, giving Yang a kiss on the cheek before returning to her seat, beaming.

'That's really very good of you, Yang,' agreed Diane, smiling. 'How exciting, Stacey. But the big question is, what are you going to wear?'

'Oh,' she said, clutching her head. 'I was going to ask you, if I managed to sort out the babysitting nightmare. Would you have anything? You always look so amazing. I thought . . . well, I thought you might lend me something.'

'Of course I will,' grinned Diane. 'It would be my absolute pleasure. Will you let me do your make-up too?' she asked.

'Really?'

'Only if you're comfortable with that. I love doing other people's make-up. Chloe used to let me do hers, but she doesn't let me anywhere near her now. Doesn't even wear much, to be honest.'

'I would love that,' said Stacey. 'You're so much better than me. I can't believe it,' she said, looking round the table. 'Thank you, Yang. Thank you, Diane. Really, this is amazing. Can't wait to tell Will.'

'Looks like you shall go to the ball,' grinned Jerry. 'No pressure on the rest of us now over Secret Santa,' he said, looking round the table.

'You know you said you were in a choir earlier?' said Jolene.

'Er, yes?' replied Jerry, suddenly looking nervous. 'What of it?'

'Can we have a chat later? You might be able to help me with something, and maybe then I could perhaps help you with some ideas for your Secret Santa?'

Jerry nodded. 'Yes,' he said. 'All ideas would be most welcome. I'm stumped.'

'Great,' said Jolene, grinning. 'Really great.'

Just at that moment Stacey's phone buzzed angrily on the table.

'I'm sorry,' she said, looking at it. 'It's the school.'

'Take it,' said Diane.

Stacey picked up her phone. 'Hello.'

Everyone watched as she nodded, then sighed, her eyes darting around the room. Then she said, 'Tell her I'll do my best, but I can't promise.'

She put the phone down. 'Sorry about that,' she said. 'Grace insisted they call me. She's refusing to go on stage if they don't.' She turned to Yang. 'I can't believe I'm asking you this, given what you've just offered to do for me, but Grace wanted to make sure that I'd asked you to go to her Nativity play this afternoon to watch her sing the "Donkey Love" song. I told her last night that you wouldn't want to go and that you're at work, but she won't listen. I honestly don't know what I'm going to do with that girl.'

Yang looked at Stacey. 'I'll come,' he said.

'What!' said Stacey. 'No, really, you don't have to.'

'Can I go?' Yang asked Diane. 'I came in at six this morning to plug in all the numbers from the survey. Can you let me off a little early?'

'Er, yes,' she said. 'If you want to?'

Yang looked at Stacey. 'I'd like to come and see Grace sing in a Nativity play. Never watched one before.' He shrugged. 'Feel like I've missed out.'

Stacey stared back at him, blinking.

'Good lad,' said Barney, nodding.

'Thank you,' she said to Yang, clearly baffled by his desire to go. 'You'll make her Christmas.'

215

Yang shrugged. 'Why wouldn't I want to go and see a young child murder a song I wrote?' he said.

'Yeah,' said Jerry, giving him a curious look. 'Why wouldn't you?'

Chapter 21

The bus journey to Grace's school had been fraught. The traffic was insane and, despite his best efforts, Yang couldn't keep Stacey from fretting that they were going to be late.

'She'll kill me if we're late,' said Stacey.

'It's OK,' said Yang. 'We can't do anything about it, so it is what it is. And we've got plenty of time.'

'But everyone will have got there early and be queuing at the door for the front seats and we'll be at the back, and what if Grace doesn't see us? God knows what she'll do. She'll kick off, I know she will, if she thinks I've not turned up.' She leaned back in her seat, clearly distressed, and Yang had no idea how to calm her down so he decided to keep quiet and say nothing.

Eventually Stacey dug him in the ribs and announced they'd arrived and they should hurry to the school. They got off the bus and immediately Stacey broke into a jog, in heels, down the road. Yang had no choice but to pick up his speed and go in pursuit.

They rounded a corner and there were the school gates looming ahead. Behind them stood a three-storey Victorian school that looked anything but welcoming. Yang was starting to wonder whether he'd made a huge mistake.

Yang edged nervously into the school hall, feeling like a total fraud. Everyone would be able to tell he wasn't one of the parents, he thought, and they'd wonder what on earth he was doing here.

They got themselves seated right at the back on the end of the row. Will was sitting a couple of rows in front and turned to wave at Stacey and frown at Yang. Yang could imagine it was quite confusing for Will to see him there, but there was no need to give him such a filthy look. The lights went down and the head teacher stood up on stage to introduce the production.

The production had something in common with all primary school nativities in that it was a well-meaning but shambolic retelling of the biblical tale. Yang struggled to follow the story as it unfolded on stage. There were children in hoods, shuffling around on stage with sheets wrapped around them, and lots of kids dressed as random animals such as donkeys, cows, sheep and goats. There were even a couple of zebras, which confused him. Then two tall boys and a very tall girl arrived wearing crowns and carrying boxes wrapped in foil, and stood behind the people in sheets and a couple of kids that were possibly dressed as camels, but equally could have been hairy mammoths. After them a mixture of boys and girls dressed as angels

218

arrived and did a song-and-dance number. Then they sat all along the front of the stage until the stage was absolutely crammed with every kid who must be in Grace's class. Finally, the two in the middle, dressed in sheets, picked a doll out of a cot in front of them, which Yang assumed must be Jesus, and held it up, and everyone turned round and pretended to be amazed. At various points during the play, groups of children would come to the front of the stage and sing their little hearts out. Some would shout, some would sing, some would refuse to sing a word, but Yang found it totally mesmerising. He couldn't take his eyes off the kids coming together and singing, then lapping up the applause as proud parents wiped tears from their eyes.

A children's Nativity play. Kids singing together in fancy dress about a story as old as time. Knowing it had been done by generations before.

Tradition.

Yang knew all about tradition.

Tradition connects us to our past and our future and, most importantly, to other people.

Yes, it can hold us back. Of course it can. It can bury us far too deep in the past, but as Yang looked around at all the glowing faces in the audience, and indeed the glowing faces on the stage, he recognised that whatever your beliefs, it really didn't matter. What mattered was being together in a shared joyful experience. Regardless of what colour or creed or, indeed, religion. Gathering together, connecting over something peaceful. That was what mattered in this world.

He glanced at Stacey, who was watching the play intently. She looked at him and smiled.

He smiled back.

He was glad he'd come.

She leaned over and clutched his hand just for a moment and grinned. She looked like she was glad he had come too.

The final number of the performance required the entire cast to be on the stage wailing 'Twinkle, Twinkle, Little Star' at the tops of their voices. All the cast took it in turns to come to the front of the stage and take their bows. Eventually the donkeys stood at the front, Grace right in the middle, scanning the crowd, looking slightly disturbed as though she thought no one had turned up to see her.

Yang couldn't help himself. He half stood up in his seat and waved his hand, hoping to get Grace's attention. She looked over and he saw the biggest smile leap to her face. She nudged the person next to her and pointed straight at Yang and told the poor little boy he had to wave as well, which he reluctantly did. Yang sat himself back down again and grinned at Stacey. He'd liked Grace smiling at him like that. Clearly pleased to see him.

The headmistress stood up and gave a speech, pointing out how well all the children had performed and congratulating the frazzled-looking teacher who sat at the side of the stage, who had orchestrated the whole shebang. Miss Shepherd (which raised a laugh) looked like she was about to slide off her chair in sheer exhaustion. She accepted the flowers offered to her with a grimace, looking as though she would have preferred a bottle of gin that she would have happily downed neat in front of everyone at that precise moment.

The headmistress then announced that they were going to end the show with a new composition from a very special child in their school who really loved donkeys and was very keen to share her song.

Yang clapped hard and watched as Grace arrived beaming on the stage with her ukulele and a chair. She sat on the chair and stared out at the audience. Yang watched her swallow. He hoped that wasn't nerves. Nerves is the killer of all creation.

She took a breath and launched into the song.

Donkey Love . . . is the best kind of love.
Donkey Love . . . is everlasting love.
Donkey Love . . . beats any kind of love.
Donkey love . . . is all you need.

She closed her eyes as she sang, slightly out of tune, really feeling the moment. It only took until the end of the first verse for parents to be exchanging looks of silent amusement. Yang tried to ignore them, willing Grace not to notice, willing her to keep her eyes closed, willing her just to enjoy it. That's what he did when he sometimes found himself gigging to a mainly empty and uninterested room. He closed his eyes and enjoyed the moment, picturing instead the Glastonbury crowd, shouting and screaming his lyrics back to him. That was

221

the way to enjoy a tough gig. With your eyes closed and pretend you were somewhere else.

There were a few audible titters now and Yang looked around sharply, wanting to shush the vicious idiots intent on crushing the poor girl on stage. He immediately spotted that Will's shoulders were heaving up and down with laughter. Stacey hadn't appeared to have noticed, totally focused on Grace as she was.

Yang glanced back over at Grace, who still had her eyes closed, but as she totally missed a high note he heard Will let out an audible guffaw. Yang couldn't stand it any more.

He leaned forward round the person in front of him and bashed Will on the shoulder.

Will whipped his head round immediately and Yang saw the tears of laughter streaming down his face. Yang saw red, pulled his fist back and punched him in the face.

Will reeled backwards, nearly falling to the floor. 'What the hell . . .?' he said, struggling to get his balance. Will lashed out at Yang and caught him on the chin, causing him to fall off his chair and land on the floor. He looked up and there was the headmistress looming over him, and he was aware that Grace must have stopped singing.

'What on earth is going on here?' shouted the head-mistress. She glared down at Yang on the floor and then up at Will dabbing his bloody lip. 'You and you, my office, NOW!' she said, striding off.

* * *

A few minutes later and Yang, Will and Stacey were sitting outside Mrs Bunton's office on cripplingly small chairs. Will was sulkily dabbing his still-bloody lip. Yang had decided he needed to be somewhere else so had put his headphones on and was listening to Blur. He felt awful. He'd ruined Grace's performance. How could he have done that? He'd performed once in a pub when a fight had broken out over a spilled pint. It was his worst gig ever as clearly the audience found the fight over spilt Special Brew much more exciting than his singing. He remembered he'd just given up when everyone turned their backs on him to surge round the two men in their fifties having a scrap. He'd packed his guitar and walked out, and not a single person had noticed, as far as he could tell. It broke his heart to think that Grace might be feeling the same as he had felt. Ignored because a fight was going on in the back of the room. And what must Stacey think of him? She looked bewildered and confused. And she had every right to be. Her colleague and her boyfriend had ended up in a fight at her daughter's Nativity. It was bad however way you looked at it. He really had screwed this up. Hitting her boyfriend was not the way to get her on side, even if Will was a complete and utter arsehole. He wished she could see that? Why was she so blinded by the smart clothes and the fancy job and the fancy Christmas parties? Why couldn't she see that behind all that, he was not a good person. And certainly not good enough for her.

A door was flung open at the end of the corridor and Mrs Bunton strode down the corridor in her cord

223

trousers, Chelsea boots, Christmas jumper and a face like thunder. She unlocked her door and held it open, indicating for them all to go in.

There were four chairs arranged in front of a desk. Will made sure he sat next to Stacey whilst Yang sat dejectedly on the end, trying to work out what his story was. He took off his headphones and hung them round his neck.

'He started it,' said Will the minute Mrs Bunton had sat down. 'I was sat there enjoying Grace's song and he just punched me for no reason whatsoever. And he's not even a parent; he shouldn't even be here.'

Mrs Bunton glared at him until he went silent. Then turned her gaze to Yang. Yang had flashbacks of when he was called to the headmaster's office at his school when he was thirteen years old because he'd been skipping chemistry.

'And who are you?' she asked.

'I'm Yang. I, er, I'm a colleague of Stacey's and I wrote the "Donkey Love" song with Grace, Mrs Bunton,' he said, reading her name off the strip on her desk.

'Creep,' muttered Will under his breath.

Mrs Bunton nearly got whiplash she transferred her look back to Will so quickly.

'What was that?' she asked.

'Nothing,' said Will, bowing his head.

'What was that?' she asked again. 'It was definitely something.'

'I called him a creep,' said Will defiantly.

'You called him a name,' said Mrs Bunton, her eyebrows arching. 'How very grown up,' she added.

'About as grown up as him throwing a punch at me during a children's Nativity play,' said Will.

Mrs Bunton turned back to Yang.

'Why did you punch him?' she asked with the sigh of a woman who has asked little boys that a trillion times.

'Because he was laughing at Grace,' said Yang. 'I didn't think that was very nice of him and not fair on Grace.'

'I was not laughing at Grace, I was laughing at your stupid song and you couldn't take it,' replied Will. 'Can so tell you're not a parent. I mean, how stupid can you get? Making an innocent child get up on stage and sing your stupid song. What an idiot.'

'There is no place for name-calling in this school,' said Mrs Bunton sternly. 'You should know that by now, Mr Caton.'

'But he *is* stupid,' said Will.

'And you're a total shitbag,' muttered Yang under his breath.

'Enough,' said Mrs Bunton, slamming her hand down on the desk. 'Have either of you thought about the example this is setting the children? Fighting! At the Nativity play! And what about poor Miss Shepherd? All her hard work in getting the children Nativity ready, only for them to be upstaged by two idiots in the audience having a fight.'

'I thought you said there was no space for name-calling in this school,' said Will.

Mrs Bunton looked as though she would punch him there and then.

'Do you have anything to say, Miss Bentley?' Mrs Bunton asked Stacey.

Stacey looked up at her, and then at Will and then at Yang. Then shook her head slowly.

'Well, for a start I think you both need to apologise to Grace,' said Mrs Bunton, getting up from her chair and striding over to the door. She opened it and there appeared Grace, looking as confused as her mother.

'Come in and sit down,' said Mrs Bunton.

Grace dashed in and sat on her mother's knee.

'I'm not in trouble, am I?' said Grace to Mrs Bunton.

'Goodness no,' said Mrs Burton. 'These two gentlemen have something to say to you.'

'You were brilliant,' said Yang immediately to Grace. 'Utterly brilliant. And I'm so sorry I interrupted you by punching Will. It was unforgivable. I am so sorry.'

Grace's eyes grew wide. 'Why did you hit him?' she asked. 'Is it because he's kissing Mummy?' she asked.

'Grace!' shrieked Stacey. 'You can't say things like that here.'

'No,' said Yang. 'It wasn't because of that. No, I punched him because . . .' he paused to consider his words, '. . . because he was laughing at me,' he said finally. 'That's all. I was stupid and I shouldn't have done it. I'm sorry, Grace.'

Grace shook her head. 'It was the best bit of the play,' she said. 'I mean, it was so funny when the shepherd did a really loud fart, did you hear it? But a real fight, whilst I was singing. And someone punching Isaac's dad. It's like a Nativity dream come true.'

'Grace!' admonished Stacey.

Yang tried to suppress a smile.

'Your turn,' Mrs Bunton said to Will.

'What's my turn?' asked Will.

Mrs Bunton remained stony faced. 'Apologise to Grace.'

'I'm sorry, Grace,' he said. 'I'm sorry that Yang's song didn't go down well with the other parents and so he hit me.'

'More please,' demanded Mrs Bunton.

Will looked at her bewildered.

'I'm sorry that because he hit me, that I hit him back,' he said.

Mrs Bunton finally nodded. 'Well, I think it's time you all went home now, isn't it? I've got enough to do without supervising the poor behaviour of parents. Having said that, the poor behaviour of parents seems to take up an increasing amount of my time. You are all dismissed, but let us be clear. I'll be keeping a close eye on you and the slightest hint of trouble and there will be serious consequences. Understood?'

'Understood,' muttered Yang and Will.

'Not sure I'll be coming back, though,' said Yang, 'so you don't need to worry about me.'

'Oh, you will,' said Grace. 'They do a summer concert every year. We need to start composing right now. I've got an idea for a song about a rabbit.'

'I'm so sorry,' Yang said to Stacey as they stood awkwardly at the school gate. Will had left the headmistress's office to go to find Isaac, and Grace had to dash back into school to fetch her coat.

'I didn't mean to ruin Grace's Nativity play,' he said.

Stacey looked angry. 'How could you do that?' she asked. 'In front of the whole school, cause a scene. It's bad enough being a single parent at the school gate, everyone judging you, looking at you, watching you with their husbands. It's a nightmare. And then you come along and hit the man everyone knows I'm seeing. What do you think that says? I'm going to be the biggest topic on WhatsApp until Christmas, you realise.'

'I'm so, so sorry,' said Yang, looking at the floor. 'I don't know what came over me.'

'And what about Will?' she said. 'What must he be thinking? What if this makes him think that dating me is more hassle than it's worth?'

'I'll do whatever you need,' Yang found himself saying. 'If you need me for extra babysitting so you can see him, then just tell me.' What was he saying? He wanted to get Will away from Stacey and yet he was encouraging it. But he was desperate. Desperate to make amends and not have Stacey think badly of him.

'OK,' she nodded. 'I might just have to take you up on that. You're still coming when we go to the Christmas ball, aren't you? If he still wants to take me, that is.'

'Of course he'll want to take you,' said Yang.

'You think?'

'I mean, who wouldn't want to take someone like you to the ball?'

'What do you mean, someone like me?'

Yang swallowed; he wasn't prepared for this. 'Well,

228

beautiful and charming and fun to be with. I mean, you're the perfect person to take to a ball, I'd say . . .' He trailed off, although unable to look away from Stacey, who was giving him a strange look.

'Can Yang come home with us?' Grace said, bounding up behind them.

'Er, no,' muttered Yang. 'Sorry, can't today. Busy. Stuff to do.'

Stacey nodded. 'Let's get you home,' she said, looking down at Grace.

'Aww,' complained Grace. 'But you are coming soon to babysit again, like Mummy said, aren't you?'

'Yes,' said Yang to Grace. 'Wouldn't miss it for the world. Looking forward to spending time with you.'

'Yippee,' said Grace. 'And thank you for making it the best Nativity ever,' she said to him. 'Everyone's talking about you and wishing you were their dad because you're so cool.'

'Are they?' said Yang.

'Yes,' said Grace. 'Everyone's super jealous because I invited the man who punched Isaac's dad. Even Nikesh came to talk to me and he's the coolest boy in our year and he never talks to me.'

'Time to go,' Stacey said to Grace. She took her hand and Yang watched them walk away. Grace turned back at the corner of the road and gave him a thumbs up and a huge smile. He thought his heart might break.

Chapter 22

The following Sunday Jerry and Carol went for brunch after church. It was a lovely little place down an alleyway just off Trafalgar Square. It had a cool vibe and didn't play cheesy Christmas music, which was why Jerry had picked it. Christmas music was just too much for him at the moment.

'Interesting sermon from the vicar,' said Carol as she sat down and surveyed the menu, glasses instantly steaming up from the contrast in air temperature between outside and inside.

'Didn't hear a word of it,' mused Jerry.

'Mind elsewhere?' asked Carol.

'You could say that.'

'Still obsessed with the man in the red scarf?'

'Not obsessed, no.'

'How many times have you been to the coffee shop this last week?'

Jerry looked up sharply. Carol looked expectant.

'Five,' he admitted.

'And has he showed?'

'No,' said Jerry, pretending to study the coffee menu.

'And what are you concluding from that?' asked Carol.

Jerry cocked his head and thought. 'I'm thinking that he's thinking about what he said to me at the candlelit carols and he's giving himself some space to reconsider and he'll be back in the coffee shop any day to tell me what a massive mistake he's made.'

'Well, you're more of a moron than I thought you were,' said Carol.

'Thanks,' replied Jerry. 'Helpful. Supportive. I can always rely on you.'

'For the *truth*,' replied Carol. 'I'm a truth friend.' She smiled as though pleased with herself. 'Did you get that? A little play on the term "true friend". I'm a truth friend.' She grinned even harder.

'You are the killer of all joy and hope,' Jerry said miserably.

'Hope!' exclaimed Carol. 'Hope, you say. Hope has you hanging out at that coffee shop every evening, jumping out of your skin every time the door opens, hoping against hope that he'll walk through the door. And can you say if you are enjoying that experience? Is that fun? Is hope bringing you joy in those moments?'

Jerry hung his head. 'Not really,' he said.

'I've had experience with a lot of men,' announced Carol, a bit too loudly for Jerry's liking. He glanced around and saw that many of their adjoining tables were staring at them. Carol seemed to be enjoying the attention.

'I've seen it all,' said Carol. 'Literally everything.' She turned to the two ladies staring at her on the next table.

'Everything,' she confirmed. 'No man can shock me any more. Once a man told me he was a heart surgeon and so he really had to look after his hands, which was why he had weekly manicures. I didn't question this, nor his neatly trimmed pubic hair. Turned out he was a porn star.'

The women's jaws dropped, as did Jerry's. Carol did not elaborate but efficiently ordered avocado on toast with smoked salmon from the passing waitress.

'He's not a porn star,' said Jerry. 'He's not the type.'

'Have you checked his nails?'

'Not really.'

'Pubic hair?'

'No! Of course not. We've never even touched, never mind seen each other naked.'

Carol stared back at him. 'It's all very strange, though, isn't it? I mean, he's not given you much to go on, has he? He could be a porn star.'

'I'm not sure they spend their time in Starbucks, sipping Eggnog Lattes and chatting to strangers.'

'Who knows?' said Carol.

'He said he worked in the arts,' said Jerry.

'Acting is in the arts. Porn is acting.'

'Is it, though?'

'Of course it is. Apparently acting turned on is the hardest type of acting.'

'Not helping, Carol.'

'Are you sure? I'm just saying you may have had a lucky escape from a porn star, that's all. Look on the bright side of all this.'

Jerry looked at her. 'Not sure there is a bright side,'

he said. 'He doesn't want me. Even when he saw me singing carols by candlelight, he still didn't want me.'

'I don't think I believe that and neither do you. If you really believed that, you wouldn't be hanging out in that coffee shop waiting for him to come back.'

Jerry shrugged. 'Perhaps,' he said.

'Like I said, I've seen everything,' Carol went on. 'Been there, done that, bought the T-shirt that says all men are bastards on it. But I'm confused on this one. Coming to a frigging candlelit carol concert to say you're not interested. No man does that.'

'He did,' said Jerry.

'Mm,' said Carol, deep in thought. 'Baffling, absolutely baffling.'

The following evening Jerry sat in the coffee shop with faint hope yet again, despite his conversation with Carol. He'd tried to go straight home, or to a different coffee shop, even, but he just couldn't do it. Couldn't quite give up on the hope that tonight would be the night. He did, however, sit with his back to the door with earphones on, deciding that he would have a heart attack if he jumped out of his seat every time he heard the door open.

He was listening to a podcast about the origins of the musical *Hamilton* when he saw out of his left eye an Eggnog Latte appear on the table in front of him.

He'd recognise that hand anywhere, he thought. And it was neat and clean, but definitely not manicured, he would report back to Carol. He looked up. Coffee-shop man was smiling down on him.

'Is that for me?' asked Jerry, trying to be nonchalant – whatever that meant.

Coffee-shop man nodded back.

'Semi-skimmed and no cream?' asked Jerry.

He nodded again. 'Just how you like it,' he said. 'May I join you?'

Hope was flooding into Jerry like a tidal wave. He swallowed, trying to stop the narrative going on in his head from overwhelming him. The narrative being that he'd arrived to tell Jerry he'd made a massive mistake and he'd actually like to invite him to ice skate with him at Somerset House, and they would make their way down there and then glide across the ice like Torvill and Dean, giggling and laughing, until Jerry would accidentally on purpose fall over and he would have to haul him up and then he would fall in his arms and they would kiss, right there on the ice in front of everyone. Yes, Jerry needed to stop these romantic Christmas thoughts and concentrate on the fact that coffee-shop man had merely settled himself down in front of him on a chipped chair and was currently unwinding his red scarf before placing it neatly on the table between them.

Jerry weighed up what he should say before he decided that he didn't need to say anything. Coffee-shop man had asked to sit with him and so he should spark the conversation. Jerry picked up his Eggnog Latte and sipped it. Yes, exactly how he liked it. He just fell in love with coffee-shop man a tiny bit more.

'So how have you been?' he asked Jerry.

Jerry wanted to be honest. Miserable, he wanted to

say, since a man raised my hopes of some Christmas romance, only to dash them by walking away.

Instead he said, remembering to angle his good side, 'Peachy. You?'

He didn't answer. He picked up his Earl Grey tea, no milk, sipped, then set it down again.

'Pretty miserable, actually,' he said.

Serves you fucking right, Jerry wanted to reply. But he didn't. He kept shtum.

Jerry watched as he scratched his head, then leaned forward and put his head in his hands. For a moment Jerry thought he was going to cry. Then what would he do? He had no idea. He found himself starting to feel sympathy for this man. This man who had played with his emotions. Bloody hell. This was not the time or the place to feel sympathy for the man who had broken his heart.

He looked up and rubbed his face before setting his hands on his knees and opening his mouth to speak.

'I wanted to come and apologise,' he said.

Brilliant, thought Jerry. He's come to apologise. What good was that going to do him?

'Now don't roll your eyes,' the man said.

'I didn't,' replied Jerry.

'You did. I can't blame you, but you did. You rolled your eyes in the same way as you did when I admitted that *Wicked* was one of my favourite musicals.'

'Well, you deserved it then. How can you say *Wicked* is a favourite when you have *Hamilton* and *Six* and *The Book of Mormon* and *Cabaret* to pick from? I mean, get real, *Wicked* is good, but it ain't that good.'

'All right,' he grinned. 'Calm down. I should have known better than to raise the issue of musicals when I needed to say something important.'

Jerry's hope went through the roof again. Something important? That had to be good, right? Like, really good. He tried to control his breathing and not look hopeful. He took another sip of Eggnog Latte.

'I need to apologise for not explaining my situation properly last week.'

Jerry's hope flopped again. Explaining a 'situation' was not what he needed to hear. A situation sounded set, settled, stuck. If he'd said he wanted to explain the situation he *was* in, then that would have more hope to it. Instead, he was reading that nothing had changed whatever his situation was, and so hope was out of the window again. Jerry became aware that as he was thinking this through, coffee-shop man had started speaking again and he wasn't listening. He suddenly stopped speaking and Jerry was aware he hadn't heard a word he'd said.

'I'm so sorry,' said Jerry. 'Could you repeat that? The background noise, you know . . .'

He took a deep breath. 'I said that I'm married.'

Deep and utter confusion, followed by anger. Jerry was now totally in the moment.

'What do you mean, you're married?'

'You know what I mean by married.'

Jerry rolled his eyes again.

'Well, actually no, you don't know what I mean by married. Because . . . well, there is something else, you see . . .'

'How long have you been married?'

'Twenty-one years.'

'Fucking hell!' said Jerry, leaping back as though someone had hit him. 'Twenty-one years and you're dangling me on a bit of string. What the hell are you doing?' Jerry got up to leave. He'd heard enough.

'No, wait, you don't understand.'

'Don't understand? Oh, I'm not stupid. I totally understand. Getting a bit bored, were you? Thought you'd try a bit of flirtation, did you, to spice things up a bit? Have you been going back to your husband and telling him all about this guy in the coffee shop who's into you and you're just having a little play? Messing with his feelings in the interests of spicing up your marriage?'

'It's not been like that at all. You really don't understand.'

'Oh, I do. It's a tale as old as time. What happened? Did you bottle it? Were you about to come up with the line – "I'm married but we live separate lives, my husband doesn't understand me"?'

'I was going to tell you that I'm married but we live separate lives, but I wasn't going to tell you that my husband doesn't understand me because, well, because actually I think my *wife* really does understand me. Well, sort of . . . a big part of me, although obviously not this part of me because I barely understand it myself. Which is why I've been such a jackass, because I'm still trying to make sense of it.'

Jerry sat down with a thump.

'You're married to a woman?'

237

'Yes.'

Jerry was floored. It explained so much and yet it explained nothing at all. That was the last thing he had been expecting.

'How come?' was all he could say.

Coffee-shop man shrugged. 'I fell in love. We were young. This was twenty-five years ago. Being gay was still very much . . . well, you had to be very brave, braver than now, to come out then. And . . . me and my wife just got on really well and so that's what you did, didn't you, back then? You found a girl that you got on well with and married her. I loved her. I still do, but it's like a platonic thing really. I was always aware that I did have feelings for men as well as women, but it was easier to suppress them. Easier to fall on the side of women. It made for a more straight-forward life, I guess.'

'So what? You think you're, like, bisexual?' asked Jerry.

He shrugged. 'I guess that's what you'd call it these days. If you had to put a label on it. Not sure that's helpful, though. Makes everything too defined. I mean, how do you define love? It's such a broad and varied thing. There are so many different types of love. All I know is that when I was in my twenties I loved and wanted my wife. I know I did. But we've grown apart. We don't make each other happy any more. And . . . and something about you makes me think that you could make me happy.'

Jerry shook his head. 'Why are you telling me this now?' he said. 'Why come back here tonight?'

Coffee-shop man stared at his fingers before raising his eyes to look at Jerry.

'Because walking out of that church, without you, is the hardest thing I have ever had to do. I cried all the way home on the Piccadilly Line.'

'That's a long line.'

'It sure is.'

'How many stops?' asked Jerry. He hoped it was double digits. Double digits crying had to be worth something.

'Maybe twelve, maybe thirteen.'

'Good,' Jerry found himself saying.

'A hen party also got on at Charing Cross and tried to console me until Leicester Square. They invited me to join them to go and see *Magic Mike* at the Hippodrome, but I just couldn't face it.'

'You would never have got in.'

'They had a spare ticket. Crystal from Epping couldn't make it because she'd already passed out at the bottomless afternoon tea.'

'Wow,' said Jerry. 'Poor Crystal.'

'I guess.'

'So what did the hen party ladies tell you to do?'

'They told me to get off the tube and head straight back to the carol concert and sink to my knees in front of you and beg you to go out with me.'

'Weren't they on your wife's side?'

'You would have thought, wouldn't you? They said they were always on the side of true love. The only side to be on.'

'But you didn't come back,' said Jerry.

'No,' he said. 'I decided I needed to talk to my wife first. Only I got back and she was all upset about Christmas stuff so I couldn't do it to her. I couldn't add this to her Christmas hell.'

'Christmas is a kind of hell, isn't it?' said Jerry.

'Sometimes,' he replied.

'So . . . where does that leave us this Christmas?' asked Jerry, agonising over the fact that his dream Christmas seemed to be coming and going out of his future like a yo-yo.

Coffee-shop man scratched his head. 'I think it leaves us at me sorting my life out over Christmas with the hope that, come the new year, I'm in a very different place. And I know that might sound like I'm fobbing you off, but I have a lot to do. I need to do right by my wife, somehow. To be honest, I don't think she'll be devastated about the end of our marriage; I'm sure she's unhappy too. I have an idea of how I might be able to give her the life I know she really wants, to help her through this mess I've made of our lives, but I need to make that happen.'

'It's a lot to take in,' said Jerry.

'I know. And I thank you for your patience. Sorry, sounds as though I've been keeping you on hold for forty-five minutes. But I'm asking you if I can keep you on hold for just a little longer so that when I do come back for you, next time I can do it with a clear conscience.'

Being on hold, especially over Christmas, felt like Jerry's worst nightmare but he could appreciate his honesty as well as his torment. He knew he was being totally and utterly genuine with him and he had to give him credit for that. As well as the fact that he would hold in his heart, throughout the difficult Christmas period, the words, *Because walking out of that church, without you, is the hardest thing I have ever had to do*. He literally couldn't wait to tell Carol. It was by far and away the most romantic thing anyone has ever said to him and he would cherish the memory of those words coming out of someone's mouth about him, for the rest of his life. He'd waited this long for him, so maybe he could bear to wait until after Christmas.

Jerry nodded his agreement on the plan. He picked up his mug of cold Eggnog Latte and tapped it against his tea.

'Merry Christmas,' he said. 'I'll see you on the other side.'

Chapter 23

'You really are my fairy godmother,' said Stacey when she pulled the door open to Diane at 5 p.m. on the night of the Christmas ball. Diane was clutching several coat hangers over her shoulder and holding an enormous make-up box. Stacey felt her heart leap in excitement.

'No need to thank me,' said Diane, pushing past her into her tiny hall, long gowns in billowing dry cleaning plastic trailing behind her. 'I was thinking about this all weekend. It's kept me going. Now where can I set up?'

'Set up?'

'My mirror and make-up case. We need some good light. Yes, in here is perfect. Hello, young lady,' Diane said to Grace as she piled into the lounge. 'Want to help me set up a make-up station in here?'

'Absolutely,' said Grace, leaping off the sofa where she had been watching cartoons. 'Are you a real fairy godmother,' she said, eyeing up the dresses draped over her arm. 'You look like a fairy godmother.'

'Does that just mean I look old?' asked Diane, draping the gowns over the back of the sofa.

'Erm, I'd say glamorous old,' replied Grace.

'Grace!' said Stacey.

Diane laughed. 'Do you know what, I'll take that as a compliment. Now, why don't you go and try on some of these, Stacey, and me and Grace will tell you which one to wear.'

'Don't I get to choose?'

'Of course not, Mummy. You must let the fairy godmother choose, with my help, of course,' said Grace.

'OK,' said Stacey, grinning and grabbing the dresses. 'Give me a minute.'

'I would offer you a cup of tea,' said Grace to Diane, 'except I've been told to not touch the kettle since I put my goldfish in it because it was shivering.'

'Shivering?' asked Diane.

'Yeah, it was swimming all wobbly – you know, like he was shivering.'

'What happened when you put it in the kettle?'

'Well, I sort of forgot about it and the next morning Mum made a cup of tea and poured dead Fred into her mug. She wasn't happy.'

'Was she fond of Fred?'

'No, it just ruined her tea.'

'OK then, great,' said Diane. 'I'll pass on the tea, I think. Ah, here she is.'

'That's a no, then,' said Grace as Stacey appeared in the doorway.

'Hang on,' said Diane, approaching Stacey. 'Actually, I think your daughter is right but only because, as

243

expected, you're slimmer than me so you need to try the more fitted dresses, the ones I wear need some serious body-shaping underwear underneath in order for me to get into them, although you'll be absolutely fine. Go and put the red one on. It looks tiny but there's plenty of stretch. And it's short but not too short, especially with your legs.'

'I've seen that one – there's no way I'll fit in that,' said Stacey.

'Trust me, if I can get in it, you can. Off you go.'

Diane and Grace settled down on the sofa to wait. Grace switched the telly on again and they watched a cartoon, enjoying it so much that they didn't spot Stacey when she first came to the door. She had to step in front of the TV.

'Oh, yes,' said Diane. 'Now that's much better. How do you feel?'

Stacey grinned. 'I like it. Sexy and sophisticated. I think this is perfect. I think this is the sort of thing that other women will be wearing, don't you?'

'I don't like it,' said Grace, folding her arms in a sulk.

'Why not?' said Diane.

'I don't want to say.'

'But she looks super in it. Your mum has an amazing figure. She should show it off.'

'No, she shouldn't.'

'Why not?'

Grace looked up at Diane. 'Because Will will want to kiss her and stuff, and I don't want him to kiss her.'

Diane glanced at Stacey. Stacey shrugged.

'How do you feel in that dress?' she asked Stacey.

'I feel really good.'

Diane nodded. She looked back at Grace. 'You know, Grace, you're absolutely right, you shouldn't wear clothes for other people. But your mum feels good in this so I think that maybe we should let her decide what she wants to wear?'

'Are you saying that as a fairy godmother?' asked Grace.

Diane thought for a moment. 'Such a good question. Do you mean, what would a fairy godmother say to wear?'

'Exactly,' replied Grace.

Diane looked over at Stacey, who looked expectant.

'Do you know, I think a true fairy godmother would say don't wear something too short.'

Stacey looked at Diane quizzically.

'Just a hunch,' said Diane. 'A fairy godmother would suggest a longer gown, more elegant and easier to wear. I mean, I know I spend half the night when I'm wearing that dress tugging it down – now what's the point in that? Go put the silver full-length one on and let's see what happens.'

'If you're sure?' mumbled Stacey, turning round.

'Good decision.' Grace nodded at Diane.

Eventually Stacey came to the door for the third time, just as all the Christmas ads came on TV. Grace and Diane looked up and both gasped.

'That's the one,' nodded Diane. 'That dress says that Will needs to take you to meet his parents before he tries anything on. The red one just screamed, take me now!'

'I agree,' nodded Grace.

'What do you think?' Diane asked Stacey.

Stacey nodded, her eyes slightly glossy. 'I feel amazing. I never thought I could look like this. I look like a grown-up. Like a princess.'

'Right,' said Diane, 'come and sit down and let's put some grown-up make-up on you. So I think a touch of sparkle is in order, don't you?' She picked up a couple of eyeshadows and showed them to Grace. 'This one or this one?'

Grace considered them both carefully, then looked at her mum. 'Pink sparkle,' she said seriously. 'I don't think Mum can carry off the purple.'

Diane was really enjoying herself. It reminded her of playing dressing up with Chloe when she was young. It was probably her favourite mother-daughter time. Pity Chloe didn't want to spend that time with her mother now. She'd barely seen her since she'd been home, she'd been so busy showing her new boyfriend off to her friends.

'OK,' said Diane, taking a deep breath and preparing to create. 'We'll base the make-up around that pink eyeshadow.' She figured her love of make-up and dressing up came from her performing days. Getting ready to go out for an evening was just the same as preparing for the stage, really. In Stacey's case it was the grand stage of Will's glamorous office Christmas party. Quite an intimidating stage, when Diane thought about it. To go somewhere where you didn't know anyone apart from the person you were with, to perform as the perfect girlfriend – now, that took some doing. Diane had done it many times for her husband. Accompanied him to industry gatherings as his wife. It was a tough gig. Being somewhere because of someone else and not in your own right. Not that she had done it recently, she recollected. Perhaps the industry events had dried up or perhaps Leon had just stopped inviting her.

'Close your eyes,' she said to Stacey.

Stacey closed her eyes and Diane looked at the canvas. She saw a young woman in her prime. She saw none of the lines that had appeared on her own face over the last few years. She saw fresh blooming skin. She saw how her face used to look: smooth, glowing and line free. She saw lustrous dark hair with no hint of grey. She saw everything she used to be and now wasn't. Perhaps that was why Leon had been tempted elsewhere. Was it a fresh-faced younger model who had been drawn to his distinguished looks? It hardly ever happened the other way round, did it? The fresh-faced young man drawn to the laughter lines of the older woman. The face worn by time and stress and the difficulties that life throws at you. Looking at Stacey reminded her of looking in the mirror all those years ago, full of life and promise and optimism, and now here she was on the other side, wondering what had happened to that feeling.

Diane got to work but really it took no time at all. It was amazing how much quicker it was to make a line-free face look dazzling. She added the final touch of lip gloss and then handed Stacey a mirror.

'I think you'll be the belle of the ball,' she said with a sigh, noting Stacey's delight.

'Wow,' Stacey said, turning her head left and right to look from all angles. 'I actually look, well, very glamorous and sophisticated. You're a miracle worker, Diane. Truly.'

'You're glamorous, full stop. You just needed me to bring it out.' Diane could almost feel herself tearing up at the sight of Stacey's excitement. How she longed to be in her shoes again. 'Any man would be proud to have you on their arm.'

'Really?'

'God, yeah.'

'But this party is bound to be full of really glamorous women, right? Bankers have tiny blond girlfriends, don't they? Not mums with scars and worry lines!'

Diane shook her head. Why did women always see themselves and their bodies in a bad light? Always. Why did they compare themselves constantly? What was the point? All Diane could see was a beautiful, smart young woman, and all Stacey could see was someone who had already failed at life. Instead, she had her whole life ahead of her. If only, thought Diane.

'My mother would hate this dress,' said Stacey.

'Why?' asked Diane.

'She'd say it was flashy, way too flashy.'

'I don't see flashy,' said Diane. 'I see . . . I see you . . . a young woman with her whole life ahead of her, looking stunning, but knowing there's a whole load of stuff inside of her that is so worth everyone's while. Someone who could do anything she wanted to if she put her mind to it.'

Stacey stared back at her open mouthed. 'I bet you're an amazing mum,' she said.

Diane laughed. 'No idea,' she replied. 'Currently my daughter doesn't seem to want to be anywhere near me, so you tell me. She's even ditched me for Christmas. The new boyfriend's family is much more appealing, apparently. Christmas Day is going to be dire.'

'She must be mad,' said Stacey. 'I'd give anything to be with a mother who wanted to be with me at Christmas. All I get is disapproving looks and requests for handouts. I wish I had an excuse not to see her at Christmas.'

'Christmas can bring out the worst in families,' said Diane.

'It so can. It would just be nice to spend it with someone I actually cared about and who cared about me. Still, that's Christmas, I suppose. At least I've got this ball to go to. I'll just have to spend Christmas Day trying to remember what a fabulous time I had with my Prince Charming.'

Diane nodded. Diane really hoped she had a good time. And she prayed that this guy really did turn out to be Prince Charming. She was worried Stacey had way too much riding on him and it would inevitably be him that would let her down.

Grace wandered back in, chocolate biscuit in hand. She gaped when she saw her mum fully made up and hair in an updo.

'You look amazing, Mum,' she said. Then she let out a deep sigh. 'Just make sure he's worth it.'

Diane had to agree with this very wise seven-year-old. She'd performed her role very well as the fairy godmother. Perhaps too well. She'd swooped in and transformed Cinderella so she was ready to go to the ball and attract Prince Charming, because obviously Prince Charming was only going to be attracted to someone who looked like a princess and not a scruffy scullery maid, despite the fact that they were exactly the same person.

Bloody Cinderella, thought Diane. Fairy-tale clap-trap that teaches all girls they must be beautiful and they must spend their lives trying to get a man to fall in love with them. That is the main objective in life. Forget all your other achievements. Forget all your other wonderful traits. No, to be loved by a man is your highest accolade.

Diane could feel her blood starting to boil as she looked at Stacey. Stacey deserved love – of course she did – but not the desperate kind she was possibly seeking. Not the 'take anyone who will have me' kind of love. Not the 'anything is better than being alone' kind of love. She deserved the real deal. The two-way street. The non-compromising, 'take me as I am' kind of love.

Stacey was gathering her things now. She was picking up a black leather bag that she used for everyday in the office, which didn't match her outfit at all. Diane reached down for the sequin-covered clutch she had bought specifically to go with the outfit Stacey was wearing.

She offered it to her, but grabbed her hand as she reached out to take it.

'Listen to your daughter,' said Diane. 'Be sure he's worth it, be sure he's worth you. Be sure you're not just choosing bad company over no company. Be sure he sees you, Stacey. Smart woman, diligent colleague, wonderful mother, not just a pretty woman in a sparkly dress.' She let go of her hand.

Stacey looked a little startled but she nodded. Diane prayed she had listened.

'Can I just say you're the best fairy godmother I have ever met,' added Grace.

'Met many, have you?' asked Diane.

'Don't be ridiculous!' said Grace.

As if totally on cue the doorbell rang.

'Your carriage awaits?' asked Diane.

Stacey glanced at her watch.

'No, actually. Yang, I hope,' she replied.

'Yay,' replied Grace, dashing to the door.

'Such a great idea of Yang's to babysit as his Secret Santa,' said Diane. 'Wish I could think of something that good.'

'Well, yeah,' said Stacey. 'It's very kind of him.'

'Hi,' said Yang as he dumped white plastic carrier bags on the coffee table.

'Did you bring those cracker things?' asked Grace, diving into one of the bags.

'Yeees,' said Yang.

'I'll get some plates and stuff. You said you'd teach me to use chopsticks this time.' Grace careered out of the room.

Diane watched as Yang noticed Stacey was all dressed up.

'Wow,' he said, looking genuinely stunned. 'You look amazing. Like . . . yeah . . . great.'

'Thanks,' blushed Stacey. 'All Diane's work. She's a marvel. There was no way I could scrub up like this without her.'

Yang looked at her. 'You always look great,' he said. 'Always.'

Stacey hesitated. 'Thank you, Yang,' she replied.

'It's true.' He shrugged again, then wandered into the kitchen after Grace.

'We need a lot of kitchen roll if I'm teaching you chopsticks,' they heard him say to Grace. 'Or do you have a dog?'

'In a flat!' replied Grace. 'Dogs don't do lifts.'

'Fair point. Better get the kitchen roll out, then.'

Diane looked at Stacey. She couldn't believe how at home Yang appeared to be in Stacey's flat and how relaxed he was with Grace.

'They get on well,' she said, indicating the pair in the kitchen.

'Oh God, yeah, Grace never stops talking about him,' said Stacey. 'She adores him.'

Yang and Grace arrived back in the lounge, clutching plates and kitchen roll.

'Don't you need to go now?' asked Grace.

'Yes,' said Diane. 'You're right. I have a hot date with the remote control.' She began to gather up her things.

'Will's coming here and we're getting a black cab into town,' said Stacey.

As if on cue, almost as though they were in a panto-mime, the doorbell chimed stage left.

Grace booed in much the same way as someone would if Cinderella's evil stepmum had just arrived.

Diane watched Yang smirk at Grace.

Stacey brought Will into the lounge whilst she collected her things. He stood in the doorway and jiggled his keys in his pocket, glaring at Yang, whilst Yang glared back. He did look extremely handsome. Diane could totally understand why Stacey was swept away by him. His tuxedo was immaculate, with elegant silk lapels matching his silk black tie. He was clean shaven and his hair was coiffured to within an inch of its life. His expensive aftershave was making its way into Diane's nostrils and she could almost feel herself swoon.

'This is Diane, my boss,' said Stacey. 'She came over to lend me a dress and do my hair and make-up, because, well, she does sophisticated, which I've never been much good at.'

Diane watched as Will looked Stacey up and down then turned to Diane.

'Decent,' he said. 'Thanks for that. Shall we go?' he said to Stacey.

Diane held her breath as Stacey paused for a split second, maybe waiting for a compliment to be directed at her but it never came.

'You go,' said Diane. 'I'll see myself out. Go on. Your taxi will be waiting.'

'OK, right, bye then. Bed at eight, Grace. Thanks, Yang. You're one in a million.'

'Have a good time,' he replied, but Stacey had slammed the door behind her. She was already gone.

Chapter 24

Stacey didn't think she could be any more excited. She felt giddy and giggly, as though she was about to embark on the most magical journey of her life. She felt the magic of Christmas again like she had done when she was a child. As she rode through the streets of London in the back of the black cab, she saw the Christmas decorations as though she was seeing them for the first time. The awe and wonder of them was blinding as she clutched Will's hand. She couldn't understand why she hadn't noticed before how beautiful her home city was. As they rode over the Thames she almost gasped at the reflection of the lights in the river, looking far down towards Tower Bridge and St Paul's and the skyscrapers beyond. It looked like a painting, it was so jaw droppingly beautiful. She must have been given a new set of eyes. She had never seen London like this, she could have sworn. She had never seen the magic of Christmas like this before. This grown-up Christmas night out felt as if she had been spirited away to a magical wonderland for a few hours, and the reality of life was quietened for the moment.

She leaned over, squeezing Will's hand. 'Thank you for inviting me,' she said. 'Honestly, I can't believe I'm going to a Christmas party at the Tower of London. It's just amazing.'

Will shrugged. 'Not sure it will be as good as the Shard last year, if I'm honest. Apparently the food isn't as good at the Tower, but then again the Shard does have a Michelin-starred chef so it's going to struggle to match up to that.'

Stacey shook her head and thought of the Accounts Department's usual Christmas Coffee celebration, when she might treat herself to a ginger spiced latte rather than having her usual tea. She wasn't having to rate the relative merits of luxury Christmas venues year on year. But maybe if it continued to go well with Will, then she would be sitting in a cab this time next year wondering whether this year's party would be as good as the one last year at the Tower of London. Now, wouldn't that be a thing.

'That reminds me,' Will said, clutching her hand and looking into her eyes as they whisked past the Savoy. 'I wanted to ask you something.'

Stacey held her breath. Perhaps he was going to ask her to spend Christmas with him. How brilliant would that be. Finally, a Christmas with romance attached. Oh, how she would love that.

'When you're out buying presents, could you get something for Isobel? For some stupid reason we still get each other gifts, but I never know what to get and

I haven't got time to go shopping, and you'd be much better at choosing than me. Is that OK? It would be doing me such a favour. Just whilst you're out and about. No need to make a special trip.'

Stacey stared at him. That didn't sound like something she wanted to do at all. Buy his ex-wife's Christmas present? No, not really.

He put his head on one side 'Honestly, you would be such a life saver,' he continued. 'It would give me more time to look for something for you.'

'OK,' she said slowly, not wanting to break the mood. She'd shelve her feelings on this request for this evening.

'Wow, you're so amazing, you know. You really are,' he said, holding her tight and moving in for a kiss. She couldn't resist. Why did he have to smell so good? They kissed long and hard in the back of the cab and for a moment Stacey thought she had been transported to a Hallmark Christmas movie.

They were zipping along Embankment now, possibly one of the most magical parts of London on any day of the week, but the addition of Christmas trees lit up brightly along the river bank added extra fairy dust. Stacey could see couples walking along hand in hand like you often saw in the movies. She'd like to do that. Maybe she and Will could take a stroll down to the river later and take in the glory of the city after a few glasses of champagne and a smooch on the dance floor.

Eventually the infamous turrets of the Tower of London came into view. Majestic, robust, strong. What a sight, in contrast to the multitude of skyscrapers, she'd just passed, Stacey thought. One of the oldest buildings in London still dominated the skyline, with its unique towers and turrets. The cab driver dropped them at the public entrance and Will jumped out before offering his hand to help Stacey step out of the cab, which she did with as much elegance as she could muster.

'I feel like a queen arriving home,' she giggled, looking up at the floodlit Tower. Will bent low and kissed her hand. 'For tonight,' he said, 'you will be my queen, my beloved.' Stacey giggled again. This was more like it.

Will took a thick card out of his breast pocket and showed it to the man on the gate, who nodded them through in stately silence. They walked along a walled pathway towards an archway between two imposing towers, above the dry moat. Stacey felt as if she was literally going back in time as the noise of the city grew distant and the quiet calm of the Tower of London took over. Her heels clicked loudly on the stones and echoed as they entered a short tunnel. At the other side a Beefeater stood to greet them with a tray of mulled wine in festive cardboard cups.

'You might need this to fortify the rest of your journey onward to the White Tower, the oldest building within the Tower walls,' he told them.

'Thank you,' said Stacey, gratefully taking one of the cups. 'It smells wonderful,' she added, blowing the steam off the top.

'Now follow the signs. It's a five-minute walk, so tread carefully over the cobbles and don't stray off the path, whatever you do,' he grinned.

'A five-minute walk,' muttered Will. 'You'd think

257

they'd be able to get us closer to the venue in a cab, wouldn't you?'

'Well, I guess they weren't thinking about access for corporate parties way back in the eleventh century,' said Stacey. She'd been reading up on the history of the Tower as she had been so excited, and thought it might be a useful conversation point if she got stuck for what to say to Will's colleagues.

'I guess,' said Will.

'Nice touch, giving us a shot of mulled wine to accompany us on our way,' said Stacey.

'Mm,' replied Will. 'Never been a fan of mulled wine. It's just red wine watered down with orange juice, isn't it? I don't get it. Ian had better have ordered some decent champagne for arrival drinks.' He put his paper cup down on an ancient wall.

'You can't leave that there,' said Stacey.

'Why not?'

'Well, it's litter.'

'They'll have cleaners coming round. We're guests. I have it on good authority that the firm has paid a lot of money for this party so we can leave someone else to clear up. Come on,' he said, putting his arm round her. 'Let's go find a real drink.'

They continued to follow the cobbled road along the ramparts of the towers. It was eerily quiet, as though they were the only ones there, as though they had got the dates totally wrong or had been lured there under false pretences. It felt a little more like the latter as their footsteps echoed round the hushed walls.

'This is the Queen's House on the left,' said Stacey. 'Henry VIII built it for Anne Boleyn, apparently, which sounds romantic, of course, but it's also where she spent her last night before he had her beheaded.'

'Brutal,' said Will.

'Well, it was, especially as he'd moved heaven and earth to have her. I mean, the man set up an entire new religion just so he could marry her. And yet they were only married three years and he ordered her to be beheaded! I mean, that is some turnaround, isn't it?'

'Didn't she, like, sleep around?' asked Will.

Stacey shrugged. 'Maybe, but Henry VIII was the most unfaithful man known to life. He wasn't beheaded, was he, but poor old Anne was. Women couldn't get away with anything in those days.' Stacey felt herself shiver. 'Not that it's much different now.'

'Yes, it is,' said Will. 'A woman can have sex as much as she wants now – no one gives a damn.'

Stacey raised her stuck-on eyelashes. 'She can. She might not be beheaded like Anne, but she's still judged. Believe me, I'm a single mum, I know. But Freddie, Grace's dad – no one's judging him, as far as I can tell. And all I can see on Instagram is his family fawning all over him and his engagement. Not a thought for the child he's fathered.'

Stacey felt the outside world closing in on her suddenly. It had broken through the fortress of the Tower of London and was threatening her magical evening. She couldn't allow that to happen. She needed to forget the fate of poor Anne Boleyn and enjoy her evening of fun and frivolity.

259

'Traitors' Gate,' she said, nodding down towards the grim-looking wooden structure to her left. 'They used to bring traitors here by barge and imprison them in the Tower.'

'Nice,' sighed Will. 'This venue has all the atmosphere you need for a cracking good Christmas party.'

'I wonder if the traitors could hear the members of the household partying. How weird would that have been.'

'Not as weird as you giving me the entire grim story of the Tower of London on our way to a party.'

'Sorry,' said Stacey. 'Sorry. Just I find the history amazing. Imagine, we're going to eat and dance and be merry in the very spot where Henry VIII and Anne Boleyn did. Doesn't that give you the chills slightly? Doesn't that feel amazing?'

'I'd rather be at the Shard,' said Will. 'They do the best Espresso Martini you have ever tasted there by a country mile. Don't think we'll be getting one of them here.'

Eventually they were directed along a narrow corridor, through a small door and down a narrow staircase into a large grey-stone-wall-lined room with magnificent arches on each side. A large fire roared at the far end and beside it stood a tall and extremely wide Christmas tree twinkling with white lights. Round tables stretched out in front of them, bedecked with candles and sumptuous festive decorations. A warm festive glow filled the room as well as the hum of chatter from the guests lingering around a bar on one side of the room. Waiters glided effortlessly with full trays of tall glasses filled with bubbling golden wine. One of them greeted Stacey at the bottom of the steps and handed her a fizzing glass with a nod and a smile.

She took a glass gladly and sighed. This was heaven. She turned to smile at Will and clinked his glass. 'Merry Christmas,' she said to him. She could feel herself starting to well up, she felt so full of Christmas cheer. Here she was, in one of the most historic buildings in London, bathed in fairy lights and feeling the warmth of an open fire on her cheek. This was the most festive she had felt in a very long time. She could almost look forward to Christmas, feeling like this.

'Jacko is over there with his girlfriend,' said Will. 'He DM'd her on Instagram. She's an underwear model, or so he says. She doesn't look much like one, though. I reckon he's talking out of his arse as usual. Let's go over and find out. You ask her what she does for a living when I introduce you.'

Will was striding off towards a group gathered round the Christmas tree before Stacey could say anything. She didn't want to know what Jacko's girlfriend did. She didn't care. And equally, she didn't want to be talking all night about the fact she worked for the council. That would be sure to ruin the warm glow she was feeling.

'Jacko, mate,' bellowed Will, slapping his colleague on the back. 'How long have you been here? You look like you've had my share of the champagne already.'

'Well, if you don't get here bang on, then old Charlie will only neck it, won't he? Now, who's this?' he asked, eyeing up Stacey.

'This is Stacey,' said Will. 'She's the mum of one of Isaac's friends.'

Stacey felt her heart sink. Not the way she wanted to be described. A mum was not her main descriptor tonight, surely? And Grace would be horrified if she heard Will describe her as a friend of Isaac's. She clearly detested him.

'Nice to meet you, Stacey,' said Jack, nodding his head. 'This is Bianca. She's an underwear model.'

Stacey's jaw dropped slightly. She wasn't sure if she would want to be introduced as an underwear model either!

'Used to be,' said Bianca, giggling. 'Like two years ago. I do promotional work now. It's warmer.' She laughed as if she'd made an hilarious joke. Jack and Will also laughed like she had made an hilarious joke. She was wearing a dress not dissimilar to the red one that Grace and Diane had told her to take off because it was too short. Bianca did look stunning in it and her hair extensions nearly touched her hem. It almost looked like she was wearing a winter cape.

'Well, that sounds like the underwear modelling world's loss,' said Will. 'Can I get you ladies another drink?'

'Lovely,' said Bianca.

'Thank you,' said Stacey.

Jacko and Will turned and left to go to the bar, leaving Bianca and Stacey alone.

'This is pretty cool, hey?' said Bianca, looking round her surroundings. 'Best I've been to this year, I reckon.'

'You been to a lot of parties, have you?' asked Stacey.

'Oh, yeah,' grinned Bianca. 'It's why I keep "underwear model" in my bio, if I'm honest. I'm never short of invitations over Christmas, funnily enough.' She winked at Stacey. 'I'll let you into a secret. I only did it once and that was for thermal underwear.' Bianca threw her head back and laughed. 'Gets them every time,' she said.

'You and Jacko, you're not like girlfriend and boyfriend then?' she asked.

Bianca laughed her heartiest of laughs so far. 'God, no,' she said. 'In his wet dreams. No, I make a point of not being involved at Christmas. Means I can come and go as I please, get taken to every party there is going, have a good time and still get to be wrapped up in my jim-jams on Christmas Day with my mum and dad and baby brother. Just the way I like it. Who needs a man at Christmas, anyway?' she continued. 'All they expect you to do is buy all their Christmas presents for them, send all their cards, do all the donkey work that Christmas brings to women, whilst they swan about having a good time. No, believe me, not having a man at Christmas is the way forward.'

Stacey blinked back. She didn't know what to say. Bianca had zapped all the romance out of a Christmas romance just like that!

'How about you?' asked Bianca. 'You been with that Will guy long?'

'No, not long,' said Stacey. 'I mean, I think we're together, but you know it's hard when there are kids involved. Hard to commit.'

Bianca nodded. 'Christmas will sort you out. You'll know if he's committed when it comes to this time of year. He brought you here. That's a pretty big commitment, right? Has he asked you what you want for Christmas yet?'

'No,' replied Stacey. She had been rehearsing her response to that question for a while. 'Nothing special,' was going to be her modest reply. 'Don't go to any trouble. Maybe some perfume would be nice.'

Bianca pulled a face. 'Ask him what he wants and watch his face, that will give you a clue, darling. He can't ask you for something decent if he's not planning something decent for you. Now, here they come. Don't mention the thermal underwear, will you?'

Will and Jacko approached with four glasses of champagne in their hands, killing themselves laughing about something.

'About time,' said Bianca, grabbing a glass. 'Thought you'd skipped off to France for these babies.'

'You all right?' asked Will.

Stacey looked at him. 'Fine,' she said.

'We're about to sit down, apparently,' he told her. 'I'll apologise now for my table. My department's so boring but we were told we had to sit together. But it's just for the meal and then we can ditch them.'

He took her hand and led her across the room to a round table at the far end. People were already hovering behind chairs, waiting for everyone to arrive so they could sit down. They looked generally older than Will and a bit fierce. Stacey looked over her shoulder, wishing they were sitting with Bianca. She seemed like fun.

There were little name tags on the place settings, and when they found their spots on the table of eight her label read: 'Will Taylor Plus One'. She felt her heart drop. So far at this party she appeared to have no identity. She was a mum and a plus one. Did she belong anywhere other than to be the supporter of other people?

She sat down and turned to the person sitting to her right, determined to get to know them and make sure they got to know her. She'd been invited, after all, and had just as much right to enjoy the party as anyone else here.

'Hello,' she said to the older woman sitting next to her. 'I'm Stacey. I'm here with Will.'

'Hello,' beamed the woman back. 'Very nice to meet you. I'm Carol, as in Christmas carol, so you got lucky tonight. I also sing in a choir so I could be this table's very own carol juke box – name me a tune.'

Stacey opened her eyes wide. Carol was full on. She glanced over to Will, who was already deep in conversation with a woman next to him.

'Come on,' said Carol. 'Tell me your fave. I bet you are a "Silent Night" type of person, hey? Like a bit of misty eyes during the festive season, or maybe "Away in a Manger"? You got kids at all? Always a favourite with mums, "Away in a Manger".'

'"Little Donkey", actually,' said Stacey, feeling almost afraid of this force of nature.

'Now there's an ugly carol.'

'My daughter loves donkeys,' replied Stacey, 'so I hear it on repeat from about September.'

'You poor thing.'

'It's the worst one, isn't it,' said Stacey, 'carol-wise?'

'It's right up there with "In the Bleak Midwinter", I have to say. Any song with "bleak" and "moan" in the first two lines is not helping bring joy to the season. So you've come with Will, have you?' she asked, nodding at Will.

'Yes,' said Stacey.

'Why?' asked Carol bluntly.

'Erm, because he asked me,' said Stacey.

'You a single mum?' Carol asked.

Stacey nodded, no idea where this conversation was going.

'Well,' said Carol, picking up the bottle of red in front of them and pouring them each a glass. 'You and me both, lady,' she grinned. 'So settle in, I'll get you through this shitshow. You have no reason to feel afraid or alone.'

'It's OK, I'm with Will. You really don't need to look after me.'

'Oh, I do,' said Carol, taking a large gulp of wine. She leaned back in her chair and observed Stacey for a moment. 'Believe me, I do,' she continued. 'I've worked with Will for a few years now, throughout his break-up and divorce. He brings a single mum every year to this party and they all look the same as you. Beautiful and grateful. Just be wary of whatever fairy tale you may have in your mind for tonight.' She put her hand over Stacey's and whispered in her ear, 'But don't worry, I'm here to look after you. And if at any point you feel the need to make a quick exit, you just say the word, and I'll get you out of this fortress. Now excuse me for a minute whilst I chat to the poor woman on my other side to see what her story is.'

Stacey sat bewildered. Who was this mad lady? The ghost of her Christmas present or something? She almost pinched herself to check that she was real. She turned back towards Will to ask him what his take on Carol was. He was still talking to the lady next to him so she put her hand lightly in his knee for reassurance. He put his hand down and squeezed it and turned to Stacey.

'Rachel, this is Stacey,' Will said to her. 'She's a mum from Isaac's school.'

'Hi,' said Stacey. For the first time in a very long time Stacey actually wanted to say she worked for the council, that she had a career as well as being a mum, but perhaps no one was going to ask her what she did for a living here. Perhaps her long-length dress just shouted 'mum' and therefore rendered her invisible in this crowd, and certainly unlikely to have anything interesting to say outside of what food allergies her child had or what reading band they were on. Mums can only talk about kids, right? They have nothing else interesting to say at all.

'Do you work with Will?' asked Stacey when Will gave no descriptor for Rachel. Was she a colleague? A plus one? Or also a mother of someone and therefore needed no further explanation.

'I do,' said Rachel, 'but I'm up in the Manchester office. I thought I'd see how these southerners party for a change,' she said, grinning at Will.

'We showed you lot how to party in Copenhagen that time,' said Will. 'Beth went off particularly early, I recall. Such a wuss.'

'She has young kids,' replied Rachel. 'She wanted a full night's sleep more than anything in the world. The rest of us made up for her, though. I seem to remember us totally shouting you lot down in karaoke.'

'No way,' grinned Will. 'Your rendition of "Islands in the Stream" emptied the bar.'

'You and Henry singing "Don't Stop Me Now" dragged in the cats from the entire neighbourhood.'

'We were awesome.'

'You were properly bad – like, Coldplay bad.'

Stacey watched without really listening as they went back and forth, firing insults that totally went over her head. She watched as their body language defied what they were discussing. Massive grins on their faces, hands gesturing wildly, shoulders arching towards each other. A lively animated conversation they were both thoroughly enjoying. Stacey shrank back. Will didn't defer back to her again but carried on his conversation with Rachel. They were roaring with laughter over some shared joke now. Something to do with a chipolata at a buffet breakfast in Frankfurt. She sank back in her chair and gazed around the room. The noise levels were high, spirits were even higher. She sighed and closed her eyes for a second, trying to summon up her spirits from earlier.

She was at a wonderful party in a wonderful place – she *must* enjoy herself.

She felt something move at her shoulder and as she opened her eyes a plate appeared in front of her. It looked beautiful but it was small. A single scallop in a shell with something foamy on it. She hadn't dared eat since lunchtime for fear of what figure-hugging dress Diane was going to bring for her. She was absolutely starving and the scallop in front of her was probably going to be gone in two mouthfuls, if that. She looked around and waited patiently whilst everyone else received their single scallop, and then waited for the first person to pick up their cutlery before she dared pick up her own. She could see a basket of bread rolls in the middle of the table but dared not be the first to reach for them because obviously if she did then she would be labelled Will's greedy pig girlfriend, wouldn't she!

Thankfully Carol stood up and grabbed the basket, placing it firmly between her and Stacey.

'There is no way I'm going to survive on one scallop. Here, have some bread.' She picked a roll out for herself and then offered Stacey one. Stacey had never been so pleased in her life to grab hold of a bread roll. She could almost cry and she was very tempted to hug the marvellous creature she was sitting next to, and she wasn't referring to Will.

She divided her scallop into four pieces and tried to make it last as long as possible, dreading the moment when she looked down at her plate – empty – knowing that she would look up and she would be the first one to finish and would be mortified. She did eventually look up to find that Carol had long finished and was on her second roll. Will, however, hadn't started his yet as he was still talking to Rachel. She was very tempted to swap his plate for hers and tell him he'd eaten it without noticing because, to be fair, she had pretty much eaten hers without noticing too. He did eventually take a breath and glance down at his dish and then at her.

'Was it good?' he asked.

'Delicious,' she said.

He tucked in. His demeanour had totally changed from when they arrived. He was buzzing and smiling. Like the night had suddenly turned around for him. One of those nights when you bump into someone you don't expect to and it transforms your evening into one full of potential, hope and optimism. An evening that suddenly held new romance in the air. She remembered those special evenings from her late teens. You might trawl from bar to bar to bar, looking for the slightest hint of new romance, and when you found it, well, your night took a totally different turn. You lit up like a Christmas tree when romance came knocking. Just as Will had lit up from the moment he'd sat down next to Rachel.

Of course, the effect on Stacey was the opposite. Her lights went down to the bottom rung of the dimmer switch. Her night was now so gloomy she could no longer see straight. She tried to turn herself up again. Told herself she should still enjoy the evening, despite the glow coming from Will being aimed at Rachel and not at her, but she wasn't sure she could do it. She just could not turn her lights up. She closed her eyes again, trying to summon up the Christmas spirits, find a way through what was turning into a Christmas nightmare.

She felt something at her shoulder again. It was Carol's hand. She turned and looked at her.

'Not tonight,' she said, 'but sometime, you'll realise that that is a Christmas blessing.'

'What is?' asked Stacey.

'That,' said Carol, waving at Will fawning over Rachel, his scallop hardly touched. 'You will realise that actually she's your Angel Gabrielle, who has arrived to rescue you from, well, from Will, actually.'

Stacey stared at Carol.

'Who are you?' she asked.

'I'm your brand-new truth friend,' she said. 'Do you like that? I came up with it the other day, talking another friend down from the slippery pole of romantic hope. I'm not only a true friend, I'm a truth friend. Do you get it?'

'I get it,' said Stacey.

'I think we could all do with a truth friend. There aren't enough of us to go round,' added Carol.

'Did your other friend listen to you?' asked Stacey.

Carol thought hard about this question. 'I suspect not,' she said. 'I suspect he heard me and it was helpful, but he still did what he was going to do anyway, which was to still go hanging round, hoping for this guy to show up.'

'Hope does that to you,' said Stacey with a sigh.

'Hope and loneliness. You can't trust hope but you can rely on loneliness.'

'Not sure that makes any sense,' replied Stacey.

'Neither am I, but it sounds kinda good.'

'So what do I do now?' asked Stacey.

'You be my plus one and eat the free food, drink the free drink, dance like no one's watching and then go home and start all over again.' Carol picked up her glass and held it up to Stacey's and they clinked a cheers as she attempted to brighten her lights just a little as she felt her very happy Christmas slip through her fingers.

Chapter 25

At the end of the meal, which Stacey spent most of listening to Carol's random stories of her life, Will suddenly touched her hand. Stacey turned to him to see that Rachel had disappeared, her seat empty.

'Sorry, Stacey, I didn't mean to ignore you, it's just that I haven't seen Rachel since the summer conference.'

'It's fine,' she said, desperately trying to remember Carol's wise words. That Rachel was actually her Angel Gabrielle flown in to save her from a doomed relationship. Will looked at her and squeezed her shoulders. 'You really are a wonderful person,' he said, in exactly the same tone as one might say 'It's not you, it's me,' when you are trying to gently dump someone.

'Thanks,' sighed Stacey.

She looked at Will just as the DJ put 'Last Christmas' on as a prompt to get the dance floor filled. She'd had such high hopes for this relationship. Will coming along felt like she finally had a life again and now it was all slipping through her fingers. She bit her lip to try to stop a tear from falling down her cheek.

'I'm actually really tired,' she said. 'Can we have just one dance and then I might call it a night? I'm sorry. You stay, please, but I'll head home, if you don't mind.'

She was very aware that she had just handed Rachel to him on a plate, given him a Get Out of Jail Free card, added certainty to his night of hope. He lit up even further right before her eyes.

'Of course,' he said, getting up and taking her hand, way faster than was polite. 'If you feel tired you get yourself home. I'd better stay, though. Would look bad if I left so early.'

'It would,' agreed Stacey. 'Come on – I've got a dance in me. At least let's do that before I leave you to it.'

George Michael and Andrew Ridgeley had brought people flooding onto the dance floor just as the DJ had intended, and Stacey could feel one of her Christmas wishes coming true. To be at a Christmas party in a magical place dancing to 'Last Christmas' with a handsome man. Pity the handsome man wasn't hers. Will grabbed her hands and raised them above her head, grinning away. He looked elated that his Christmas dream had suddenly come true. She'd never seen him so smiley. Oddly, she didn't mind. Why was that? Was it because she'd spotted that Will had never spoken to her the way she had watched him speak to Rachel? He had never lit up like that in her company. Never. And she realised that was what she wanted. What she deserved. Just like Diane had said: whoever it was, he should be worth it. The real dream was to have a man light up like a Christmas tree for you. And clearly Will wasn't that man.

She saw Carol at the edge of the dance floor, dancing with a nervous-looking young woman. She wondered if this is what Carol did. Saw it as her job in life to stop women falling for the wrong guys. Or even guys falling for the wrong guys, if her story about her friend was anything to go by. Whoever Carol was, Stacey was glad she had met her. It almost felt as if she had had two fairy godmothers looking after her this evening.

She forced a grin as 'Last Christmas' came to an end. Time to exit stage left. It had been swell for a moment. The anticipation had been exciting, and just being in this place, at Christmastime . . . well, that was amazing, but she found she was oddly looking forward to going home. And being with Grace, knowing that Grace would be full of happiness at her night with Yang. And that she would have had a lovely time. And actually Stacey was looking forward to seeing Yang. Knowing he would be pleased to see her, even though Will couldn't wait to see the back of her.

'Well, I guess that's it,' she said, taking a step back. 'I just need to get my bag from the table.'

'I'll see you out,' said Will, taking her hand and leading her quickly off the dance floor.

Rachel was in her seat when they got back to the table.

'Stacey's leaving,' Will told Rachel. 'But I'm staying.'

'Oh, I'm sorry to hear that,' Rachel replied, looking at Stacey.

'I'm shattered,' she explained. 'Not used to late nights, you know. I have a young daughter back at home so it means Yang, our babysitter, can go home early, too, so you know, it's all good. It's all great. I'll leave you to it.' She glanced up at Will, aware she was waffling and overexplaining.

'Yang is the guy I was telling you about,' Will said to Rachel. 'The one who thumped me at the Nativity play. Total maniac. Just because I laughed at a kid singing his stupid song.'

'A kid?' questioned Stacey. 'Not just a kid. You mean my daughter.'

'Yeah, yeah,' said Will, still laughing. 'You should have seen him,' he told Rachel. 'It was hilarious. I mean, half the audience was laughing at Stacey's daughter. And then this chubby little guy punches me right in the middle of it. And we get hauled into the headmistress's office. I mean, you couldn't have written it. So funny.'

As Stacey watched Will recollecting the Nativity play, laughing yet again. She could quite understand why Yang had hit him. She'd actually like to hit him herself right now.

She knew it was pathetic but she couldn't help herself. She picked up a glass of wine and threw it in Will's face.

'What the . . .!' he exclaimed, spluttering.

'That's for Grace, Yang and me,' she said. 'That's for laughing at Grace at the Nativity play, that's for laughing at Yang now and that's for taking me for someone that you could just string along and pick up and use as and when I was useful for you.' She turned to walk away.

'Hey, I never . . .' continued Will.

Stacey turned back. 'Let me just say this,' she said, catching Carol watching out of the corner of her eye. 'Don't ever pick on a lonely woman again. Every single mum out there is worth more than you. So I don't want to see you pulling a fast one with any of the single mums outside the school gate ever again, do you hear? I cannot believe I'm saying this. But stick to the younger ones who have the time to be messed around and don't have the children who shouldn't be messed around with. Ones like her. Have a lovely evening with Rachel. I hope you enjoy each other's shallow company and are able to walk away tomorrow with a clear conscience.'

She took a step back and faced the both of them. Rachel was looking very uncomfortable and Will looked in shock.

'Merry Christmas,' she said. She turned and stalked towards the exit. Carol was waiting with her coat at the edge of the dance floor.

'You go, girl,' she said, slipping her coat over her shoulders. 'You just made my night. Keep walking, don't look back. I can tell you now that they looked crushed. You own the night, princess. Now just keep on walking.'

Stacey didn't look back. She held her head high and kept walking up the stairs, then down the corridor and then out through the heavy door and into a cobbled courtyard. She kept strutting, knowing she was not running away: this was truly a victorious exit. She carried on right along the moat walk until she got to the exit where a Beefeater tipped his hat as she left the castle. She climbed into a hackney carriage and leaned back on the seat as she watched the towers disappear into the night air. She wondered exactly what Will and Rachel were thinking or doing, still captive in the Tower. She found that she didn't really care.

Eventually, the cab pulled up outside her block of flats and she looked to see lights glowing from her sitting room. With any luck Grace would still be up, knowing Yang would have been a soft touch when it came to bedtime. She thought about the good time her and Yang must have had together and found herself looking forward to joining them.

Stacey thought about all the amazing things she had seen that night as she got in the lift. The London Eye lit all the colours of the rainbow, the Thames reflecting all the pretty lights along the Embankment, the Tower of London, resplendent with Christmas decorations. She had celebrated Christmas in the same space as some of her favourite queens from history and yet her most favourite sight of the evening greeted her as she walked through the door of her own home.

The lounge was transformed. A dozen or more Chinese lanterns hung from the ceiling above Grace and Yang, sitting either side of the coffee table, cross-legged on the floor. An array of takeaway boxes sat between them. There was no other lighting apart from the emergency torch that usually sat on the shelf in the kitchen. Christmas tunes were blaring out from somewhere and Grace was crying with laughing as she attempted to pick up a prawn with chopsticks. They were having so much fun they didn't even hear Stacey come in.

'Room for a small one?' she asked, kicking her shoes off and dropping to the floor.

'Muuuum!' screamed Grace. 'What are you doing home?' Grace threw herself at her mum and enveloped her in a massive hug. A hug from her daughter had never felt so good.

'Was it rubbish?' asked Grace. 'Was Will rubbish? Did he not ask you to dance? Did he dance with someone else?'

Stacey stared at her daughter. 'Pretty much all of the above,' she said.

'Excellent,' said Grace, punching the air. 'Just what I asked Santa for.'

'I'm sorry,' said Yang. 'Sorry to hear that.'

'You know what,' Stacey said. 'I'm not, actually. As a wise woman told me tonight, better to be alone than lonely with an arsehole. Or something like that.'

Yang's face broke out into a grin. 'I think you're the wise woman tonight,' he said.

'Finally got there,' she agreed.

'Better late than never,' he said.

'Jesus, Mum, you can't say arsehole,' cried Grace. 'If you can say arsehole then I can say fuck. Know what I mean?'

Stacey laughed. 'I know what you mean. I'll mind my language in the future.'

'You just do that. You can't just come swanning in here after a night out and think you're God's gift, young lady.'

'You are funny,' said Stacey.

Grace grinned. 'Thanks for coming home, Mum,' she said. 'We were missing you, weren't we, Yang?'

'Absolutely,' he agreed. 'Here, have some chopsticks. Grace is in desperate need of further tuition.'

Stacey smiled gratefully at him. She looked up at the beautiful Chinese lanterns gently swaying above them.

'You put these up for Grace?' she asked.

'Grace said she'd never been to a Chinese restaurant so I thought I'd try and bring a Chinese restaurant here. It's just a few lanterns, but you get the jist.'

'It's amazing!' said Grace. 'And I've nearly learned how to use chopsticks. Watch this.'

Stacey watched as Grace violently stabbed a prawn until it was pierced through. She held it aloft triumphantly.

'Really excellent technique,' said Stacey.

'Have you eaten?' asked Yang.

'Barely,' replied Stacey, eyeing up the food spilling out all over the coffee table.

'I'll get you a plate,' said Grace, leaping up. 'We can have a Christmas Chinese party here. The three of us. Much better than the one you were at.'

'Sorry your night didn't go well,' Yang said when Grace left the room.

Stacey looked at Yang thoughtfully. 'It wasn't what I thought it would be but, nonetheless, a successful outcome. Made me realise a few things.'

'Good,' replied Yang. He looked down and skilfully scooped up a prawn before looking back at her. 'You were always way too good for him, you know.'

'I think I realise that now. But thank you for saying that. You didn't have to. And I totally understand now why you hit him.'

'He was just being so mean to Grace. I couldn't let him do that.'

'But to actually hit him?'

'I know. Surprised myself, actually. Not like me at all.'

Stacey recalled Will describing Yang as short and chubby and it made her blood boil. He wasn't short and chubby. He was, well, he was just Yang.

'You deserve someone great. Really you do,' said Yang.

'Well, that's really good of you to say.' She paused. She suddenly felt bad for the way she sometimes treated Yang at work. 'Look, Yang, I realise that I'm not always the nicest to you. I'm sorry if I've taken out my anger on you for all the privilege you have, being male in the workplace. You didn't deserve that.'

'It's OK,' he shrugged, looking down.

She realised at that moment how kind Yang had always been to her and she had not always returned the courtesy.

'Look, you must have better things to do than spend your evening with a seven-year-old girl and her miserable, rejected mother. If you need to get off then obviously we won't keep you.'

'Well, I, er, I promised I'd do fortune cookies with Grace so, you know, it's fine. I'll go after we've done those.'

Stacey nodded.

'Thank you,' she said.

'What for?'

'For being Grace's friend. For being patient with her.'

Yang nodded. 'It's funny how you find the people you like in the strangest of places, isn't it?' he said.

'It sure is,' replied Stacey, looking at him. 'It sure is.'

The three of them did fortune cookies, squealing with laughter at the weird sayings. Yang started to make up some of his own, all containing the word 'donkey', which Grace thought was the best thing ever. Stacey thought they were pretty funny too. Then suddenly it was somehow approaching midnight and Stacey fleetingly thought what could be happening now if she had stayed at the party. She strongly suspected she'd be talking to Carol because Will would have mysteriously disappeared somewhere with Rachel. It felt highly unlikely that she would have been swaying along to a romantic Christmas tune before having a romantic stroll along the riverside.

She announced that they had better clear away, which Yang insisted on doing with Grace, allowing Stacey to go and change out of her dress. She hung it up on the side of her wardrobe, thinking wistfully that even the most stunning of dresses hadn't made her dream come true. She changed into her pyjamas, took off her make-up and brushed out her hair. She looked in the mirror: the princess had gone. Back to single mum, council worker Stacey.

She walked back into the lounge and there she found Yang and Grace on the sofa, both fast asleep.

She smiled, then sat down next to Yang, rested her head on his shoulder and promptly fell asleep too, thinking the after-party had been so much better than the actual party.

Chapter 26

Diane was all alone in her office. It had long since gone dark and the rest of her team had already left to go to the event at the London Eye. It had been such a strange day. She'd expected Stacey to arrive in that morning, brimming over with news of the party at the Tower of London, starry eyed at how wonderful it had been. Except she had barely mentioned it. When Diane had asked how it had gone, she had merely shrugged. Said it had been fine, just fine, and thanked her for all her help with getting ready before handing back the sparkling dress carefully packaged in a suit carrier.

'How was Will?' asked Diane. 'Did he sweep you off your feet?'

'Something like that,' said Stacey, but her body language said anything but. Diane glanced over at Yang to see if he could shed any light on what had happened, but he merely shrugged, put his headphones back on and stared into his screen. She was clearly going to get nothing out of him either.

Jolene, however, had bounced into the office that morning full of beans, dressed in a full-on elf costume, excited about that evening's event at the London Eye. Diane admired her enthusiasm and, to be fair, she appeared to have everything under control. She'd been down to brief the mayor on proceedings the day before and he had even called Diane to tell her what a magnificent job Jolene was doing. Diane wouldn't be surprised if, when it came time for Jolene to move on from the Accounts Department, she was offered a placement in the mayor's office.

Diane had watched silently as Jolene had stood on a chair that morning and briefed everyone on the timetable for the event. She'd run through everything in a very professional manner, despite the fact that she was wearing an elf costume. Even Barney appeared to be hanging on her every word as he proudly modelled the Father Christmas outfit she'd found for him. Yes, Jolene had proved to be a real asset to the team, despite Diane's major misgivings when she had arrived. Her enthusiasm and drive to get things done were traits that the council desperately needed. She would go far if she could maintain that and not get bogged down like most people seemed to in this building. Maybe her positive mental attitude would keep her going in this difficult work environment. Even her Secret Santa Project had had a positive impact. Much as they had all griped and groaned about it, it had made them think about Christmas in a different way; brought them closer together, somehow. After her briefing on the London Eye event, Jolene reminded them of their commitment to the Secret Santa Project and that they were only a day away from the deadline of the Christmas Coffee celebration.

'And don't forget it's nearly Christmas, guys,' Jolene had said, clapping her hands together. 'I'm going to come in early tomorrow and get some atmosphere going ready for Christmas Coffee and the Secret Santa Project,' she announced, grinning from ear to ear. 'Really can't wait. If anyone needs any help getting theirs done I'm happy to be of assistance. Please just ask.'

Not that Diane had nailed hers yet, of course. As soon as she'd done this damn structure that was next on her list, she'd put her mind to it.

Everyone had set off for the London Eye in the late afternoon, with Diane promising to join them as soon as she could. Deadline day for submitting her new structure to HR was fast approaching and she needed to find space to think about it. Should she actually make the call and suggest cancelling next Christmas? She had all the data now to make it look like a valid suggestion, but she wasn't sure if she could be the one to pull the plug on Christmas in the borough. She needed to weigh it up against making a member of her team redundant. The blank organisation chart sat in front of her but all she had managed to do so far was to put her name at the top.

She knew she should not treat it personally, that she should work out the best structure to deliver what her department needed her to. However, these were people's lives she was dealing with. How could she not treat it personally? Making people redundant was always personal.

She got up from behind her desk and took a walk around the open-plan office where her team worked. Barney's desk was fastidiously tidy, with paper files lined up neatly in a row. Barney was the only one in the office who still insisted on paper files, saying that he needed to feel his filing system as well as see it. She'd tried telling him it was a waste of paper and he needed to file on his computer but he ignored her, telling her that he could always put his finger on whatever document he needed and the way he did that should not be questioned. Barney really was stuck in the past and probably the most obvious one to be asked to leave. But there, pride of place, was the picture of his dead wife next to his tidily arranged files. This was a man still grieving. A man who lived alone, a man not ready to be put on the rubbish pile of life. Getting rid of Barney would be condemning him to abject loneliness, and the thought of that during the season of goodwill to all men chilled Diane's very soul.

Stacey's desk was dominated by a large digital display clock. The badge of a single mum constantly trying to pack too many responsibilities into not enough time. Stacey reminded Diane of herself when Chloe was young. The weight of responsibility hanging heavy on her shoulders alongside the shock of living a life purely to the benefit of others, without a moment to herself. Diane wanted to make Stacey's life better, not worse. That's why she was so flexible with her hours. She had total empathy for the position young working mothers found themselves in, and really she couldn't bear to put Stacey on the job market, knowing that another empathic boss like her was going to be really hard to find.

Yang's desk held no personal trophies, nothing. A completely bare space apart from his computer. Yang barely brought his personal life to work. Diane felt she knew nothing about him outside of this building. But he was by far the most essential employee in this department. He consistently overachieved in his role without really trying. His knowledge of the complicated systems and processes used by the council was second to none and the team would truly sink without him. He could conjure up a spreadsheet to solve a difficult accounting problem out of nowhere. And his knowledge of computers – well, it was like having their own IT specialist in their department. And given the utter direness of the IT support function, Diane didn't know how they would manage without him.

Jerry's was another tidy desk, but with the odd personal touch. A plant and a very elegant pen holder. Jerry was their conscience. Despite the fact he wasn't a national, Jerry really cared about where taxpayers' money was spent. His morals were second to none and he was a constant reminder that it was public money they were dealing with and so it should be cared for diligently and carefully. True, Jerry could probably get a job at any big finance company, but she suspected he liked working for the council because he felt what he did mattered. He felt that he was helping the nation that hosted him by taking care of its money. And he was very respected in the council. Diane feared that if she got rid of Jerry it would be seen as getting rid of the very person who was the main threat to her job.

She sighed and sank down in Barney's chair. The one he'd probably sat in for at least the last twenty years. What on earth was she going to do? Whatever she did, she was going to ruin someone's Christmas. She felt totally and utterly exhausted. A tear escaped her left eye.

'Penny for them?' said Kev from HR, peering round the door.

'Not worth a penny,' sighed Diane, brushing the tear away.

'I thought I'd come and see how you're doing. I saw that you haven't submitted your new structure yet. You're the last one.'

Diane stared at him. 'Perhaps I'm taking it more seriously than the other *male* heads of departments,' she spat. 'Perhaps the men find it easier to ruin someone's Christmas.'

'I don't think that's a fair stereotype, is it?' said Kev. 'I'm sure they've all had sleepless nights over it.'

'I very much doubt it,' said Diane. 'Men don't seem to let life affect their sleep in the same way that women do.'

'I do sometimes wake up in the night,' said Kev. 'I mean, I don't have the night sweats or anything that perhaps you're suffering with.'

'Will you please ban all men in HR going on the Menopause Awareness course? Discussing menopause with you makes me want to hurl.'

'OK, sorry. I was just trying to be empathetic.'

'Please be less empathetic.'

'OK. I'll try. If you think I should.'

'Anyway, what have you got that keeps you awake at night?'

'Erm, well, if I'm not trying to be empathetic, then it's often my fantasy football league team. Especially if it's the day before big games. And I'm top of my league at the moment but you know that can slip through your fingers so quick.'

'Fantasy football keeps you awake at night?'

'If I'm being honest, then yes, yes it does.'

Diane hauled herself out of Barney's chair. She'd had quite enough of this conversation. She walked towards the door and grabbed her coat off the rack.

'So when will you have your new structure?' Kevin asked.

'It will be on your desk tomorrow morning. Now I must go and support my team, who are not getting paid for this, I might add, as we set up an entirely pointless photo op for the mayor.'

'Oh, yes. Is that the London Eye thing?'

'Yes.'

'Can you send me a picture? It'll be good for the internal newsletter.'

Diane paused. 'Shall I include the team member we are about to get rid of or not?'

'I think that's entirely up to you, isn't it?' said Kev.

Jolene was trying hard not to panic as she stood in front of the London Eye at 5.25 p.m. It was rotating gracefully as ever, the black sky lit up with stars behind it. It looked stunning, but as the mayor bore down on them they were missing quite a few of the key players for his photo op, including the really key players: the school children. Despite working very hard to make sure she had everything nailed down, including people actually turning up, Jolene was rapidly realising she had no control over that. Her heart was racing so fast she thought she might actually have a heart attack.

Stacey was on her mobile, frantically trying to get hold of Grace's teacher, but didn't appear to be getting through. Yang was nowhere to be seen. He'd said he had a job to do before he left work an hour ago, but promised he'd be there.

Diane had just arrived, looking splendid in a sparkling silver outfit. Jolene had been relieved to see her arrive just five minutes before and even keener to get her to phone her husband to find out where the bloody hell the elves were! They hadn't arrived either. At least Barney was in County Hall, next door, getting his costume on. He would be waiting for the children when they finished their trip. If they made it. Jolene thought she might be sick. Diane was still on the phone to her husband, chasing the elves, as the mayor approached with Jerry, who had volunteered to escort him here, along with Barbara, the General Manager of the London Eye.

'They're coming,' said Jolene, hopping up and down on one leg as they approached. 'They're definitely coming.'

'Where are the children?' asked the mayor, looking round, bewildered.

'That's who I mean,' said Jolene. 'They are coming. Stacey's just on to their teacher now.'

Barbara glanced up at the giant wheel rotating slowly above them. 'We really need to get you on the two capsules coming in now,' said Barbara, sternly. 'I promised you the last two capsules of the day. That's all. I can't keep the wheel running for you until they arrive. Closing time was briefed this morning. You must catch those last two capsules.'

'They are literally seconds away,' said Stacey, coming off the phone. 'We should see them running down the South Bank any minute. Unforeseen circumstances, the teacher said.'

'What about the elves?' asked Jerry. He looked towards Diane, who was frantically nodding. She put down her phone. 'Just got off at Waterloo. They're going to leg it. Leon says not to worry.'

'Leg it?' said Jerry. 'But they're little people – how fast can they leg it?'

'Leon says they're running as fast as they can, you know, given the circumstances.'

'There they are,' shouted Jolene, feeling a massive sigh of relief run through her. She could see a crowd of children rushing towards them. All dressed in their Nativity play costumes. It was quite a sight to see the entire Nativity scene running at speed along the South Bank, pushing the crowd to one side as they did so. And was that Yang also dashing up at the rear? What was he doing with them? He'd not mentioned he was going to the school. She didn't have time to question, however. They just needed to start loading the children onto the pods.

'This way,' she shouted, jumping up and down. 'This way.'

'Only twenty-five per pod,' said Barbara, dashing forward. 'They can't all get on one pod.'

'Right,' bellowed Jerry, stepping forward. 'Stand in line, everyone. An orderly queue now. That's it. Now Barbara and Diane, you get on and I'll count the children on. That's it, Mary, you push to the front of the queue. Every woman for herself. That's it, keep coming.'

Jolene strained to look towards the train station, hoping against hope to see some elves running round the corner. If she thought it would have helped, she'd have dropped to her knees and prayed. Why had she ever started this crazy plan? 'Please, baby Jesus,' she said, looking up towards the sky, 'bring me some elves.'

'There they are,' cried Stacey. 'Look, the elves are coming.'

'Thank you, Lord,' breathed Jolene. She turned to Jerry. 'You get on this one with the mayor and I'll count the rest on the second one, OK?'

'Will do,' replied Jerry, chivvying on the mayor and boarding the capsule as the door closed behind him, allowing a couple of elves to just scrape in. One capsule loaded. One to go.

'Right, the rest of you, in here,' said Jolene as the next capsule gliding serenely into the station, nothing like the way she was feeling. The last thing Jolene was feeling was serene.

The shepherds and angels filed on, clearly the kids with the less sharp elbows, followed by a menagerie of farm animals.

'I'm Grace,' said a small girl dressed as a donkey, getting on with Stacey.

'Oh, lovely to meet you,' said Jolene. 'Enjoy your flight.'

'I will,' sang Grace, stepping onto the pod.

'Loving the donkey,' the teacher whispered as she passed Stacey. 'Lovely touch.' She was pointing somewhere behind her. Jolene looked to where she indicated and she was pointing to Yang, who appeared to be leading a donkey. A real live donkey!

'Oh my God, that's amazing,' said Jolene. 'Wow. Where did you find a donkey? That's going to look brilliant in the photographs.'

'Knew you'd love it,' said Yang. He grinned. 'You can't have a Nativity photo without a donkey, can you?'

'Absolutely,' said Jolene. 'Of course you can't.'

Jolene didn't think to question whether a donkey would be allowed on the London Eye. It never even crossed her mind, and luckily for her Barbara was already loaded onto the first capsule so could not intervene with her loading policy.

However, a woman in a fluorescent tabard tapped her on the shoulder.

'No animals are allowed,' she told Jolene.

'What do you mean, no animals?'

'Only assistance animals.'

Jolene only needed to blink once before she came up with an answer.

'This is an assistance donkey.'

'Really?' said the lady.

'Of course. A donkey is the original assistance animal. A donkey assisted the pregnant Mary to the inn.

Without the donkey there would have been no safe arrival of the baby Jesus, so you see this is an assistance donkey . . . and I cleared it with Barbara and the mayor nearly a month ago. Look, she's in the next pod, and I can assure you she'll be very upset if you don't allow the assistance donkey on to this special flight to see Santa.'

Jolene turned and enthusiastically waved and gave a thumbs up to Barbara, who was now about twelve feet above them. She prayed she couldn't see the donkey under the awning. Barbara waved back.

'She also cleared the elves, if you're interested, if you really want to be that picky,' said Jolene.

The woman looked at her then shook her head. 'Look, it's my last day,' she shrugged. 'On your head be it.'

'Thank you,' said Jolene. 'Yang, take the donkey on its maiden trip to see Father Christmas.'

'You are a superhero,' he whispered to her as he sneaked past with the donkey.

'I'm so sorry,' said Leon, coming up at the rear with the elves. 'Every drunk person out on a Christmas do wanted a picture. It's taken us so long to get here.'

'You're here now. I'm still ever so grateful,' said Jolene. 'Jump on. Let's all go see Santa Claus, shall we?'

Jolene was the last to jump on as the kids all crowded to the edge of the capsule to take in the spectacular view. They started to rise in the air and Jolene looked around in relief. This should be the easy bit, as long as the donkey behaved. Photo op at the end with Santa and she will have achieved what she promised: an unforgettable ride to see Santa Claus. And an amazing photograph for all to treasure for ever!

Chapter 27

'Looks like the rest of the elves made it,' said Diane, peering down towards the capsule below them. 'I can see the kids jumping on top of them. Jesus, I hope they're all right.' She looked around at the kids enraptured by the view. The teacher had them fully under control and spotting the main sights, such as Buckingham Palace and St Paul's and the Shard. The mayor was busy talking to Barbara, which was good. Hopefully that would keep them both busy. Diane allowed herself to heave a sigh of relief. Everyone was in their place and they would get the photo op that the mayor was so desperate for. She could relax just for now. That had been quite hairy for a moment.

'Is that a donkey?' gasped Jerry, appearing at her shoulder and pointing down into the next capsule. 'It can't be, can it?'

Diane followed his gaze and there, in the next capsule, appeared to be a donkey, a real live donkey.

Diane gasped. 'Oh my God,' she said. 'Who on earth brought a donkey?' She looked nervously over at

Barbara, who thankfully for now was still talking to the mayor.

'Looks like Yang,' said Jerry. 'What the hell is he doing?'

Diane shook her head. 'I don't understand.'

'Is that a donkey?' said Stacey, appearing next to them. 'Tell me that isn't a donkey.'

'It's a donkey,' said Jerry.

'Oh God,' said Stacey, burying her head in her hands. 'It's bound to be Grace. She's obsessed with donkeys. I mean *obsessed*, but how? She does stupid stuff all the time, but a donkey . . .?'

'Looks like Yang is feeding it carrots,' said Jerry. 'I think Yang is responsible for the donkey.'

'What!' said Stacey, looking up startled. 'Yang. What is he thinking? He'll have done it to impress Grace. Honestly, those two. It's like watching some love affair going on. I mean, he decorated the flat with Chinese lanterns, just for her. It looked amazing. But a donkey? That's insane. And for what? Just to impress a seven-year-old girl?'

'Perhaps it wasn't the seven-year-old he was trying to impress,' said Jerry, raising his eyebrows.

'What do you mean?' asked Stacey.

Diane nodded. 'Do you know what, very perceptive, Jerry. I think you might be right.'

'What are you talking about?' asked Stacey.

'Look, we need to focus,' said Diane. 'We have to make sure Barbara doesn't see the donkey. Why don't you go and keep Barbara and the mayor distracted,' she told Stacey. 'We've half a chance of getting the

298

donkey off the capsule without her noticing if you can keep her on that side of the capsule.'

'OK,' said Stacey, breathing heavily. 'I'll do what I can. Yang owes me for this.' Stacey went to sit next to Barbara and the next thing they heard was her complimenting her on her coat.

'Yang likes Stacey, doesn't he?' said Diane.

Jerry nodded. 'The donkey really does make it totally obvious, even if it doesn't to Stacey. What a guy, going to those lengths,' he said, peering at the other capsule again to check on the donkey. He stepped back in astonishment. 'That's weird,' he said, looking over at Diane.

'What? Weirder than seeing a donkey on the London Eye?'

Jerry peered through the glass again. 'What's he doing there?'

'Who?' said Diane, also peering out.

'Coffee-shop man,' said Jerry. 'You know, the guy I told you about. He's there in the capsule. So weird.' He started to gesticulate wildly to grab the man's attention.

'Where is he?' urged Diane, straining to see. 'I can't see any men apart from Yang and my husband, who came with the elves.

'There he is, look. There. I'd know that red scarf anywhere.'

Diane did a double-take. She looked towards the other capsule again, just to check there wasn't another man there wearing a red scarf. But there was only Leon. Her husband.

She felt her heart pound instantly and her breath quicken. All the blood drained from her face. She felt faint. She looked again for another red scarf but couldn't see one, and in any case, it all made perfect sense as she looked back at Jerry. Well, kind of. The world spun around her whilst she spun around the world on the capsule in the greatest capital city in the world. Jerry stared back at her and she felt the world stop as they gazed at each other. She tried to process desperately as they looked into each other's eyes. Jerry? Jerry was the mystery woman.

'The man in the red scarf is your husband?' said Jerry.

Diane nodded. 'The man in the red scarf is coffee-shop man?'

Jerry nodded.

Diane knew the capsule must be noisy – they were with over a dozen kids, for goodness' sake. But she couldn't hear anything. The world had gone silent. Her body had gone numb. She turned back to look out at the other capsule. Leon was staring straight back at them. He was gently shaking his head as though he couldn't believe what he was seeing.

'How?' Jerry had mentioned the gentle courtship in the coffee shop. She had thought it had sounded so romantic, so very understated. So mature. She'd almost been jealous. The person she had pictured, however, wasn't her husband. It was someone younger, better looking, in fact; someone who had his life sorted. Certainly not her husband who appeared to be in a complete emotional turmoil.

And yet she wasn't surprised. Not really. Not surprised that it was a man who had captured Leon's heart. It was a cliché, but he did work in the theatre and had been surrounded by gay men all his life. He'd always been in touch with his feminine side in an understated and subtle way. But if he was gay then why had he married her? Why had he gathered her into his life? That was what she needed to know. Somehow she could totally fathom the why of Jerry and Leon, but she could not fathom the why of Diane and Leon. That she would need help with.

'I'm so sorry,' said Jerry, trembling. 'I . . . I . . . had no idea. I . . . I only found out he was married last week. If I'd have known, I would have walked away sooner, so very much sooner. I never in a million years would have put you in this position. I . . . I don't know what to say.' She watched as he looked down towards Leon. Leon was pacing up and down. Diane looked back at Jerry.

She was waiting for the feeling of relief that she was set free. The feeling of relief that she had been disappointed not to get when Leon announced that he had been tempted by an affair and was not planning to take it up.

But the relief wasn't coming. The shock of it being Jerry was too much to process right now.

'You'll have my notice on your desk in the morning,' Jerry said Diane. 'At the very least, I can take that problem away from you.' He turned and walked to the opposite side of the capsule and joined in the game of trying to spot where Santa lived. Diane turned back to look at Leon. He was gazing up at her.

'Sorry,' he mouthed.

*   *   *

The capsule host announced that their flight was nearly over and maybe they had arrived at the North Pole and Father Christmas would be waiting. All the children jumped up and down in excitement. They had walked onto the capsule in central London and miraculously arrived thousands of miles away, where Santa lived. Diane considered that she had travelled the greatest distance of all. From wife to . . . well, had she ever really been a wife at all? What had they been doing all these years, the pair of them? Had they ever been a proper husband and wife? Had they merely been a convenient pairing? What had she ever meant to Leon?

'Hope you all enjoyed your trip,' shouted Jolene as everyone filed off. 'Time for a special photo with Santa Claus.'

Diane spotted that there were a couple of photographers waiting and Jolene was desperately trying to herd everyone into one spot so she could deliver on the all-important photo op for the mayor.

'This way, everyone,' said Diane to the party from her capsule. She figured the sooner they got the photo over with, the sooner she could tackle the great big fat elephant that had suddenly descended into her life.

But the donkey was having none of it.

'Can we have the donkey in the middle of the photo with the mayor and Santa?' asked one of the photographers as Yang struggled to guide the donkey away.

Diane looked over to see that Barbara seemed to have muscled her way into the photo opportunity, standing right next to the mayor. She was beaming from ear to ear. The mayor seemed to have completely charmed her, or perhaps she had charmed the mayor, making sure he was on side for any future developments the visitor attraction might want to make. She didn't seem to be fazed by the presence of a donkey; she must have assumed that it had arrived purely for the photo shoot. Thank goodness.

'We need to get this photo done quickly,' Diane said to Jolene. 'We should get these children out of the cold.'

Jolene did a brilliant job of getting an almost complete Nativity scene to surround the mayor, alongside Father Christmas, his elves, the General Manager of the London Eye and a donkey. Two of the shepherds and a sheep gave a flat refusal, but hopefully no one would notice their absence. The mayor beamed in a weird fashion and, the minute the picture was taken, grabbed the photographer and proceeded to give him chapter and verse about all his achievements as mayor that year.

Diane watched as Jerry studiously ignored Leon by keeping himself busy helping Jolene with the children before herding them into the main building.

The time had come. Leon had stood to one side, his hands firmly in his pockets whilst Diane supported her team, but now it was the time to confront the matter.

She stood still. There was no way she was walking towards him. He needed to come to her. He walked towards her and they stood facing each other as the festive cheer swirled around them.

'I'd like to say that I can explain, but I'm not sure I can,' said Leon. 'I'm sorry. I'm so sorry that this is happening and if I could have done anything to stop it I would, but I met Jerry and somehow my life fell into place.'

Diane stared back at him.

'Did that not happen the day we got married?'

'Oh God, it did,' said Leon. 'Of course it did. Well, at the time it did. Me and you . . . well we felt inevitable.'

'Inevitable? Bad things are inevitable.'

'I didn't mean that. I just meant that us two getting married – it made so much sense.'

'Like choosing a solid career path?'

'No, just, well, we were in the same industry, we understood each other, we got on, we fit.'

'What about we loved each other?'

'I did love you, I do love you, really love you,' said Leon, 'but . . . but . . .'

'Somewhere along the way you fell out of love with me?' said Diane.

'I guess,' replied Leon, looking away ashamed, 'or started to love you differently.'

Somehow it wasn't the devastating blow that she expected it to be. Somehow she wasn't surprised. She figured it was because she knew that she had also somehow fallen out of love with Leon.

'Have you always been gay?' she asked.

Leon bit his lip. 'The honest answer is, I'm not sure. I guess I grew up having feelings for men but I also had feelings for women and so I guess I suppressed the liking men part because, well, it just made life easier. Times were different when we were in our twenties, weren't they? I suspect if I had been born in

304

this generation then I would be classed as pansexual – attracted to the person and not the gender – but that sounds like such a weird thing for a fifty-five-year-old man to be saying. It's what the kids say, if they bother to define themselves at all. Doesn't seem to matter any more, does it, but we just didn't have the language back in the day.'

'So you did fancy me?' asked Diane. She had no idea why this was important, but somehow it was.

'Of course I did,' said Leon. 'You were Diane fucking Shenton, the whole world fancied you. Even the gay men.'

Diane had to smile. It was a relief to hear. She remembered that when she was all dressed up in her theatre garb Leon would often refer to her as a gay icon. Perhaps that's what had appealed to him when he married her. Anyway, she couldn't bear the thought of being married to someone who hadn't fancied her for all these years.

'But now you fancy Jerry more?' said Diane. It was a question she never in a million years thought she would be asking.

'As totally unbelievable as that sounds – and I cannot believe I am saying this, and the twenty-year-old Leon would think I'm insane – but yes, yes, I do.'

'And I cannot believe I've been competing with my colleague all this time. He told me about you,' she told him. 'I know about your coffee-shop courtship. How I didn't guess, I have no idea. For Christ's sake, he even told me that *Wicked* was your favourite musical. How that didn't give it away I have no idea.'

'I'm sorry,' he said again.

'He told me how you made him feel. How when you talked to him he felt like the most important person in the universe. He told me that no one had ever made him feel like that.'

The conversation she'd had with Jerry about her husband came flooding back as she stood in front of Leon, their marriage disintegrating around them.

'He told me that you never touched,' she whispered. 'You never touched and yet he felt really close to you. Is that how you feel about him?'

'I do,' said Leon, after a moment's pause. 'I thought I was going to tell you, when I came home the night Chloe was back.'

'After you'd been to his carol concert.'

'Of course, yes, you would know all about that. I was going to tell you, but you were so upset about Chloe leaving us for Christmas I couldn't leave you too. I was so confused. I decided I would wait until after Christmas. Spend Christmas with you so you weren't alone, and then tell you.'

Christmas, thought Diane. She'd forgotten about Christmas. The relief had been starting to appear at the edges of this catastrophe. She'd just begun to feel the signs of some sense of freedom, and then the prospect of Christmas was presented to her in all its gloom. The last-minute jobs reared their heads. She had to decide who to put out of a job, she had to sort out a bloody Secret Santa, she had to wave goodbye to her daughter, and on top of all that, deal with the dissolution of her marriage. If her head wasn't swirling before then it really was in turmoil now. The Christmas period just got a whole lot harder. She felt close to tears and it wasn't because of this evening's revelations – although those no doubt contributed – it was because of bloody Christmas.

'I also had another reason for waiting to tell you,' said Leon. 'See, I realised, when you sang on stage the other day, and when we talked the other night, just how much you've sacrificed for my career.'

Diane bit her lip hard. Now there was something to mourn. Her lost career. She looked away.

'I wanted to try and do something to make up for that,' he said.

'How can you? My time is up. To be honest, it was up before I had Chloe. No one wants mothers in the theatre. Bringing up children and the theatre just don't match.'

'But you're not bringing up Chloe now,' said Leon.

Diane laughed. 'The second least wanted type of person in musical theatre is a middle-aged menopausal woman.'

Leon looked at his watch.

'Am I keeping you,' asked Diane bitterly.

'I'm sorry, but I'm supposed to be meeting someone.'

'Someone else?' fumed Diane. 'Sorry if your wronged wife is holding you up.'

'Will you come with me?' asked Leon.

'What do you mean, come with you?'

'I didn't want to tell you before I had it in the bag. This was not how I planned it but I'm meeting someone about your Christmas present; well, about your future, really.'

'What do you mean, my future?'

Leon looked pained. 'I don't want to promise anything, but if you come with me it might help. But we have to go now. Look, I'll explain on the way, but it might just make your Christmas.'

'What? Drag it out of this shit show of a Christmas where none of my immediate family want to spend it with me.'

Leon nodded. 'It just might.'

Chapter 28

'I'm so sorry,' said Stacey, going up to Grace's teacher.

'What about?' asked the teacher.

'Well, the donkey,' said Stacey. She somehow felt responsible even though it was nothing to do with her. But she had introduced Yang to school life, and so far he had punched another parent and conjured up a live donkey on a school outing. She had no idea what had got into him since he'd met Grace. It was coming to something when your seven-year-old daughter was responsible for leading your adult colleague astray. She needed to have a word with Grace.

'What are you doing, asking Yang to bring a donkey?' said Stacey when she eventually found her daughter.

'I didn't ask him to bring Diago,' said Grace. 'He brought him all by himself. Isn't that amazing?'

'What?' said Stacey. 'You are kidding me, aren't you? You're behind this.'

'No, Mum. I wish. I mean, what a genius idea, to bring a donkey. Wish I'd have thought of it.'

'Genius idea?' questioned Stacey. She'd see about that.

*   *   *

'What the hell do you think you're doing?' shouted Stacey at Yang.

'Just feeding Diago,' said Yang, looking startled. 'He likes carrots around this time, apparently.'

'I don't mean what are you doing now! I mean, what are you doing bringing a donkey? What were you thinking?'

'I was, er . . .'

'Donkey's kick, they poo, they really are not suited to visitor attractions, and you could have ruined Jolene's whole event. What if they'd cancelled it all because you were stupid enough to bring a donkey? It's so irresponsible! Were you just trying to impress Grace? You could have made donkey noises and she would have been impressed. You didn't have to do any of this to get her attention?'

'I wasn't trying to impress her,' said Yang.

'Then what were you doing?'

He looked away. Then back into her eyes. 'I was trying to impress you.'

'What?'

'Stupid idea, I admit. Using Diago. Sorry, mate,' he said, ruffling the donkey's ears. 'I didn't mean for you to get involved in all this.'

'Involved in what?' asked Stacey.

'Me, trying to get your attention.'

'We work together, Yang. You get my attention every single day.'

'Not that type of attention,' he said. 'I mean the other kind of attention. The kind of attention you gave twatty Will.'

310

'Don't call him twatty. I mean, I have to agree, but all the same, don't call him twatty.'

'It's mine and Grace's name for him.'

'What are you trying to say, Yang?'

Yang let out a massive sigh and looked at the ground.

'I thought bringing you a donkey might impress you because I'm just not impressive. I can't impress you with my looks or my charm, or cool clothes or anything like that. I'm just short and I've eaten too much Chinese food and I have a bit of a nerdy personality, and so I thought maybe if I brought a donkey then you might see me; you might be just be a bit impressed finally with something to do with me.'

Stacey swallowed. She thought she knew what Yang was trying to say but she could barely believe it, and she didn't know how she felt about it, not quite. Very nearly, but not quite.

'I don't understand,' she said. 'Make me understand.'

Yang looked at her like a rabbit in the headlights. 'I don't know what else I can say,' he said.

'Please try,' pleaded Stacey.

Yang looked down, shuffling his feet. The donkey nudged his arm, then licked his face. Yang gently pushed the donkey's head away.

'What I'm trying to say is,' said Yang, 'and forgive me for stealing a line from the most romantic movie of all time . . .'

'*Mission Impossible?*' asked Stacey.

'No! Really? Not even close, but let's not go there.' He took a deep breath and looked her in the eye. 'What I'm trying to say is that, I'm just a boy, standing in front of a girl, with a donkey, asking her to love him.'

This was a shock. This was big. Bigger than she'd thought.

'Well, actually . . . *like* would be a start,' stumbled Yang, blushing a shade of puce. 'Liking me would be great, would be wonderful, would be amazing, would be a start. Sorry, I didn't mean to scare you. You look really scared.'

Stacey stared at him, open mouthed. She was totally speechless. She had no idea what to say. She had no idea that Yang's feelings ran that deep. It wasn't too long ago that she was regularly blaming him for all the failings of men in general. How can this have happened? How?

Yang was looking at her, face fallen. She watched as Diago nudged Yang's arm again and Yang put his arm around his neck.

'Time we went, old chap, I think,' said Yang. 'Time we both went back to where we belong.'

'Yang,' said Stacey as he turned away. 'It's . . . it's a lot.'

'I know,' he said. 'It's too much.' He gently turned Diago round and led him away along the riverside to wherever he had come from.

Chapter 29

Diane paused by the coffee machine. It was the last day in work before Christmas and Kev appeared to be having some trouble. His brow was furrowed and he was staring deep into the machine abyss. Suddenly he pulled his leg back and kicked it before leaning his forehead against the glass.

'Everything all right, Kev?' she asked.

'Oh God, you didn't see me do that, did you?' he gasped. 'I didn't do that. I gave a disciplinary to someone for kicking a recycling bin last week so it's hardly setting the right example, is it, if I'm caught kicking the coffee machine?'

'It's all right, Kev,' she said, laying a hand on his shoulder. 'I won't tell anyone.'

'Oh, thank you, Diane, thank you.'

'Are you OK, though?'

'I'm fine, I'm absolutely fine,' he said. He coughed and put his tie straight. He looked up and spotted she was wearing a Santa hat. A look of confusion spread over his face before he gathered himself. 'I was on my way to see if you had arrived, actually. I know it's so hard, but I really do need your restructure this morning. If you want to sit down and talk it through . . .'

'It's done,' said Diane with a grin.

'Really?'

'Yep. I was on my way to give it to you. Here it is.' She held up a single sheet and handed it to him. He looked at her in shock, then took it from her and spent a few moments scrutinising it. He screwed up his face, then looked back at Diane.

'This is it? Your new department organisation chart.'

'Yes,' she nodded.

He looked at it again in utter confusion, then back to her.

'I know that the menopause can lead to brain fog and lapses in cognitive ability. Are you sure that you want to submit this chart in your current mental state?'

'I am not in a mental state, Kev. And you really need to stop blaming the menopause for all my actions. Yes, it is having an impact on my life but I am more than capable of telling you if I think it is affecting my work life. Now, as far as this chart goes, I have never thought more clearly in my life, so you can go and add that to your restructure presentation and report that the Accounts team are very happy to have indeed reduced their head-count by one person. Now I must go and share the news with the rest of the team. We're having our annual Christmas Coffee this morning as well as exchanging our Secret Santa gifts, and I'm sure they will all be keen to know what the outcome of the restructure is before we break up for Christmas, don't you?'

Kev was staring at her, open mouthed.

'Are you sure you are feeling OK?' he asked her.

'Do you know what?' she said. 'The honest answer is that I do feel a little strange. A hell of a lot has happened within the last twenty-four hours but . . . but . . . for the first time in a very long time I woke up and was looking forward to coming to work. Now isn't that a thing?'

Kev looked at the chart again and frowned.

'I'll be here if you need me,' he said.

'Thanks, Kev, but I think I can handle it.'

Jerry and Jolene had been in the office since 8 a.m., preparing for Christmas Coffee. They had been liaising over the last few days and agreed to help each other out with their Secret Santas, which had been extremely productive. Part of the agreement was that they would both come in and add a few more decorations to get everyone in the mood.

'Bloody hell,' said Jolene, taking a step back when they had finished. 'This looks amazing.'

'Too much?' asked Jerry, looking round at the tinsel garlands hanging from the ceiling and the fairy lights zigzagging across the room. It wasn't his usual taste, but he figured over the top was the only way to go. And that was what Jolene wanted. 'Hang on a minute,' he said, diving for a socket switch. 'You need to see the full effect.' A light hit a glitter ball rotating silently in the middle of the room. He flicked the main light off and the effect was complete. The office was transformed into a magical sparkly, star-lit otherworld. It was pretty dazzling.

'Wonderful,' said Jolene. She noticed that Jerry looked a bit teary, a bit red eyed. She hoped he wasn't coming down with anything. He switched the main lights back on and stopped the spotlights.

'Are we all set?' she asked him. 'Is everything in position?'

'I believe so,' nodded Jerry. 'We're good to go.'

Barney wandered in and didn't acknowledge the transformed room in the slightest. He sat down in his chair holding a very large red bow. He smiled at Jolene. Actually smiled.

'You all set?' asked Jolene.

'As ready as I'll ever be,' he said. 'Is one of those for me?' he asked, nodding at the Christmas coffees that Jerry had popped out for earlier.

'Shall we wait until everyone's here?' said Jolene. 'We need to start properly.'

'OK,' sighed Barney. 'Just love cold coffee.'

Yang slid sheepishly in, looking exhausted, as if he hadn't slept all night. That was not good, thought Jolene. He needed to be wearing a smile.

'Well, at least there's no pressure on you today,' Jolene said to Yang. 'Not like the rest of us. You already nailed your Secret Santa, looking after Grace for Stacey.'

Yang sat on the edge of his desk and dangled his feet, looking at the floor. 'S'pose,' he shrugged.

Sweet baby Jesus, thought Jolene. This did not bode well at all.

Stacey arrived finally, in a rush as usual. She dumped her bag on her desk and pulled her coat off. 'Sorry,' she said to Jolene. 'I just could not bring myself to wear a Christmas jumper. I've just got too much on my mind.' She stood in the middle of the room, her eyes darting everywhere. She looked more harassed than Jolene had ever seen her. 'I mean there is so much going on and . . . and . . . well, one of us could be out of a job by the end of today.'

Jolene swallowed. She'd kind of forgotten about that. That might put a severe dampener of things. Maybe that was why Jerry and Yang looked so miserable too.

'You have no need to worry,' announced Jerry. 'It's going to be me going. Guaranteed. So none of you need worry. Let that be my extra little Secret Santa present to you all.'

'No, Jerry,' exclaimed Stacey. 'What are you talking about? It's not going to be you. Diane totally relies on you.'

Jerry looked up at them all. 'It's complicated. I can't explain, but I can absolutely one-hundred-per-cent guarantee that Diana will be getting rid of me.'

'Never, ever predict a lady,' said Diane, walking in behind Jerry.

'Diane, can I have a word, please?' said Jerry, going very pale. 'Just before—'

'Absolutely not,' said Diane, brushing him off. 'I believe it's Secret Santa Project time, is it not, Jolene?

I've put my best Christmas earrings in so we'd better make a start, hadn't we?'

'Er, yes,' said Jolene. 'Yeah, let's do it. Do you want to hand out the Eggnog Lattes, Jerry?'

'Yeah, I guess,' he said, looking at Diane warily. He quickly handed out the paper cups and then stood nervously beside Stacey.

'This is delicious,' said Yang. 'Cold eggy milk with a back note of cinnamon. Yummy.'

'Cheers, team,' said Diane, raising her cup. 'Merry Christmas to you all.'

'Not going to be a very merry Christmas for one of us, is it?' said Stacey miserably.

'Shall I start?' said Diane cheerily.

'You've given it away if you announce you're going to start,' said Jolene. 'It's *Secret* Santa!'

'I think the secrecy in our Secret Santa disappeared a long time ago, don't you? Right when Yang offered to babysit for Stacey.'

Yang and Stacey were standing on opposite sides of the room both staring at the floor. Stacey had what looked like an anxiety rash spreading up her neck to her face. She was clearly extremely stressed.

'Well, anyway,' continued Diane. 'I don't mind announcing who I got. So I picked out . . . drumroll, please?'

Jolene was the only one to manage a drumroll.

'I got . . . Jerry!'

'Oh my God,' muttered Jerry. 'I am so dead.'

What was wrong with him, thought Jolene. He was acting very strangely.

'Jerry,' said Diane. 'I have to admit I didn't give much thought to what my Secret Santa was going to be until last night.'

'Diane, I . . . I'm so sorry . . .'

'Hush. Don't fret. Because with a little help from my husband, I realised exactly what I should give you.'

Jerry was trembling and was covering his face with his hands.

'Here's the new structure,' she said, holding a piece of paper towards him.

Stacey gasped.

Jerry uncovered his eyes and looked directly at Diane for the first time. He nodded as though accepting his fate. As though he was about to be led to the gallows. Jolene had no idea what was going on.

Jerry looked down at the chart for a moment. Then he turned it over to look at the other side as though he thought something was missing. Then he scrutinised it again. His brow furrowed.

'I don't understand,' he said. 'Have you given me the right one? You must have made a mistake.'

'Let's see,' said Stacey, grabbing the piece of paper off him. She looked up at Diane immediately. 'What is this?' she asked. 'Where are you?'

Jolene peered over Stacey's shoulder and saw the top line of the structure where you would expect Diane to be. Except she wasn't. She was nowhere to be seen. In her place was Jerry, along with her job title, and then Yang and Stacey reporting into him with Barney with a dotted line to Stacey.

'Hopefully, somewhere in the Pacific is where I'll be,' smiled Diane.

Actually she was grinning. She was like a new person. What on earth had happened?

'I don't understand,' said Jerry. 'After last night, surely you should be getting rid of me.'

'What the hell happened last night?' asked Stacey. 'Christ, I'm so confused. Am I drunk? What is in these Eggnogs? I so don't know what to think any more. It's like the world has turned upside down.'

'A lot happened last night, didn't it, Jerry? Maybe you should explain.'

'Really?' he asked.

She nodded and folded her arms.

He turned to everyone. 'You know the coffee-shop man?'

'Yeah,' said Stacey.

'Turns out he was Diane's husband all along.'

Everyone gasped.

'What! Hang on a minute! How? Oh my God, but how the hell did that happen . . .?'

Everyone was clamouring with questions, shouting over one another. Until Barney boomed over everyone else.

'You stole Diane's husband and now she's promoting you?'

'I didn't know he was Diane's husband,' said Jerry. 'I would never ever—'

'I know,' said Diane. 'I know that.'

'You seem really weird about it,' said Stacey.

Diane let out a sigh. 'I do feel weird about it. That's

a good way of describing it. Because I know I should be distraught, but I guess the truth is that Leon and I haven't been happily married for a very long time. So I kind of feel relieved, but still upset. Does that make any sense?'

'Human beings are weird,' said Yang, glancing at Stacey.

'But he's a man?' said Barney, pointing at Jerry. 'And your husband was married to you. A woman.'

Diane nodded. 'I know, Barney. Not what I was expecting, really. Difficult to understand. But look at it this way. I didn't get jilted for a hot sexy young female. I think I'd much rather it be a middle-aged man with dodgy stubble.'

'Sorry,' said Jerry, his hand flying to his chin. 'I forgot to shave this morning. I was in a right tizz.'

'Not surprised. You just stole the boss's husband and her job!' said Yang with raised eyebrows. 'How does anyone pull that off?'

Jerry looked completely nonplussed.

'Leon gave me his present last night,' said Diane. 'And it's the best Christmas present I have ever had. It's going to change my life.'

'An air fryer?' said Jolene. 'My mum says it's changed hers.'

'No, not an air fryer. Do you remember that video you took of me singing on the stage with the elves?' she asked Jolene.

'Yeah,' said Jolene. 'You were amazing.'

'You sent it to Leon, didn't you? Well, he sent it to a friend of his who casts singers on cruise ships. He took me to meet him last night. One of his singers has just got pregnant. He needs maternity cover and fast. And I'm in!' A massive grin swept over Diane's face. 'I'm going to sing my way around the Pacific Ocean. I leave on Boxing Day.'

Jolene screamed. 'Oh my God, the love of your life! You told me that in the theatre. That singing was the love of your life. This is so amazing!'

Diane's eyes were flooded with tears. 'I'm going to sing again,' she said, clutching Jolene. 'I'm going to sing again.'

'I . . . I'm in shock,' said Jerry. 'I . . . how is Leon?' he asked, looking the most confused anyone had ever looked, ever.

'He'll be in touch, I'm sure,' she said. 'At an appropriate time. Possibly when I'm on a boat somewhere in the Caribbean.' She grinned.

Jerry looked down at the chart again, then back up at Diane. 'You are the most amazing person I have ever met,' he said with tears in his eyes.

'Just you make sure you look after this lot,' she told him. 'I need to know I'm leaving them in safe hands.'

'Of course,' said Jerry. 'I'll look after everything and . . . and if you ever want to come back, well, I would step aside in an instant.'

'Thanks,' said Diane. 'I won't, but thanks anyway.'

'Well, now that it appears that those who want to stay here are staying,' said Barney, 'it seems like a good time to do my Secret Santa.'

'Ooh yes, Barney,' said Jolene, keen to move things along. She couldn't wait to do her Secret Santa. Albeit she wasn't sure if she could top Diane's.

They all went quiet as Barney reached round and picked up the bright red bow on his desk and stuck it to the back of his chair. Then he looked up and slowly rolled the chair towards Jolene.

'It's all yours,' he said. 'Welcome to the team.'

Jolene was speechless.

'I'm glad you're here,' he said. 'You've made such a difference. To the team and to me.'

Jolene couldn't believe what she was hearing. The man went out of his way to make her feel like an idiot and that she didn't belong. He was actually giving her his chair.

'But what will you sit on?' she asked.

'Oh, don't worry about me. I have contacts in Facilities. I'll get a chair.'

'Of course you will,' said Jolene. 'Thanks, Barney. I can't tell you what this means.'

'I'll have it back when you move to a different department and forget all about us,' he said.

'I will never forget all of you,' she replied, looking round at everyone smiling at her. Things were so different from when she had arrived.

'Oh, and one other thing,' Barney said, getting an envelope out of his pocket. 'I'm not sure if this is allowed because I had to pay for it, but I've signed you up to go to the pottery class that Bella goes to. You said you liked pottery and, well, actually I've signed myself up as well. If that's OK?. Figured I need to start doing something with my evenings. If you don't mind me coming too.'

'Of course not,' gasped Jolene. 'That would be brilliant.

You're going to love it, Barney, I promise you. Once you get your hands on that wet clay it's the most amazing feeling.'

Barney raised his eyebrows. 'If you say so, Jolene.'

'My turn, I think,' said Stacey. She took some deep breaths. She looked like she was calming down and the rash had disappeared from her neck. Albeit her eyes were still darting all around the room as if she didn't know who or what to look at. 'Well, at least I can give this one now,' she said. 'I wasn't sure, but now it's all OK.' She took an envelope out of her bag and gave it to Diane.

'If you sacked me I was going to give you something else, if I'm honest, no idea what. A piece of my mind perhaps.' She gave a small grin. 'But this is all good now.'

Diane opened the card inside and a big smile spread across her face. 'I would love that,' she said, taking Stacey in her arms.

'I'm ditching my mum's Christmas this year,' Stacey told everyone. 'I'm having Diane over. She's looked after me way better than my own mum since Grace was born. So it's only fitting that she spends Christmas with us, especially as her own daughter is disappearing.'

'I'm so honoured,' said Diane. 'Let me know what I can bring, won't you? Let's make it really easy and just slob on the sofa all day and eat chocolate and have girlie chats with Grace.'

'Sounds perfect,' grinned Stacey. 'Can't wait.'

'So who have we got left?' said Jolene, looking round the room. 'Mine and Jerry's?'

'I haven't had anything yet,' said Barney.

'Just be patient,' said Jolene.

'I've already done mine,' said Yang, still looking down in the mouth.

'Yep, got that, plenty of babysitting, well done, Yang,' said Jolene. 'So shall we do Jerry's then? Are you ready?'

'As I'll ever be,' he said. 'So Yang. I drew you and I need you to go into Diane's office and put on the outfit I have laid over the chair.'

'It's not a turkey, is it?' he sighed. 'You're not going to make me look stupid, are you?'

'No,' said Jerry. 'Not at all. Promise. Just go in there and get changed. Don't forget the shoes.'

Yang slid wearily off the desk and wandered into Diane's office. He walked in and then peered out again.

'Are you sure about this?' he asked.

'Absolutely sure,' replied Jerry.

He shut the door behind him and Jerry leaped up. He flipped off the main lights and flipped a switch at a socket, transforming the office into the perfect fairy-lit grotto, complete with the glitterball bouncing multi-coloured lights all over the room.

'Wow,' said Stacey. 'That's beautiful.'

'Good,' said Jerry. 'That's good, glad you like it. You ready, Yang?'

The door opened and out stepped Yang in full tuxedo, including bow tie. He looked immaculate. Jerry had even left him a comb to do his hair. He looked as if he was from the Rat Pack.

Diane let out a wolf whistle. 'Looking hot, baby,' she grinned.

'You look amazing,' said Jolene.

'Proper smart,' said Barney, nodding.

Stacey said nothing, just stared with her mouth open.

'Is this it?' asked Yang. 'You bought me a tux? You weren't supposed to spend anything.'

'No,' said Jerry. 'That is not it. I borrowed the tux, but we all now need to go for a little walk and the rest of your Secret Santa will be revealed. Coats on, everyone.'

'What about me?' asked Barney. 'I haven't had mine yet.'

'You will,' said Jolene. 'Patience, Barney, patience. It's you next, actually. But you need to come with us.'

Chapter 30

Barney grumbled gently the whole way there, whilst Yang looked embarrassed to be out in broad daylight wearing a tuxedo. Jolene led the way and took them on a slightly circuitous route in the hope of putting Barney off the scent, but when they eventually reached the gates of the park he stopped short and gave Jolene a look. She took his hand.

'It's OK,' she told him. 'I promise.'

As a light sprinkling of snow drifted down, they walked hand in hand together through the park gates. Everyone in the group fell silent, walking behind Jolene and Barney until they rounded a corner and Barney's wife's bench came into view.

Barney stopped short and gasped. Standing around the bench were members of a choir, song books open and singing 'O Come, All Ye Faithful'. Jerry walked round to join them as Carol handed him a song book and his clear tenor voice added to the beautiful sound.

Barney clutched Jolene's hand tightly as tears streamed down his face.

Tears also streamed down Jolene, Diane, Stacey, and Yang's faces as they clustered round their colleague Barney.

They stood in silence as the choir got to the end of the song, at which point the tiny audience burst into thunderous applause. Jolene stepped towards Barney, holding a large Christmas wreath that one of the choir members had kept safe for her.

'You told me how you wish you could have had a proper send-off for your wife, Barney. We're all so sorry for your loss and we wondered if you would like to say a few words, then lay this wreath on Linda's bench as we sing her favourite carol, which I believe was "Silent Night".'

Barney looked at her speechless.

'Thank you,' he finally mouthed, before taking the wreath and gathering himself.

He turned to face everyone.

'I really wasn't expecting this,' he said, tears making his eyes glisten. 'Linda was the love of my life. I miss her every moment of every day. Although I sometimes think she loved Christmas more than me,' he grinned. 'You remind me of her,' he continued, nodding at Jolene. He looked up at the choir and then at the Christmas wreath. 'This is perfect,' he said as he broke down in tears again. 'She would have adored this. Her dream send-off, if there is such a thing.' He looked up into the sky. 'Merry Christmas, my darling,' he said. He kissed his hand and blew his kiss into the sky. Then he stepped forward and laid the wreath on Linda's bench as the choir sang.

Silent night, holy night
All is calm, all is bright
Round yon Virgin, Mother and Child
Holy Infant so tender and mild
Sleep in heavenly peace
Sleep in heavenly peace . . .

As they moved through the song, Barney joined in, followed by Diane and then the rest. They all stood with their arms round each other and thought of their loved ones and silently wished them all a merry Christmas.

As the last note died in the snowy air, Jolene made an announcement.

'May I thank Jerry so much for bringing his fellow choristers for this very special performance. But we have one more Secret Santa to complete. Over to you, Jerry.'

Jerry stepped forward and cleared his throat. 'Let's fast forward to midnight Christmas Eve, shall we?' he said. 'We've all had a lovely time, wherever we've been, and it's coming to crunch time. The time when you ask for what you really, really want for Christmas. Come and join me, Yang. Over here.'

Yang looked around in shock, then walked slowly towards him, looking extremely nervous.

'Now, you're on the dance floor and there's one lady here and all she wants for Christmas is to dance to this song with a nice man, so why don't you go and take that lady by the hand and let's grant her that Christmas wish, shall we?'

Jerry turned round to indicate to Carol, who was holding a xylophone. She began to ping out the opening bars of Mariah Carey's famous song as Jerry nudged Yang towards Stacey.

Carol shouted over to Stacey, 'Yoohoo, remember me, your fairy godmother from the Tower? I think this one's a keeper,' she said, nodding her head towards Yang. Stacey gave Carol a small nod then turned to face Yang.

Yang still looked bewildered, and for a heart-stopping moment he hovered in front of Stacey, then offered his hand and mustered the immortal line – 'All I Want for Christmas Is You'.

It looked as if she was going to stand frozen to the spot for a moment, but then she softened and she smiled.

'Why didn't you just tell me?' she said. 'It would have saved you the trouble of babysitting my crazy daughter, unnecessarily going to a school Nativity and taking a donkey on the London Eye.'

'I wouldn't have missed any of that for the world,' he said.

'Neither would I,' she replied as she stepped forward and put her arms around his neck.

Jerry pulled Diane into the choir line up as they all began to sing the ultimate romantic Christmas song. The rest of them swayed along, all misty eyed and tearful.

Jerry scrutinised Stacey. Yes, she was looking totally into Yang's eyes. They might kiss. Maybe not now, but soon. Jerry had just nudged them a bit closer and he knew that was the best Secret Santa ever for Yang. He would have to take it from there. Jerry's work was done.

The song came to an end and everyone jumped up and down and cheered and hollered, and to Jerry's delight, Stacey kissed Yang. Briefly but square on the lips. This really was an excellent start to Christmas.

'Last song then, guys,' said Jerry, looking round. 'You're all troupers, you know that. We thought we should end this exclusive little show with what we understand was another one of Linda's favourite songs. Are you ready, guys?' he asked the choir. They all pulled out hand bells from behind them and started shaking them. They launched into singing about snow falling and children playing and love and understanding as they did a joyous rendition of Shakin' Stevens' 'Merry Christmas Everyone'.

Jolene grabbed both of Barney's hands as they began to dance to the joyous tune. She was delighted to see Yang and Stacey do the same, whilst Diane stayed beside Jerry and added her epic voice to the choir. Other park visitors had begun to gather round and some even started dancing too, such was the infectious joy of the occasion.

Eventually they came to the end of the song as everyone chanted 'Merry Christmas Everyone' at the tops of their voices and hugged and kissed.

Well, Yang and Stacey did anyway. A long slow one. Not just a peck on the cheek. The perfect Christmas kiss.

Acknowledgements

In October 1993, I started my first day on a graduate training scheme much like Jolene in *The Secret Santa Project*. I remember it vividly, but little did I realise that I would meet some of my closest friends through that job. Relationships with colleagues can grow into very special friendships, and I would just like the opportunity to thank some of my colleagues over the years who have given me so many happy memories.

Gemma, Catherine, Phill, Rosie, Graeme & Keeley, you made my time at The British Shoe Corporation an absolute ball – so many highlights – but special mention has to go to getting Margarita Pracatan announced over the tannoy!

I moved on to work at Alton Towers in the late nineties. A place where everyone worked extremely hard but also had a lot of fun. Ali, Liz, and Rich were there from the start, alongside Deardo and Gary supporting us as suppliers – brilliant times. And finally, Nikki and Duncan. What a team! An absolute privilege to work with you both at The Tussauds Group.

Pregnant with my first child, I moved to the US for three years with my husband's career which is when I started writing my first book. As an author I have accumulated some amazing colleagues too. I have Madeleine Milburn to thank for giving me my start, then Araminta Whitley and top woman, Peta Nightingale, who helped me with my success in self-publishing. The wonderful Jenny Geras got me into book shops whilst at PRH and then supported me whilst at Bookouture. Now I have Hannah Todd to thank for giving excellent agent guidance and Kate Bradley of HarperCollins for navigating my past four books through the publishing process. I have loved getting to know you all and greatly value your support and friendship. I must also mention again Rich Swainson who I first met whilst working for Alton Towers but who became a valued colleague again when he produced the most amazing book trailers for my self-published books. Please look up on YouTube our epic creation in Lego for *No-one Ever Has Sex on a Tuesday*. Making those films together was an utter joy and I was so glad that brought Rich back into my life. Sadly, Richard passed away last year, and I know he is desperately missed as a colleague and friend by many, many people.

It is such a privilege to be a writer; however, I do miss the human connection of going out to work every day. I have, however, been lucky enough to be part of a fabulous group of writing colleagues who regularly meet and support each other, laugh together and try to make sense of the life of a writer in whatever way we can. Jo Barndon (writing as Anna Stuart and

Joanna Courtney), Julie Houston, Sharon Sant (writing as Tilly Tennant), Debbie Raynor and Helen Conway: you are a very special group of women whom I love spending time with and who help me enormously in my working life.

Finally – as always – I have to thank my wonderful family, Bruce, Tom and Sally. I would be nowhere without you. Thank you all for your patience, guidance and support as I play out my working life in front of you!

If you loved *The Secret Santa Project*,
read on for an excerpt of
Tracy's funny and uplifting novel,
The Wife Who Got a Life . . .

1 *January*

I wouldn't say I was unhappy. I was just normal.

Neither happy nor unhappy. Somewhere in the middle, just trying to get from day to day without much thinking about how cheerful I was. To be honest, I actually hadn't given it much thought at all until my sister gave me this 'Motivational Diary' for Christmas. A diary! I mean, I hadn't written a diary since I was a teenager and needed to pour out my angst about Paul Backleton and his inability to see beyond my acne, braces and fluorescent Eighties wardrobe.

I was insulted to start with. Why on earth did she think I needed a Motivational Diary? She lives in California and passes her time mostly up to her neck in yoga poses and kale smoothies and somehow she thought this qualified her to tell me how to run my life. I'd specifically asked her for the sing-along version of *The Greatest Showman* for Christmas, thinking that pretending I was singing and dancing with Hugh Jackman might provide the necessary escape required from another largely dissatisfying family Christmas, but clearly she hadn't listened. On opening the disappointing diary, I immediately sent her a text to express my disgust as I topped up my festive calorific intake with Ferrero Rocher.

A Motivational Diary – WTF?!

Within moments she was FaceTiming me.

You knew it was serious when you sent someone a text and they replied by video-calling you. It meant that serious, maybe even complicated words needed to be said that could not be covered by text-speak or emojis. She was, of course, glowing with health and sunshine whereas I was muted by grey skies, skin puffed out by too many carbohydrates, my up-do frazzled by too much time over a hot stove and an unsightly rash around my neck caused by my 100 per cent acrylic Christmas jumper.

'Before you even start,' she said, 'I know what you're thinking. This diary is some hippy crap that my sister's got into because she lives in LA.'

Funnily enough, that was exactly what I was thinking.

'Well, it's not. My girlfriend Janelle, you know the one who's married to the cousin of the Foo Fighters' drummer; well, she gave me a Motivational Diary for my fiftieth birthday and it's changed my life, honestly Cathy. It's made me put myself first. Made me think about what makes me happy, and that's really hard for people like us.'

'What do you mean, "people like us"?'

'You know: female, a mother, a wife.'

I gave that one a moment's thought.

'If you say so,' I replied eventually, grabbing my eighth Ferrero Rocher of the evening.

She peered at me through the phone and I hoped she couldn't see the gravy that had dripped down the fluffy snowman on my chest.

'All we do is fit around other people's lives,' she continued. 'While we let ourselves go.'

Harsh, I thought.

'We let other people live the way *they* want while we adjust our way round them. Well, it's time to put yourself first, Cathy. Work out what you want to achieve to make yourself happy before it's too late.'

'What makes you think I'm not happy?'

'How was Christmas?' she asked.

'Oh, you know, the usual over-panicking and under-delivering. I've spent weeks in the endless cycle of buying food, then buying even more food in case there's not enough food. Then buying presents followed by buying even more presents in case there are not enough presents. Then hours alone in the spare bedroom wrapping way too many presents before spending hours alone in the kitchen cooking way too much food. Two activities that – as you well know – I hate and am terrible at. It's been great, really it has. An absolute joy, as usual.'

'Might I say you sound a little depressed, Cathy?'

She was making me mad now.

'No, I'm not! I've had a perfectly normal Christmas, Lizzy. That doesn't make me depressed.'

'If that's your Christmas then you *should* be depressed,' she replied. 'Of course it could also be the menopause kicking in. That might be why you are feeling a bit down.'

'Jesus, Lizzy! I was feeling perfectly fine about my typically disappointing Christmas until you put me on the counselling couch and overanalysed it.'

'I'm just saying that at your age you need to be monitoring for symptoms of the menopause. Anxiety and depression can be a part of that.'

'*You* are making me anxious, Lizzy, not my reproductive system!'

'Are you having night sweats yet? Or difficulty sleeping, vaginal dryness, reduced sex drive?'

'Are you reading this from a leaflet or something?'

'No. I have a web page open.'

'Look, I haven't seen any sign of the menopause yet. My periods are all still perfectly normal.'

'You're still having periods!' gasped my sister. She looked truly horrified. As if I'd told her I was an axe murderer.

'Yes! They still keep coming, monthly, like they're supposed to.'

'But why aren't you on the pill, Cathy? I went on the pill straight after I had Alicia. I can't have had a period in eighteen years.'

I paused, flummoxed for an answer to what I realized was a perfectly reasonable question.

'Well, I guess, well, I thought about it but . . . but I never got round to it. I was just kind of distracted by, you know, life.'

'Distracted by other people's needs and not your own, you mean,' said Lizzy. 'You see this is exactly why I have sent you the Motivational Diary. So this kind of self-neglect doesn't happen.'

'I'm not self-neglecting,' I told her. 'I'm perfectly fine.' I reached for my ninth Ferrero Rocher.

'Look, you don't have to put anything difficult in there,' she said. 'Just some simple stuff that will make all the difference.'

'So what have you put in yours then?' I asked her. 'What's your January goal?'

'Well er . . . well, actually I've decided to train for a marathon, but that doesn't mean . . .'

I laughed. Of course I did.

'I'm not doing it,' I said firmly. 'I'll only disappoint myself and then I'll be really unhappy.'

She sighed and leaned back, folding her slim bare arms and revealing the clear blue skies behind her.

'If you say so,' she said. 'But don't come crying to me next year when you're miserable. Just give it a go, sis. Please.'

'I'm not miserable,' I told her. 'Well, I wasn't until I spoke to you.'

My reaction to this phone call was obviously to reach for several more Ferrero Rochers and go into a deep sulk. What did my sister know about my life? I *was* perfectly fine. Plus I knew where that 'Motivational Goals' mumbo-jumbo got you. Self-loathing and disappointment, that's where. Having goals meant increasing your expectations, and that would always lead to dissatisfaction and unhappiness. My approach, I felt, was much more useful, and it didn't require me to sit and scratch my head over a list of things that I was never going to get around to.

It was so much easier to just lower my expectations instead.

I realized some time ago that – so far in my life – creating expectations had only led to disappointment. I could count on the fingers of one hand when my expectations have actually been exceeded.

1. When I was twelve years old and ate my first pizza in a proper Italian restaurant rather than the frozen four-pack kind from the supermarket. I thought my head would explode.
2. How painful childbirth was. I genuinely thought a JCB had entered my uterus.

That was it.

Now if there was a centipede that happened to have

fingers and toes, they would not have enough fingers and toes to count how many times things have not met my expectations and therefore how many times I have experienced the low dull gloom of disappointment.

So that was why I would *not* be writing a list of 'Motivational Goals'. I knew where they led. So no thank you, Lizzy. I was perfectly fine. Life was fine. I didn't need any stupid goals to make me miserable.